AFTER THE SHUT UP RING

CATE C. WELLS

This book is a work of fiction. Names, characters, places, and incidents are the product of the author's imagination or are used fictitiously. Any resemblance to actual events, locales, or persons, living or dead, is coincidental.

Cover art and design by Clarise Tan of CT Cover Creations
Edited by Nevada Martinez
Proofread by The Blue Couch Edits, Jess Jaeger, and Kayla Davenport

Special thanks to Noelle Benach, LCPC, CST, Jean McConnell of The Word Forager, Pepper Knight, Grace C, Jess T, Jen S, Elizabeth L, Allyssa B, Sara B, Erin G, and the CCW Street Team

❀ Created with Vellum

AUTHOR'S NOTE

This book is not going to be for everyone. It's *meant* for everyone, but you might not be in the headspace, and I want to give you a heads up.

A few spoilers—Angie, the female main character, has HSV-2. She is coming out of a bad relationship, and she's navigating visitation issues with her ex. Both main characters experienced the loss of a parent before the story begins.

1

ANGIE

"Ready for this, sweetheart?" Tyler says, gazing at me, his blue eyes twinkling.

I'm beyond ready. I've been dreaming about marrying him since I was fourteen years old.

He clears his throat, and the corners of his lips twitch like he's stifling a smile. A trickle of dread drips down my spine. I know that look.

The hall is deathly quiet. Our guests lean forward in their seats. They can't wait to hear this.

My breath is shallow from nerves, but I can still smell the booze coming out of Tyler's pores. He partied hard last night and started early today. Good thing he wasn't the one who had to walk down the aisle. He wouldn't have been able to do it in a straight line.

"Uh oh," he says, patting his pockets. My heart leaps into my throat. Did he forget his phone?

"Oh. Here it is." He laughs and holds it up. A few people chuckle. My heart sticks where it leaped.

Everyone's been joking about Tyler writing his own vows, but it was his idea. He didn't want a preacher to marry us. He wanted his friend Duck, who got ordained on the internet, to do the ceremony. Duck said he would, but he didn't want to do too much. Tyler promised him fifty bucks and said we'd write our own vows. Duck said, "Bet."

My best friend Madison said Tyler's going to burp his vows like he does the lyrics to Kid Rock's "Bawitdaba" every time he chugs a beer. I thought he'd be more likely to forget them in the car or in his other pants. I asked him earlier when we got to the Elks Lodge, though, and he said not to worry.

Actually, he said, "For once, can you not worry?"

Now he's scrolling and scrolling. Did he accidentally delete his vows?

"What's going on?" I whisper.

"Oh! Here they are!" he says brightly. He's playing around.

I can hardly swallow past my heart in my throat, and he's joking.

He flashes a smile at our girls sitting in the front row. "Ready for Daddy's vows?"

"Yes, Daddy," Tamblyn answers obediently. The crowd goes *awww*, and my chest eases.

The girls are sitting in the front row with Madison's mom, Miss Dawn. Tamblyn's spindly legs stick straight out of her ruffled petticoats. She's munching Goldfish crackers from a bag on her lap. Ivy is twisted around and folded over the back of her white plastic folding chair, chatting to my aunt.

Tyler's mom is on the opposite side of the aisle, casting a stink eye at her grandbabies and muttering to her sister. I just know she's saying that the girls wouldn't be eating Goldfish or turned around in their seats if they were sitting with *her*. She's right, they wouldn't, but they'd be bawling because she'd yelled at them about some petty thing, for sure.

For the hundredth time today, I wish my mom was here, that she'd turned it around in time to see this day. I'm wearing her angel pin under the hem of my dress as my "something old." I even kind of wish I knew how to get in touch with Dad. Walking down the aisle alone sucked.

"Well, without further ado," Tyler says, lifting his phone. He frowns, swipes, and taps. It must have timed out. His frown deepens, and he taps some more. He entered his passcode wrong. A few folks chuckle again, and he scowls. Tyler doesn't like to be laughed at.

His groomsmen are getting restless beside him. They don't look so great today either. They've gotten haircuts, and their rented tuxes are pressed, but they all have bloodshot eyes and that greasy sheen you get when you're still drunk and hungover at the same time.

Tyler taps and scrolls, seriously searching this time, and folks begin to shift and whisper in their seats. I hope none of the chairs give. They're not the sturdiest, but they came free with the hall rental.

Thank goodness, Tyler finally finds what he's looking for. His whole head has turned red—you can see it through the buzz cut he got yesterday. I guess it's too much to ask that this day go smoothly.

Smooth isn't what Tyler and I get. The condom broke nine months before high school graduation, and we got Tamblyn instead of senior week at the beach. Then, his parents were supposed to move to Florida and rent their house to us, but his dad got busted banging an IT girl from his office, so he got fired and lost his retirement package. After his parents did counseling with the priest, they decided to stay put. And then there was all the drama with Ivy's ears and the tubes.

Nothing ever breaks our way, but we're still together,

almost eight years after he asked me to his freshman homecoming, and that says something.

Doesn't it?

My stomach refuses to settle. I've got wedding day jitters, only instead of butterflies, I've got a huge bird of prey stuck in my guts, flapping its wings, trying to get out. Like an osprey or something.

"We are gathered here today because I finally gave up and let Angie here win," Tyler starts, his voice low and stilted. He's not used to reading out loud. He pauses for laughter, but I don't think anyone heard him.

He coughs and continues louder. "We've been together a long time, and today's the day, as they say."

My gaze wanders to my babies again, and then, like I always tend to do, I search out Brandon, Madison's older brother. He's sitting behind his mother, a few seats over, stiff and solemn per usual. He looks hungover, too, even though he didn't go to the bachelor party last night. Tyler made a point to invite him—I heard him do it—but Brandon said he had to work.

When I was in eighth grade, I had a massive crush on Brandon, but he was a year ahead. Plenty of high school guys, including Tyler, would give us middle school girls the time of day, but he wouldn't.

I used to see him all the time at school and Madison's house. Now that we're grown, though, I only see him in passing. He usually makes me nervous, but for some reason, today, the sight of him grim-faced in probably the only button-up shirt he owns, makes my stomach ache.

Tyler coughs, and my gaze flies back to him. Good Lord. What am I doing staring at other men on my wedding day?

Tyler goes on. "Ever since we started talking back in high school, I knew that one day, you would drag me down the aisle. I mean, I fought the good fight as long as I could, but in the end, you wore me down." He waits a beat, and his groomsmen snicker. There's a chuckle or two from the men in the audience.

I should have known Tyler wouldn't be able to be serious. Honestly, I'm relieved he has something prepared. In the back of my mind, I was half afraid he'd pull a stunt like that groom in the viral video who just said something like "I vow to ride it like a pony every night" and called it a day.

And Tyler's right. I've waited for this moment for a long time. Every Christmas and birthday and Valentine's since Tamblyn was born, I held my breath for a ring, and now finally, after so many tears and so much pain and disappointment, it's finally happening. We're going to be a real family. *This* is what I've always wanted.

"Plenty of people here thought we wouldn't make it, but here we are." He gestures around the hall like he wrote stage directions in his vows.

It sucks to be reminded, but he's right. Tyler and I were young when we got together, and we had our growing pains. No one is their best self at sixteen or nineteen or even twenty-one. We had a lot of responsibility when most people our age were out at the bars. Tyler resented that, and he made some hurtful choices, but at the end of the day, he came home to me. To *us*.

This is our new beginning. Life is going to be easier now. We're in the duplex. He's finally got the truck he wants. Ivy gets her tubes out in a few months. All the drama is behind us.

I smile up at him. He's so handsome that sometimes I still can't believe he ever asked me out. He was so popular, with his good hair and his boy-band face. I really am lucky. I've seen the DMs Madison gets from her matches in the dating apps. It's rough out there—way rougher than I've got it.

Tyler shoots his boys a look over his shoulder and then smiles back at me.

It's a strange smile. He must be nervous, speaking first in front of everyone we know.

He reads on. "So today, I'm going to make you the happiest woman in the world. You're welcome."

There are a few more laughs this time. Everyone thinks Tyler is funny. He says the things other people are afraid to say—or that they know they shouldn't.

"They say that marriage is give and take," he continues. "I promise to give it to you hard and take your shit with a smile, and if I can't, to gather your shit up for you and dump it on the lawn. Like a gentleman."

What? My mouth sours, and my throat tightens. Why would he bring that up?

That was *years* ago now. I was expecting Ivy, and they ran some routine tests, and when the tests came back, it was a whole thing. My hormones were out of control. I lost my temper and screamed at him that I'd had enough. He went crazy and threw all my stuff out on the front lawn, since technically, the house belongs to him and his dad since he co-signed. Then he drove off in his truck and didn't come back all weekend.

Mr. Neudecker from next door helped me carry everything back inside because it was starting to rain, and I was so far along, I couldn't really bend over to pick things up. Tyler and I worked it out, though. We forgave each other. We don't talk about it anymore.

Except when he's drunk and mad at me.

And he brings it up now? Here?

Tyler is still smiling down at me, and my shoulder muscles knot as I place it—it's the smirk he gets when he's about to give someone what he thinks they have coming to them. My stomach bottoms out.

"They say when you're married, you should never let your wife go to bed angry, and I promise I won't. You can sleep on the sofa." He pauses again for laughs. Duck snorts. His best man Keith snickers. None of the other guests laugh this time. My face catches on fire.

He looks over at his groomsmen, his eyes lighting with glee. When he turns back, he's not really seeing me. He's focusing all his attention on keeping a straight face as he says, "When you said I had to write my vows, I looked up marriage on the internet, and it said communication and a sense of humor is key, so I promise to listen to you when you run your mouth and laugh at your jokes, which as everyone knows, aren't nearly as funny as mine."

Another pause. His boys laugh. The sound echoes off the dingy white ceiling tiles. The other sixty people in the hall become very, very quiet.

Tyler glances at our guests, his eyebrows pinching together. I know him so well; I can read his face like a book. He doesn't understand why they aren't laughing, too. This is hilarious. He's hilarious.

He shrugs off the mystery and plows on. "Anyway, seriously though, we've been together a long time. We have two beautiful girls together, and our family makes my life perfect."

A few guests murmur their approval, and the tension in the hall eases. *This* is what vows should sound like. Later, they might cluck disapprovingly about what he said before, but they'll also smile fondly and shake their heads. *So handsome. Such a joker. Can't even be serious at his own wedding.*

I should be relaxing, too, as I scrub the words from my short-term memory before they have the chance to stick. I should be taking the joke, doing whatever mental gymnastics is necessary to smooth it over in my head.

This isn't bitter disappointment puckering my mouth.

This isn't shame twisting in my guts or humiliation crawling across my skin.

I should be getting over it *as* it happens. That's how this relationship works. He steamrolls me. I peel myself off the floor and bounce right back into shape.

"Now you've got my last name and my ring, and I promise that you've also got my heart, 'til death do us part —" He stops, his baby blue eyes so clear and gleeful and oblivious to anything except these lines he's delivering.

I need to ignore what he's doing right now, in this very moment, but as I look into his bright, shining, eager eyes, my heart sinks. He's not done.

My body braces.

His smile breaks wide. "—as long as you have dinner on the table on time and keep it tight." He winks at me. "Of course, if you don't, I'll just do what I did when you let yourself go after Tamblyn and Ivy—"

He's not going to say it. Not here. Not in front of everyone.

"I'll just shut my eyes, slap that fat ass, and"—he slaps his thigh and pumps his hips—"ride the waves in!"

His groomsmen chant the words along with him—*ride the waves in*—and then whoop at the top of their lungs.

The words drive into my soft belly like a fist. The humiliation follows in a sharp, blistering blast. I'm speechless and stuck on a rickety riser in front of everyone I know.

He planned this. His boys knew their line. They were waiting for their cue.

No one else is laughing. Duck flips through the two grimy index cards he's holding like he had the miraculous foresight to write down what he should say to transition from "ride the waves in" to my vows.

Miss Dawn, down in her seat, and Madison, standing at

my elbow, are both gaping, matching expressions of horror and disgust on their faces.

Tyler's mother flattens her lips in disapproval. His dad looks like a raccoon who got caught in the trash, frozen and in denial. His aunt clutches the cross she wears around her neck.

Everyone looks like they want to die from secondhand embarrassment, and at the same time, as if they cannot possibly peel their eyes away. Several folks are recording on their phones, including Tyler's cousin Aiden. He calls himself a content creator. He's got a hundred thousand followers just for jumping his four-wheeler over ditches in his parents' backyard.

Has he gone live? I bet he went live.

Dear God. This is going to be on the internet. People are going to feel sorry for me. Thousands of strangers are going to comment.

How could she marry him after that?

That's what you call a shut up ring.

She can't act surprised. Guarantee that she knew what kind of man he was before she got to the altar.

And I did, didn't I? After eight years, how could I not?

But I didn't worry about that. I worried about the centerpieces and Tyler's cummerbund and whether the stupid balloon arch would tip over. I was so freaked out about everything matching—the girls' hair ribbons and Tyler's mother's dress and the groomsmen's boutonnieres.

I stare around the hall, and damned if everything doesn't match down to the bows on the sides of the wobbly plastic folding chairs at the end of each cockeyed row. Everything is the exact same shade of powder blue. Perfect.

What have I done?

I wanted a family and a happy-ever-after so badly. Didn't I drag him down the aisle? Didn't I hold on and refuse to let go no matter how he fought, or what he said? And in the end, didn't I *wear him down*?

I did this to myself.

My stunned gaze settles on my girls. They're both watching me with wide, worried eyes. Ivy's head is tilted to the side. Tamblyn's grubby little fingers keep conveying Goldfish to her mouth, one at a time, in slow motion. She chews and swallows like it's her duty—if she just keeps acting normal, then this moment will pass and everything will be okay again.

Oh, God, I know exactly who she learned that from.

How much do they understand of what their daddy said?

"Mama," Ivy mouths. She knows I'm hurt somehow, and she wants to come to me, but she also knows that she's supposed to stay in her seat and be quiet, and the conflict plays out on her soft, sweet face.

From the corner of my eye, I see Aiden pan the camera from me to her.

One day, she'll see this, and she'll understand every word of it. They both will.

They'll be ashamed of me.

Like I'm ashamed of myself.

My fingers curl into useless fists. My ears ring. What do I do?

Smile.

Play it off.

Grab the girls and run.

Duck tugs at his collar. "Uh, Angie?" He coughs. "It's your turn."

My head swivels back to face Tyler. He's still smirking, so pleased with himself. He lifts an eyebrow. Somehow, it says "What did I do?" and "What are you gonna do about it?" at the same time.

Tamblyn and Ivy lean forward, waiting for me to speak. They're paying the *closest* attention.

I have to read what I wrote in my best handwriting on the pretty stationery I bought just for this. I have to pretend like I still believe what I wrote even though everything I am just cracked open and fell to pieces on the floor.

What am I going to do?

No one is ever going to love me like Tyler. No one is going to want me but him. I'm damaged goods.

I've tolerated his shit for years, and I'm going to have a problem with it now? In front of all our friends and family?

This dress costs five hundred dollars. It was on sale. No returns.

Chicken piccata and flank steak are heating over Sterno cans in the kitchen at the back of the hall. The smell blows through the vents with the air conditioning, mixing with the stale cigarette smoke that seeped into the paneling decades ago.

This is happening. All I have to do is keep going. Eyes on the prize. Our little family. All I've ever wanted. I just need to do what I'm expected to do.

I can do that. I can do *anything* for my family.

Like show my little girls how to eat shit?

I don't know where the voice comes from. It's not mine. It's loud, though, and so help me God, it's right.

"Angie?" Duck prompts.

I open my mouth, and some scrap of spirit, some spark of self that hasn't been ground into the dirt quite yet, rises up inside me and says, "No," loud and clear enough to be heard in the very last row.

My eyes bulge. Did I really just say no?

I did. And I meant it.

No.

"What?" Tyler's eyes bulge, too.

I look away from him to Tamblyn and Ivy. They're wearing their listening ears better than they ever have before. I can't let them think this is okay.

I look up and stare at the buck's head mounted on the wall at the rear of the hall. His blank expression doesn't change while I stumble ahead.

"It's not okay to talk to people like that," I say, striving for the mom voice I cobbled together from the lady at library story time and gentle parenting influencers on the internet. "Those kinds of words hurt my feelings, and my feelings matter. It's not okay to hurt the people you love. It's not okay to embarrass them on purpose. You don't have to accept that."

The stuffed buck's head gets it. I draw in a deep, shaky breath and glance down. Tamblyn and Ivy are watching me, round-eyed as owls, like I'm a tightrope walker. They're *listening*. I hold their gaze, and I keep going.

"Everyone deserves to be treated with kindness and respect by the people who love them." I look straight at Aiden's phone. If this becomes my digital footprint, I don't want my shame to show. I want my girls to think I meant to put my foot down. "And it is *never* too late to speak up for yourself."

Tyler snorts. I make myself turn to face him. He's sneering at me like I'm crazy. In a second, he'll scoff and say I'm talking shit, making a fool of myself, acting stupid again. Then, he'll get angry.

Panic floods my bloodstream, screaming at me to take it back. Apologize. Cry. Throw myself on his mercy. Do whatever it takes to keep him. No one else will ever want to be with me. No one will want to touch me. I can't handle life alone.

Madison grabs my hand, and she steps closer so I can feel her body at my back. "Don't you dare blink now," she hisses in my ear, squeezing my fingers so hard that my knuckles ache. "You're almost home free."

Tamblyn mouths, "Mommy." Ivy stays sitting, but she reaches out her hand toward me.

I'm not alone.

"I won't marry you," I say, forcing myself to look Tyler in his bright red face. "I won't do this. No."

I enunciate each word like I'm talking into an automated phone system, and I need to make my answer very, very clear. Like my *life* depends on being understood.

"Angie, what the fuck?" Tyler spits through his teeth. His boys shift and mutter so I know what they think of me. They can call me fat at my wedding, but I better watch what I say to their boy.

I paid for their boutonnieres. I paid for the flank steak, and they all picked the steak. Tyler didn't pay for anything but his tux rental because he spent all his money on the down payment for his truck.

"I won't marry you." It comes out easier each time I say it.

"This is *bullshit.*"

"Uh. Maybe do you want to, uh, take a minute, and uh, talk?" Duck's neck flushes where it bulges over his too-tight collar. He actually sounds uncomfortable.

"I'm not marrying him."

"This was *your* fucking idea." Tyler grabs me by the upper arm, his fingertips biting into my skin.

Among the guests, a chair screeches on the tile, clattering as it hits the floor. A murmur fans out through the crowd. I glance over. Brandon is standing. Is he going somewhere?

Tyler's grip tightens, forcing my attention back to his tomato-red face. His mouth twists, his lips peeling back from his teeth. His forehead furrows into ridges like that alien from *Star Trek*.

He's hideous, and he's furious, and usually, I'd be terrified and backpedaling so fast I'd leave tire tracks, but this is *my* wedding day—I paid for it all, I picked it all out—and apparently, I'm going to burn it all down.

"Well, I changed my mind," I say louder.

I take it all back. Every *I love you* when I meant *please don't leave me*. Every *it's okay* when it wasn't. Every *I don't mind, it doesn't matter; don't worry about it, it's fine; it was good, really good, I liked it, I promise*.

His lip curls, and he lets me go, shoving me backward as he does, but Madison's right there, so I don't even stumble.

"Fuck this shit," he says. He turns on his heel and storms out the emergency exit. Despite the warning in big red letters, no alarm goes off. His boys file after him, trotting like a pack of well-trained dogs.

Duck shrugs at me and follows them. The emergency door swings shut in slow motion, the rusty hinge letting out a long, screeching creak.

I look for my girls. Miss Dawn has somehow gathered both of them onto her lap, and they're clinging to her, watching me. They aren't scared. I know when my girls are scared. They're not sad, either, or angry.

I can't quite nail down the look in their wide eyes, but if I had to say, it's close to how they looked when we saw a chick hatching from an egg at the state fair last summer. That kind of stunned wonder.

I straighten my back and lift my chin. Madison winds her arm through mine, and we face the rows of shocked guests.

"What do you say we crack into that open bar, folks?" Madison says, and like a starting pistol, the guests burst into conversation all at once.

I tremble under the big balloon arch from the aftermath of the adrenaline, my ears ringing like I got conked on the head with a concrete block. There is only one thought clear in my dumbstruck brain—why is Brandon standing up?

And why is his chair knocked over?

2

BRANDON

THE BACK DOOR OF THE ELKS LODGE SQUEALS AS IT SLOWLY shuts, and my buddy Shane saunters over carrying a dinner plate heaped high with wedding cake.

"Things are getting weird in there," he says through a massive mouthful of cake.

I grunt and continue glaring at Tyler's stupid truck.

"He still around?" Shane asks.

"He left with his boys."

The truck's a heavy-duty turbo diesel with a gooseneck hitch. What the fuck is he hauling? He borrows his daddy's boat, which is tied up at his daddy's pier. Back in high school, the team would take it out crabbing sometimes, and I didn't want anyone to catch on that I hated the motherfucker, so I'd go.

Shane comes to stand beside me and stares at the truck like he's trying to figure out what I'm looking at.

"Surprised it doesn't have a window decal that says *douchebag*," he says.

"Doesn't need it."

Anyone could tell it's driven by a dickhead just by looking, if not from the lift or the aftermarket rims or the pristine bed lining, then from the big ol' pipe for rollin' coal. So fucking stupid.

Why would you remove your particulate filter, install a whole new injector, and lay out hundreds of dollars just so you can spew black smoke on a hybrid or a guy on a bicycle? Those folks are clueless about trucks. They have no idea you're doing it on purpose; they just figure your vehicle's a piece of shit.

I take a drag off the cigarette I've got pinched between my index finger and thumb. I haven't had a smoke in three years, and it's hitting like it did when I was thirteen and finishing off my dad's butts behind the backyard shed—my head swims and my hands shake.

"Got a spare?" Shane asks, nodding to the Virginia Slim I'm hotboxing.

"I bummed this myself."

Shane shrugs and shovels another piece of cake into his gob. "All the steak's gone. There's chicken left, but it's going fast."

I tap my ash onto the weed cracked parking lot and try to get my brain to work. It feels run over. I should be relieved, I guess. Instead, it's like I went twelve rounds in the ring and ended up with a split decision.

Angie didn't marry that asshole, but she was going to. If not for his unforced error at the very last minute, she'd have married him, and I was going to watch her do it.

I don't know who I'm madder at—myself or her or him—but I'm fucking furious. I don't know what to do with the energy.

I've got a half-full, three-gallon jerrycan in my truck from my last mechanic order, and Mrs. Ekholm gave me a book of matches with the cigarette. I've got some ideas.

Frankly, I'm surprised that Tyler left his truck behind—he obviously loves it more than Angie or his kids—but he probably went down to the bar to get wasted and wanted someone else to drive.

"Everybody left inside is getting drunk off their ass," Shane says. "Uncle Randy got the DJ to play Toto's *IV*, the entire album, and your mom is trying to fight him now."

"The DJ?"

"Uncle Randy." He scrapes icing off the plate with the spoon.

"I didn't know Mom hated Toto."

"I think she just hates Randy."

Probably. Randy's a dick. He heads up our gang down at the port. Shane is Randy's brother's kid, and Randy married my mom's sister, so he's uncle to both of us, but we aren't blood related. We might as well be, though. We were the two youngest guys on the gang for a long time, and that'll either make you best friends or worst enemies. Since neither Shane or I are lazy or stupid, we're tight.

Not so close that I share my fucking feelings with him, but like I said, he's not stupid. He knows who I mean when I ask, "Is she still in there?"

He shakes his head. "She and the kids left with Maddie a while ago."

"How did she look?" It feels weird as hell to ask straight out. Sometimes, it feels like I've spent my whole life acting like I'm not hopelessly gone for Angie Miller.

Shane's eyebrows go up, but he's not dick enough to bust my balls. "Shell-shocked," he says.

Makes sense. Those vows had to come at her out of the blue, even though I've never met anyone more likely to pull that kind of shit than Tyler Reynolds. He's a giant chode. And she loved him enough—or thought so little of herself—to overlook that fact until he humiliated her in front of everyone she knows.

I don't want to be angry. I'm not an angry person. But I

want to take a tire iron to the windows of that truck and that pristine bed liner. I want to yell at her, and I've never raised my voice to a woman in my life.

I brace myself and ask, "Was she crying?"

I don't need to fucking know the answer to that. Why did I ask?

Now I've got a picture of her tear-streaked face in my mind. I can feel that powerlessness again in my gut. I've only seen her cry a few times—the night when her mom was found, my dad's funeral. I'll be happy if I never see her that way again. Both times, I'd never felt more useless.

"No, she was fussing over the kids."

My lungs expand. I can breathe again.

"Maddie was pissed." Shane chuckles. "She wanted to go after him."

"Tyler?"

"Yeah, she was looking for the cake knife. Good thing he bailed. She wants blood."

I understand the feeling. Tyler was smiling when he said that shit up under that balloon arch, smirking like a little bitch. I was all ready to shut his mouth. I'd stood up. Knocked my chair over. Mom was hissing at me under her breath to sit my ass down, and then the clouds parted, and hallelujah, Angie decided she was done with his shit. I never thought it would happen.

She used to be sweet and tough. Quiet and nice, but tough. She still is, but it's a different kind of sweet and tough now. It makes you feel sorry for her instead of happy, and that pisses me off, too.

I scowl at his truck. He hurt her. He's been eating away at her for years, and we were all forced to watch. He's probably down at Donovan's, running his mouth about her to one of his side pieces right now.

I could go down there. I could shut his mouth for him. I'd feel a lot fucking better.

But then I'd break his jaw, and their girls would want to know what happened, and he'd definitely tell them because he's the type who could never take a well-deserved punch in the face like a man.

"The girls were fussing? Like crying?" I ask Shane.

"No, they wanted to get out of that puffy stuff under their dresses."

Good. I hate it when the girls cry, too. I'm not one of those guys who can't handle seeing a woman cry. Maddie leaks like a faucet, and it doesn't faze me, but if it's Angie or the girls, I can't stand it.

There was this one time when we were kids—I used to spend hours playing wallball against the side of our garage. One day, Angie and Maddie were painting their toes on the front porch steps. It was summer, and Angie was wearing short shorts, so all you could see when she sat were her long legs.

She didn't dress slutty or anything, but she didn't get new clothes very often, so her shorts would get real short and tight, and I'd started to notice. I couldn't stop noticing, even when I tried.

Anyway, Angie and Maddie were painting their nails, paying no attention to me, and I didn't like that. I got the idea that I'd let a ball get away from me, and then I'd go after it. Angie would notice me. The plan wasn't totally clear in my head.

I guess I was thinking that if I was going to be clumsy in front of her, I should make up for it with a show of brute strength, so I winged the lacrosse ball at the wall as hard as I could, and per my plan, it clipped the scoop and flew across the front lawn. And it nailed Angie.

Her scream of pain lives on a loop in my nightmares. She folded over and clutched her foot.

I don't remember going to her, but I remember sinking onto a knee in front of her on the concrete walk. Tears were pooling in her brown eyes, and for reasons that I have never figured out, she looked at me like I could fix it. Most of me felt like a total asshole, but to this day, I've never felt taller than I did when she looked at me like that. Like she trusted me. Like I was man enough to have earned it.

But I wasn't. I was a dumbass kid.

I kept saying, "Oh fuck, oh fuck." I peeled her hands away so I could see. The ball had chipped her big toenail and smeared the polish. It wasn't much of a nick. It didn't go past the nail bed, but I felt like the world's biggest asshole, and an idiot besides because I had no idea what to do.

Maddie said she'd go get an ice pack, and I felt even dumber, but no matter how bright my face got, I couldn't drop Angie's foot or look away from her. I cradled it, trying to smooth the wet polish with my thumb, which was the opposite of helpful.

Angie didn't move. She let me kneel there and hold her foot. She stared down at me, and I stared up at her. I don't know how I didn't pass out because I wasn't breathing and all the blood was rushing out of my head.

"It's okay," she'd said quietly and wiggled her toes. I fell in love. Who knows what I would have done if my dad hadn't hacked a cough from the garage door.

"Over here, champ," he'd said. "I need your help."

Maddie had reemerged from the house with one of the boo boo buddies that Mom used with her daycare kids. I was too dazed to think of anything to say, so I mumbled sorry, dropped Angie's foot, and went to my dad.

He had been changing the oil in his Mustang. This was

when he had the cough, but the doctor was still saying it was COPD.

When I got to the garage, he handed me some sockets, a ratchet, and a wrench and told me to put them back while he refilled his wiper fluid. Then he had me lie on the ground and check for leaks while he ran the engine for a minute. It was fine. There were never leaks, but Dad always checked, and he'd do a final dipstick check, too, I think because he liked that evidence of a job well done. At least, that's why I do it now myself.

When he dropped the hood, I figured we were done, but he held me back. I still remember exactly what he said.

"Remind me what grade you are going into again?" he'd asked.

"Ninth."

"And that's high school?"

"Yeah." He knew this. Ninth grade might have been junior high when my granddad was in school, but it'd been high school for a while by the time my dad went. And Dad sure as hell knew what grade I was going into. He talked enough about whether I would make varsity my freshman year or not.

"And what grade is Angie going into?"

"Eighth," I'd said, immediately understanding him.

"And that's middle school?"

"Yeah."

"Yeah," he'd repeated. "She's got enough with that mother of hers. Leave it be." He said no more. He didn't have to.

We cleaned up in silence, and like he always did after we worked on the Mustang together, he asked if I wanted to take it for a spin down to Tollgate Road and back, and of course I did. I ground the gears once or twice, and he pretended not to notice.

My dad was a great guy, and despite how it all turned out, I still take his point. I'd tell my own son the same thing. A high school kid has no business with a middle school girl. Besides, who can say things would have ended up any differently if I'd been able to shoot my shot? I had no game back then. I've got precious little now.

It's been little comfort over the years, but Dad was right. Angie was too young, and her home life was a mess. And wouldn't it be worse if she'd attached herself to me like she did to Tyler? I couldn't carry a whole other person back then, either.

I glare at Tyler's truck, and I swear I could flip it. I've got that much frustration surging through me. I could take it by the grille guard and just flip it end over end. What does he need a grille guard for in this town anyway? Is he driving through a lot of cattle herds on the way to his job at the phone store?

I must make some kind of noise because Shane side-eyes me. "Stop thinking whatever you're thinking," he says. "They've got CCTV." He jerks his head back toward the lodge.

I look behind me. There are two cameras, one aimed at the dumpsters, the other at the parking lot. "I've got a baseball bat in my cab."

Shane snorts. "You think they wouldn't be able to figure out it was you?"

"I'll stand right here. You do the cameras and then go inside. Perfect alibi."

"I'm not vandalizing the Elk Lodge for you, brother." There's already a note in his voice, though, that says he's intrigued. Shane has never met a bad idea he didn't want to get to know better. "So what, are you gonna key it?"

"I've got a dick. I'm not keying a car."

"Gonna bust it up with a bat like that chick in *Footloose*?" Shane grins.

"Not now that you put it like that."

We both sink into contemplation.

"We could move it somewhere," Shane breaks the silence to suggest. "Remember how they got Mr. Prescott's car onto the roof of the gym for senior prank? How'd they do that?"

"It was a Smart Car. They probably carried it up there." And Mr. Prescott looked like he was about to cry the next day. He took it very personally, but if he'd been absent that day, it would have been Ms. Francisco's Fiat. I sigh. "This is stupid."

I should go inside, find Mom, excuse myself, and go get wasted. Again. A piece of my liver might still be working after last night.

Shane bumps me with his elbow. "What we should do is load it on a ship."

"Send it to Dakar." My lips curve.

"Switch out the VIN plate with some old beater and just drive it on. It's a nice truck. Whoever picks it up on the other end isn't going to say shit."

We both grow silent again, considering the logistics. It's doable.

"It wouldn't solve anything," I finally say, filing the idea away.

"Yeah," Shane agrees. "He's definitely insured." He uses his finger to wipe the last of the icing off his plate and then crumples it in his hand. "I'm gonna go see if there's any chicken left. Coming?"

I grunt. We both give Tyler's truck one long, last look, and we're heading in when a kid comes tripping out the back door, his nose stuck in his phone. It's the punk who was recording during the vows. All of a sudden, my frustration has an outlet.

I cast Shane a look, and we've been in enough tight spots together that he can read me like a book by now. He grins.

We step into the kid's path.

He nearly runs into me before he notices that I'm blocking his way.

"What the fuck?" He's probably eighteen or nineteen, and he's taller than me, but I outweigh him by forty pounds. He's fit, but he's also got that nice, gooped-up hair that guys have when they care a lot about what people think. In my experience, guys with nice, gooped-up hair aren't keen to do anything that'll mess it up.

"Delete the video," I tell him.

"I don't know what you're talking about." He tries to sidestep me, but like I said, I'm bigger. I'm also quicker. He barely stops himself from colliding into me.

"You were recording during the ceremony. Delete it."

"Can't, man. I was live. It's out there now. The internet's forever." He shrugs.

I hate this kid. A punch in the face would do him good, but he's so dumb. It'd feel like punching a gerbil.

I pluck the phone from his hand. It's locked. I frown. He smirks. I hold it up to his face. It unlocks. Bingo.

"Hey, you can't do that!" He swipes for the phone, but his reflexes suck. And this is the kid who makes influencer money from dirt bike stunts? They must be videos of him wiping out. I'd pay to watch that.

I flip through screens. His background is a huge pair of fake tits. It's hard to focus on the apps with so much nipple.

"Where'd you post it?" I ask. "I know you saved it."

"Fuck you."

I tap the gear icon and cock my head. "Do we need to reset this thing to factory settings?"

I watch his expression as his shittiness goes to war with

his laziness. Downloading everything again is a pain in the ass.

"Don't do it, man," he finally huffs. "The video's already out there. You can't put the ship back in the bottle."

"It's the *genie* in the bottle, dumbass," Shane pipes up.

"Same difference," he mumbles.

"It really isn't." Shane shakes his head.

I glare at the kid. He stares sulkily upward.

"Fine." He snatches the phone back. His fingers fly, and then he holds it up way too close to my face.

Angie is frozen on the screen in her pretty dress, her face twisted and red like she's been slapped. My guts cramp.

"See?" He taps the garbage can. Then he pulls the video up on another app and repeats the process. Twice. "You know there's such a thing as freedom of speech, man," he mutters as he does it. "This is bullshit."

"Sue me," I say, taking the phone, opening his recent apps, and scrolling a ways to make sure I don't see anything but dirt bikes and his ugly mug talking to the camera.

When I hand the phone back, his fingers fly. Looks like he's changing from facial recognition to a password. Smart. "Tyler's the one who chose to make an ass of himself. You shouldn't get in the way of natural consequences, man," he grumbles.

"Angie didn't choose that," Shane says, stepping out of the kid's way.

The kid raises an eyebrow. "Didn't she?" He slides his phone back into the pocket of his tight pants. "Well, fuck you both," he says, flips us off, and strides off to his souped-up Civic.

Shane and I watch him peel out onto Sollers Point Road, only to immediately get stopped by the red light at the fire station. We grin at each other.

"I like him," Shane says. "I'd totally watch him wreck his bike in his mommy's backyard."

"Aren't you related?" I ask him. Shane's here because he's related to Tyler somehow. He was seated on the other side of the aisle for the ceremony.

"Aren't we all?"

I snort. It's true. If we're not related by blood, then we are by marriage or by virtue of our parents being friends since kindergarten. We live in a small town at the edge of a big city which none of us ever visit except for ball games and clubbing. Folks never move away, and they marry early and often. Eventually we're all gonna have six toes like Ernest Hemingway's cats.

"Chicken and beer?" Shane suggests, nodding toward the hall.

I nod, and we head back inside. The first thing I see is Mom and Randy drunkenly dancing to Toto's "Rosana." Randy's wife isn't paying them the least bit of attention, having a grand old time getting blitzed with her girlfriends. The ladies are three sheets to the wind, going by the debris radius of high heels around their chairs.

I get myself a beer and a plate of chicken. I eat standing. No one bothered to roll out the banquet tables. Whoever's working the event left things how they were for the ceremony and just brought out the food. Folks have rearranged the chairs, clearing a dance floor and a space for the kids to run and chase each other.

Honestly, the vibe is better than a lot of weddings. The muscles in my neck and back slowly relax. For the first time in months, I don't feel sick to my stomach. The nausea has been replaced by a gnawing need.

I need to see her.

Go to her. Shake her and ask her what the hell she's been thinking all these years. Kiss her. Throw her on my bed and tear off her clothes and fuck her until time goes backwards.

I want to have had the balls at sixteen to go after her.

I want to go back and pay attention in English class so I'd know what words to use.

I haven't lost her, but I've never had her, either. I have no idea how to make that happen.

Or if I should even try.

My brain knows that she didn't do this *to* me, but damn if it doesn't *feel* like she did.

I'm standing here, picking a piece of rubbery chicken clean, watching the balloon arch slowly tilt over until a kid decides to try and run through it like the ribbon at a finishing line. The balloons fold around his waist, and he tears around the hall, ducking the hands reaching out as he passes to try and pop his fun.

He's going to lose it sooner or later, to gravity or another kid's plastic fork, but he doesn't slow down. The grin of victory does not fade from his face until Randy grabs the arch from him and drapes it around Mom's neck like a boa.

Like I said, Randy's a dick.

The boy stands in the middle of the dance floor, shoulders heaving as he catches his breath, a dumb smile still plastered on his face. He might have fallen back to earth, but damn it, he almost touched the sun.

Falling is easy when you're young.

I'm not a kid anymore.

I can't be pressed about a grown woman with two kids because once upon a time she wiggled her toes and looked at me like I was her hero. That's insane.

I finish my beer and set it on a ledge. Later, when Mom corrals me so that she can drunkenly rehash the entire debacle like I wasn't there, I act like I don't notice when the kid skulks over to drain the dregs. I did the same at his age, at weddings and wakes in this same hall. Hope he likes backwash.

It's insane to be in love with Angie Miller, even now, after all these years, but I don't know what else to call this tightness in my chest.

And as the drunken debacle unfolding around me attests, she's got some shit to work out.

I say bye to Mom and make sure she has a sober ride home, and then I bail. When I'm walking out, the arch is on the floor, and kids are dropping to their butts to pop the balloons, one by one.

Not sure exactly how, but it seems symbolic.

3

ANGIE

"I CAN'T BELIEVE THAT PIECE OF SHIT TOOK THE AIR conditioners out of the windows." Madison shakes her arm like she's got bugs on it. A piece of newspaper is stuck to her skin. Her sweat is making the ink bleed.

I peel the paper off for her and ball it up, tucking it in the corner of the box with the dishes. We don't have enough of anything to waste. I'm using pillowcases to pack the girls' clothes and laundry baskets for their toys.

"They're in the garage," I explain.

Tyler was being spiteful. Packing in a ninety-five-degree house with no fans might be miserable, but he was the one who had to take the units out, and he's going to have to put them back in, and it's going to be even hotter next week. If I were petty like him, I'd have thought of something easier on myself.

"I'm gonna cut the cords off 'em before we leave." Madison hops up on the counter and starts grabbing canned goods and pasta from the top shelf.

"Don't. I'm trying to keep things civil." I pluck a plastic bag out of the butt of the stuffed bunny holder hanging from the pantry's door knob and start bagging. It feels so much like when Madison and I played grocery store when we were kids. She was always the customer, and I was always the checker.

My eyes tear up a little. They've been doing that a lot the past few days.

"How are you gonna keep things civil?" Madison pants. "He's kicking the girls and you out of the house."

"It's his house." The mortgage is in his name, and his parents co-signed.

After the debacle at the Elks Lodge, Tyler decided to go hunting with his boys since he'd already taken time off for our honeymoon. He said he wanted me out by the time he came back. I canceled the hotel I'd booked for us at the ocean. Since it was last minute, I didn't get a refund.

"They're *his* kids," Madison argues as she moves down to the next shelf. She's a machine once she gets going.

"He said the girls could stay."

"And he's gonna dress 'em and feed 'em and schlep 'em around?" Madison snorts.

"I don't want to take the girls away from their father." I didn't plan for any of this, and even though it's been five days, the magnitude keeps hitting me out of nowhere like birds crashing into clean windows.

I left my fiancé at the altar. The father of my children. The only man I've ever been with.

I did that. Me. Angie Miller. It feels like another person did it, and now I've got to pick up her mess. And pack it. In ninety-five-degree heat with no air conditioning.

What am I doing?

Miss Dawn is letting the girls and me move into her basement for now, but I'll need to rent an apartment eventually, and I've never rented a place in my name before. I don't know my credit score, but it can't be good. My limit is five thousand dollars, and it's been maxed out since I bought the dress.

I'm on Tyler's parents' cell phone plan. What happens with that?

Ivy has a follow-up with the ENT, and Tyler said he'd take off work early to drive us since it's downtown, and I suck at downtown driving. Is he still going to do that?

He's leaving my texts on read, and I'm too much of a coward to call him.

"Hey, girl." Madison squats on the counter and grabs my chin. "No freaking out now. The hard part is over."

Tears are streaming down my sweaty cheeks. When did I start crying?

"Ivy has an ENT appointment next Thursday downtown," I wail through the blubber.

"That sucks," Madison says, wiping my face with the backs of her hands, smooshing my cheeks up so my lips curve upward. "I hate driving downtown."

"And I've got a dentist appointment next Friday at four. Who's going to watch the girls?"

"Mom will." Miss Dawn's not only Madison's mom, she's also the girls' daycare mother, but I always get them by three thirty so she can get to pickleball.

"She's already doing so much for me."

"She loves you."

"I love her, too." I'm really bawling now. Snot drips down my upper lip. I fumble to rip a paper towel from the roll and wipe it up. "I'm a mess."

"Yes, but your head is out of your ass now, and it's such an improvement. I can see *you* again." Madison flashes me her wide, crooked-toothed smile, and I want to hug her so hard that her seeds come out. Her freckled face is tomato red, her copper pigtails are limp and stringy, and she's the most beautiful person on the planet.

We've been friends since the first day of kindergarten when we both sat in the seat right behind the driver on the first day. I sat there because I was terrified. She sat there so she wouldn't hit any of the boys if they annoyed her.

She's always been there for me. When my dad bailed, when my mom passed, when I came up pregnant with Tamblyn—she's always been there to grab my hand and drag me along until I could keep going under my own steam. I do the same for her, but she doesn't need me much. Life doesn't happen to her. She happens to it.

"I love you." I tug a red pigtail.

"I love you back," she says, holding up a can of chick-peas. "Did you know this is expired?"

I shrug a shoulder.

"I'm gonna leave it right here for Tyler in easy reach. So he can die of salmonella."

"That man hasn't knowingly eaten a chickpea in his life." I take the can and toss it in the trash. I don't want revenge, and I don't want my baby girls to lose their father.

I pop my eyes real wide so I don't break down crying again. There's no time for it. Tyler has work on Monday, so he'll be back tomorrow for sure. I spent too long feeling sorry for myself and eating chips on the sofa in the base-ment, cuddling with the girls, and now I'm under a time crunch. Good thing I do my best work under pressure.

Madison and I finish up in the kitchen, carrying boxes and bags out to the front lawn as we go so that we can see what we've accomplished, and what we have left to do. The girls' stuff is already out there.

I summon up the courage to pack my things next. I've been sleeping in Tamblyn's bed because I can't bear being in the master bedroom. It smells like Tyler, and it's not a stinky smell or anything, but it makes me feel nauseous and sad and panicky.

I had no idea that I was going to break up with him. I didn't even realize that was what I was doing when I made my little speech at the altar. I might have been the one who broke us up, but it came out of nowhere. I blindsided myself.

I straighten my spine, open the door, and breathe through my mouth. I just need to work quickly.

I'd packed our bags for the honeymoon, so I dump Tyler's things onto the bed and fill up the second suitcase with my winter clothes. I'm trying to take only things that belong to the girls and me, but after so long, I don't remember who bought the luggage. Since it's name brand, it was probably a gift from his mother.

It takes a few trips to bring everything down from upstairs, and with no air circulating, I'm a limp dishrag by the time I collapse on the front lawn under the young maple. I planted it myself when we moved in, and I started a tradition of taking pictures of the girls in front of it each season to track their growth. The tree is still pegged to the ground with strings.

Madison trudges out, somehow managing to carry the girls' entire play kitchen on her back. She drops it and plops herself on top of the plastic stove.

"Girl, how are we going to get all of this to Mom's in those two vehicles?" She hikes her thumb at our two subcompact beaters.

"Multiple trips, I guess. How are we going to get the girls' furniture down from upstairs?" I've accepted that I'm going to have to buy something cheap off the internet for myself, but my daughters' bedroom set was mine when I was a girl. It's well-made, and it's all I've got left of the house I grew up in. It would kill me to leave it, but it's really heavy.

"Who do we know who isn't at work on a Friday?" Madison asks.

No one.

I sigh, blowing out my cheeks, and slump back on my elbows under the patch of shade from the tree.

It's my fault that it's down to Madison and me in the ninety-degree heat. If I'd faced reality sooner, I might have been able to recruit some help, but I didn't want to ask anyone for a favor after wasting their time last Saturday at the wedding that didn't happen, so I stuck my head in the sand. Story of my life.

"Maybe Tyler will help me move it later," I say.

Madison snorts.

I open my mouth, about to argue that he might—it's such a habit, insisting that next time he might be different, like optimism, only sad—but I'm cut off by a familiar black truck pulling up in front of the house. It's a beast, the kind with a full-size bed and a second row of real seats, not just a bench.

Brandon hops out. His tan work boots hit the asphalt with a solid thud. He's a solid man.

My stomach gets weird.

I remember when he was a gangly beanpole, but he's been full grown for years now. I don't think I'll ever get used to it. It's like the kid I knew is wearing a permanent muscle suit. The pencil neck and huge puppy feet are gone, and now there's this man who makes me fidgety and awkward.

I tug at my shorts and then at the hem of my shirt. I don't know why. They're not short or riding up or anything. I'm just nervous.

Brandon frankly intimidates me now. When we were kids, he was part of the scenery, eating his cereal on the sofa or bouncing his lacrosse ball against the side of Miss Dawn's cinderblock garage, over and over for hours. Even in high school, he wasn't the type to draw attention, not like Tyler. He never had much to say, and everyone was cool with him, but no one talked about him. I was never unaware of him, but he didn't make me feel like he does now.

Like I need to squirm. And straighten up.

After graduation, he joined his uncle's gang down at the port, and now he's a longshoreman in the union. He makes a hundred thousand dollars a year after overtime with no college degree and only five years' seniority. When Madison told me, I mentioned it to Tyler, but apparently, you have to know someone to get the job, and I guess Brandon didn't feel like he knew Tyler like that.

Anyway, Brandon doesn't blend in now, not with that truck and those wide shoulders. Girls who know that I'm friends with Madison ask about him. I tell them I don't know if he's with anyone. He keeps to himself.

He's probably with someone. With the way he looks and all.

I smooth my hair, but it's hopeless. This morning, it was a messy bun, but by now it must look like I'm coming off a bender.

Brandon starts toward us, and I rise on shaky legs. I need to eat something decent. I've been living off chips, dip, and cookie batter ice cream for days.

After a few steps in our direction, he must realize he's still wearing his neon reflective vest, so he stops, peels it off, and tosses it into the bed of his truck. His biceps flex as he raises his arms over his head. His crisp white T-shirt rides up just enough to flash a strip of tan skin right above his belt and the muscle there. The obliques. My heart thumps.

Somehow, my mouth is watering, and I'm thirsty as hell.

He's wearing polarized sunglasses and a ball cap. Brown curls sneak out the back of the hat, damp and sticking to his neck. He's tan like a working man, as if it's not just the sun that's got him, but plenty of wind and dirt, too. Not that he's dirty. Well, no more than he ever is after working a ship. It's dirty work.

I see him sometimes at Miss Dawn's when I pick the girls up late, and he's coming over for dinner straight after a shift. He doesn't make a habit of it, but when Miss Dawn makes her kielbasa and pierogies, she lets him know, and he's sure to come over. She brags on it, how her home cooking brings him around.

He also mows her lawn and does whatever else she needs around the house. She brags on that, too, as well she should. He's a good son to her. He's a good brother, too, coming to help his little sister's friend move.

He doesn't say anything until he's right in the middle of the mess of boxes, pillowcases, laundry baskets, shopping bags, and plastic tubs. He surveys it all, his square jaw tight like always, and says, "Is the furniture all that's left inside?"

"Yeah," Madison answers for me. For some reason, I can't. My throat is stuck.

Tyler's vows ring in my ears. *I promise to give it to you hard and take your shit with a smile, and if I can't, to take your shit out to the front lawn for you.*

I don't like how Brandon can see all my stuff spread out on the ground. As if I've been thrown out. I don't like that he can see how little I've got when it's all laid out, and how everything is scuffed or grubby or worn.

I would've thought all my pride had been stripped from me at the Elks Lodge, but I guess I've got some left.

I shouldn't care. Brandon's an old friend. At least we've known each other for most of our lives. I should be grateful Madison called him, not worried that he can see all my half-used, soap-scummy shampoo and conditioner bottles thrown on top of a hamper filled with clean towels and a dirty shower curtain.

"I-Is this your lunch hour?" I ask, walking toward the

house, away from my stuff. He follows. He has to shorten his steps since his stride is easily twice as long as mine.

"The ship's done," he says. "I don't have to go back."

A little weight lifts from my shoulders. "Thank you," I say softly, holding the screen door open for him.

He grunts, ducks inside, and surveys the first floor. He always looks serious, but right now, his face is downright mean. Scary. I glance around, trying to see what's pissing him off.

We've already cleared out the living room. Half of the family pics are down from the walls. I left Tyler his share, as well as the old pics of his grandparents and him as a kid that I had framed for Christmas one year.

I took the curios that were mine from the cabinet, but I left the candles and potpourri bowl and whatnots. There's not much room in Miss Dawn's basement for decorations.

Is that why Brandon looks so pissed? Does he think he's going to have to wait for me to pack?

"Everything I'm taking is already in boxes out front," I tell him.

He scowls even more. "What about the TV and the couch and the rest of it?"

"That's all staying."

He glares at the entertainment center. It's Tyler's baby. He's got different shelves for his various game systems, and there's a really nice soundbar that I bought for his twenty-first birthday. The TV is ninety-eight inches.

Brandon sneers at it like it's a pile of wet dog shit.

"I just really need help with the girls' furniture." I start to lead him upstairs, but he walks over to the TV and peers around the back to check out the wires. Why are all men so obsessed with electronics?

"That's staying," I repeat over my shoulder, my foot on the bottom step.

"Tyler paid for it?" Brandon doesn't look at me when he asks; he's too busy tracing the cords with his fingers.

Yes, Tyler did. He maxed out the Visa with it. He bought a TV, and I ended up having to work out a payment plan with the hospital for the bill from having Ivy. It was a huge fight at the time.

"Yeah," I say, staring at the carpet under the toe of my sneaker. "Can we just get the girls' stuff?"

He's clearly reluctant, but he walks away from the electronics and follows me up the steps, treading close on my heels. He smells like oil and sweat and the cheap dryer sheets that come in an orange box. The higher I climb, the harder it gets to breathe. Upstairs, the air is as thick and warm as cream of crab soup.

"How come it's so hot?" he asks. His voice rumbles next to my ear, and a shiver skates down my spine.

"No AC," I say, picking up the pace down the narrow hall, praying he doesn't ask why. I don't want to say what Tyler did. I don't want to see how easy it'll be for Brandon to believe that Tyler would do such a thing. Or the pity and judgment in his eyes.

I don't want to *be* the kind of woman who would stick with such a petty man for so many years.

But I am. I was.

Another wave of realization crashes over me, draining the blood from my head. I was a clinger. I clung.

It's like I deferred all the shame from the shit I ate to be with Tyler, and payment came due at one time, in this moment, in this hundred-degree hallway, with Brandon Kaczmarek on my heels. I try to keep walking, but my knees buckle, and I reach out to touch the hallway wall to steady myself.

Brandon's hand finds my lower back, firm and sure. My breath catches. I take another, more confident step, and his hand falls. The shock of the brief touch clears my mind.

I can't drown in self-loathing, not right now. I have things to do. It's moving day, for Christ's sake.

At the girls' room, I open the door for him to go through first. He ducks his head and enters. There's no clutter in here to make him testy, if that's what was bugging him downstairs. Except for a random doll shoe on the floor and some stickers on the wall, the only things left in here are the tall dresser, the desk with a hutch, and the bunk bed.

Brandon slaps a palm on the bunk bed as if he can gauge its heft that way, and his brow furrows. My heart sinks. I've been deluding myself again. There's no way Brandon and I can carry it down the stairs ourselves, even if Madison and I both take an end together. It's solid pine and bulky besides. Tyler's boys helped him get it up, and as I recall, there was a lot of cussing and bitching.

My eyes well, but I'm not worried that Brandon will notice. Every inch of my skin is dripping with sweat. Beads trickle down my cheeks and spine and the backs of my knees. Tears won't show.

"I guess it'll have to stay for now." I sigh.

"Why do you say that?" Brandon asks, his voice weirdly sharp.

I tense. I cross my arms, my skin so slick that they slip-slide together. "It's too heavy for the two of us."

He takes off his hat, runs his fingers through his damp hair, and jams the hat back on again. His entire body is tight with frustration—his jaw, his shoulders, his arms, straight as a soldier's at his sides.

"You always give up too easy," he mutters. He's not even looking at me. He's glaring at the light switch beside the girls' desk.

The words crack against my raw feelings like a slap out

of nowhere. Brandon doesn't talk to me like this. He says *pass the butter* and *don't take Oakview home, there's black ice at the bottom of the hill* and *looks like your front right tire's low* and things like that. He's never sniped at me before.

He probably resents being here when he got off work early. I get that, but still, it's not fair to say I give up easy.

"I don't," I say, loud, so he knows I'm not letting the comment go. I always let things go, but not this time. I *don't* give up easy. I stick with things well past when I should let them go. I force it to work when a smarter, braver woman would walk away. "Are you saying that because of what I did at the wedding?"

Somehow, he draws himself up until he's even more imposing and tense. "I'm not talking about that."

"Because that wasn't giving up. That was speaking up for myself."

"I know," he says through clenched teeth. "I wasn't talking about that."

"Then what are you talking about?"

He exhales, very long and very slow. He's playing for time, but it's hellishly hot up here, and I'm bone-tired, and I want him to explain himself since he felt the need to make a remark.

"Forget I said anything."

Tyler would do that—say something mean and then refuse to clarify so I'd have to live with it rolling around in my brain with no recourse except to argue against him, silently, to myself, in the shower and on the drive to work.

"I don't need you criticizing me, Brandon Kaczmarek." I don't need *any* of this. I need to get this furniture down the stairs. I need to get everything over to Miss Dawn's and take over with the girls so she can get to pickleball. I need to take a cold shower and cry some more and figure out what I'm going to do now with the rest of my entire freaking life.

Oh, hell, this sweat fucking *tickles.* I dash it from my face with my hands and wipe my hands on my shirt. There's no help for it. It's either that or flick the drops off my fingers.

I firm my wobbling chin and glare at the thin gold chain that dangles from Brandon's tan throat and disappears under his collar. It's a cross. It's always swinging loose, and he's forever tucking it back into his shirt.

He's silent for a long moment. I refuse to meet his eyes. He can think whatever he wants about me. I can't stop him. I can't even get my feet to move from this spot.

The quiet in the room is crushing. The heat is brutal, the air is unbreathable, and I'm furious, but for some reason, for the first time in so long I can't remember, I don't feel totally, hopelessly alone.

Long past when I expect him to say anything, he coughs, catches my eye, and mutters, "I'm sorry."

I wait for the next bit—the *but*—but he doesn't say anything else. Instead, he busies himself, fetching his phone from his pocket and dialing while he experiments with his free hand, trying to lift the upper bunk from the pins that attach it to the bottom. His bicep bulges, the veins popping, but he can't lift it more than a half inch.

Someone answers his call. A muffled man's voice barks, "Yeah?"

Brandon says, "What's up? Can you and Shane come help me with something?"

The guy must say yes because Brandon rattles off my address. The conversation lasts no more than twenty seconds total.

He puts his phone away, and after a long, unreadable glance, he says, "Don't worry. It's handled."

"I'm not worried," I shoot back for some reason.

I don't know why I'm trying to fight him. He's here. He's

trying to help. I brace myself for him to sass me back. I've got it coming.

He steps toward me, digging in his back pocket. He stops when the steel toes of his boots are almost touching the rubber toes of my sneakers. He's got a blue paisley bandana in his hand. It's folded in a neat square.

"I didn't mean that you give up easy. That came out wrong. I meant that you accept bad shit too easy." As he speaks, gruff and short, he shoves the bandana into my hand.

I stare down at it numbly. "You carry a handkerchief in your pocket?"

"Yeah."

"Because you're fancy like that?" I don't know why I'm teasing. Maybe to cover up the fact that a wild mess is erupting low in my belly. He's really close. My nose is inches away from the pulse fluttering at the base of his neck.

"Because I've got manners." He grabs my wrist and raises my hand to my forehead, guiding me to blot the sweat away. I let him. The bandana smells like the dryer sheets he uses, too.

He stares down at me, and I stare up. His bottomless dark brown eyes give me vertigo. They turn my legs to jelly.

I shake my head. "If you did, you wouldn't have said that about me taking crap too easy."

"I suppose you're right." He rests his hand lightly over mine and draws it from my forehead to my cheek, along my jaw, down my neck. His hands are so much bigger than mine. They seem like a giant's in comparison.

"It's not your business—what I accept or don't or how easy." I don't know why I'm still arguing. I'm not mad anymore. I'm not sure what I'm feeling. It's like standing at the edge of the high dive. Like the slow climb to the very top of the roller coaster. It's fear, but the kind that makes your belly twist and fizzle.

Brandon lets my hand go, and it falls limp to my side. He keeps his hand raised, though. He traces the trail his bandana patted along my jaw. His thumb pad is rough, and like magic, the roughness stokes shivers that skate across my skin.

I want to nuzzle my cheek into his palm. I want to accept what he's offering. I want to care for someone and know they care for me. I don't want to be alone.

Because I'm a clinger. And a coward. And I can't afford to be anymore.

I step back, ducking my face away.

He lowers his hand and inhales, his nostrils flaring. He jerks his gaze away, over my shoulder, and scowls into the middle distance. His jaw tics. He's not happy, but for some reason, I don't have that immediate urge to placate him like I have with Tyler.

A young, gleeful part of myself that hasn't reared its head in a long, long time—the part that delights in splashing in puddles and stomping mushrooms and cracking eggs—that part *loves* that I got a reaction from him. That part wants to see what's inside of him. What he's really made of.

But there's no time for that. I made my bed. Now I have to lie in it. It's moving day. I'm moving on.

"You sure you don't want that TV?" he asks, breaking the silence and changing the subject.

"It's not mine."

"But do you want it?"

"I don't want to start any more trouble."

I steel myself and wait for him to push it, to come at me like his sister does. *You can't let people walk all over you. You've got to stand up for yourself. If you don't value yourself, no one else will.*

"Okay," he says. There's no hint of disapproval in his voice or his expression. "All you want is the furniture in here?"

"Yeah. That's all I want."

"Nothing else you'll miss?" he asks. He stares down at me, and his eyes are piercing, alive with something I've never seen before. I'm not stupid; I know he's saying more than he's saying, but I don't know what he wants me to say.

Will I miss this house? This life?

I don't know. None of this feels real. I'm not brave enough for this thing I've done.

I want to go back in time. I want another shot at growing up, a chance to figure life out before it happens to me. I want to be strong and sure and good at life like him. I want so many things, but no, there's nothing I'll miss here.

I flash him a weak smile and drag myself out of the sucking whirlpool of my self-pity. "Nothing but the maple tree in the front yard, but that's got to stay."

His harsh mouth softens at the corners. "Don't worry about this. It's handled," he says again, low and quiet and certain. And then, after the slightest beat, he adds, "Angie."

My name.

I don't know if he was going to start a new sentence, or if the word is supposed to mean something on its own, but it steals the breath from my lungs.

How is this different?

He must have said my name a thousand times.

But not like this.

For a long second, all I can do is drown in his solemn, calm, deep brown eyes. How is it that I've known him forever, but I've never *seen* him before?

Why *now* when I'm about as low as a person can get?

A thud sounds from downstairs, and Madison yelps. Brandon and I both blink and bristle as if we're coming out of a trance.

He coughs and shoves his hands in his pockets. "You can start putting shit in your car," he says to me. "I've got this."

He doesn't have to tell me twice. I scurry away like a scared little mouse and focus on what needs doing.

His boys show up before Madison and I make our first trip, piling out of a truck even bigger than Brandon's, smelling like Coors Banquet Beer, Marlboros, and bay water. They must've been fishing. It takes them two trips and fifteen minutes to get the girls' furniture down, and then they dip their chins at me, slap Brandon's shoulder, and drive off, I suppose to meet him at Miss Dawn's house.

I don't meet his eye, but when he starts piling the rest of my stuff into the leftover space in his truck bed, I help. I hand baskets and boxes and bags up to him, and he arranges it like Tetris and straps it all down when we're done.

"See you at the house," he says to me, staring at the lawn a few feet in front of my shoes.

"Yeah," I say. "Thank you again."

He grunts at me, and then he's gone. I stand there, stupid from the heat, trying to remember what I need to do next, when Madison comes to stand beside me.

She lays her sweaty face on my shoulder. I rest my head on hers. Brandon turns left at the four-way stop at the bottom of the street, and we sigh in unison.

"It's been a long day," I say.

"We're ordering pizza from Squire's when we're done, and you're paying." She nudges my arm with her elbow.

"I will," I promise. "And thank you for calling Brandon to help. I would've had to leave the bunk beds and probably the rest, too."

Madison takes a step forward, puts her hands on her hips, and arches her back to stretch. "I didn't call him," she says, smirking at me as she bends over to pick up a little girl's ballet slipper that must've fallen out of a basket. "I thought he had work today. He just showed up."

And because Madison Kaczmarek is the best friend a person could have, she strolls off to the car so I have time to digest that information and wipe the dumbfounded expression off my face.

4

BRANDON

When I pull up to Mom's, it's five o'clock, and Angie's car isn't in the driveway. She should have gotten off at three. She's been living with Mom for a couple months now, and she's got a routine.

Maybe she stopped by the store. Or the gym. Shane said he saw her down at Flex Fitness. He said she's working on a glow up, whatever the fuck that means.

I park behind Mom so Angie has a space close to the door. In case she went to the store.

The lawn could use some attention. The grass isn't too high—we haven't been getting much rain—but the edges need trimming. I'll come by with the weedwhacker this weekend.

I jog down to the mailbox in case Mom hasn't cleared it out lately. She'll let mail stack up until the flap won't hardly shut. She claims she gets everything by email now, and the post office is just leaving trash for her to throw out. The government still sends shit by snail mail, though, and she won't be too happy when they put a bench warrant out on her for skipping jury duty.

By some miracle, the box is empty. Angie's probably

been getting the mail. Mom says she's been a real help around the house, making dinner and doing all the laundry since she's living in the basement.

She even ran Mom's collection of dead batteries out to the dump on the north side of the county to recycle. I thought Mom was never gonna let them go. Pretty sure the batteries from the light saber I got for Christmas in first grade were in that haul. I loved that thing. It was like a nightlight, but I could hit shit with it.

I trip up the front steps and rap a few times on the screen door frame as I let myself in.

"In the kitchen!" Mom calls from the other end of the house.

I poke my head in the living room before I head back. Tamblyn and Ivy are perched on the edge of the sofa, skinny legs dangling, barefoot, with their mouths hanging open as they watch a cartoon with a lady in a ball gown and a white horse. Ivy has her whole hand shoved in her mouth, and Tamblyn's worrying the tip of her braid.

"Hi, Brandon," Tamblyn says without tearing her eyes away from what looks like a big moment for the lady and the horse. Ivy mumbles something, probably hi, but it's hard to tell around the hand in her mouth.

"Come back when this episode is over, okay?" Tamblyn says, then squeals as the lady leaps from a cliff to escape a stampeding bull, rescued in very good time and with a great deal of style by the horse, which suddenly sprouts glittery wings.

"Yes, ma'am," I tell her. I know when I'm outshone.

Tamblyn and Ivy are good girls. Tamblyn can smell bullshit from a mile away and has exactly zero patience for it, and Ivy could find a needle in a haystack if you asked her, just a real uncanny ability to remember where shit is and where it goes. My dad would've loved her. His biggest gripe in life was people not putting his stuff back in its place.

I get a whiff of Crock-Pot barbeque before I hit the kitchen, and my stomach rumbles. Lunch feels like a long time ago.

Mom is sitting at the table, watching one of her court shows on the little TV on the counter and drinking a beer. Her coupons are spread out in front of her in little stacks like monopoly money.

"No pickleball today?" I ask as I drop a kiss on her upturned cheek.

"Angie picked up a second shift. I told her I'd watch the girls."

"She let you?" Angie looks visibly sick whenever she thinks she even might possibly be putting someone out.

Mom shrugs. "I told her my wrist hurts, and I was staying home anyway."

"Does it?" Mom's got arthritis everywhere. It's hard to keep up with what's troubling her on any given day.

"If it doesn't now, I'm sure it will later."

"Is it bad?"

"Not as bad as a kick in the head." She winks at me. "Take care of this, would you, and get me a fresh one?" She hands me her empty bottle.

I help myself to a cold one when I fetch hers. "You're running low."

"I've got a case out in the garage," she says. I'll have to bring it in before I leave.

Mom never used to drink beer. She was more of a Bartles and James kind of girl when we were growing up, but when Dad passed, she finished off his Miller Lites from the fridge, and I guess it gave her a taste for it.

I sit at the table, pop both our caps off, plunk her bottle

in a free space between coupon stacks, and push my chair back so I can stretch my legs.

"I'll keep an eye on the girls if you want to go now," I offer. It's Friday night, and Mom's pickleball gang generally ends up at the Seahorse Inn for karaoke afterwards. It's good for her to get out.

She purses her lips and gives me a sharp look. I sigh and take a long swig. I guess we're gonna do this again.

"It's Friday night," she says.

"Yeah. Karaoke night down at the Seahorse." I play dumb.

She narrows her eyes. She knows that I'm well aware of what she's getting at. "You're twenty-five years old," she says.

"Last I checked."

"You don't need to be sitting around here."

"Got nowhere else to be." I settle back in my chair.

"*You* could be down at the Seahorse."

"Crowd's kind of old for me. Besides, you know I can't sing."

"You know what I mean."

I shrug. I understand her position. She's made herself clear enough times.

She lets out a long sigh and glances toward the doorway. Faint cartoon voices filter down the hall. She leans forward and plants her elbows on the table without regard to the structural integrity of her coupon stacks.

"How long are you planning to wait?" she asks.

I misunderstand her on purpose. "I figure if Angie gets off at eleven, she'll be here by half past."

Mom's face hardens. She means business. "You know damn well what I mean. I love Angie. You know that. She hasn't had an easy time of it. That mother of hers..." Mom could never bring herself to finish her opinion of Lisa Miller, not even when the woman was alive.

There is no one lower in Mom's eyes than a bad mother. Lisa Miller was a drunk, and towards the end, an addict, so to Mom, everything about her is just unspeakable. Still, the woman was Angie's mother, and Angie loved her. I keep my opinions off my face when her name comes up. Mom can't.

"That girl never had a fair chance, what with that loser of a father bailing before she was even in school." Mom shakes her head. "I always said there should have been some kind of program at that school for at-risk girls like her. Someone should have done something."

I should have beat the shit out of Tyler Reynolds the first time he looked at her.

"Well, that's all water under the bridge now, and I'm so proud of her for making a fresh start, but baby, she's got a long road ahead of her. She stuck with Tyler for *years*. She *worked* to keep that piece of shit. She is not a good bet. If you keep waiting on her, you could very well be waiting forever."

I shrug. "I'm only twenty-five. I got time." I give her a wink, willing her to drop it, but she's just tipsy enough that she's like a dog with a bone.

"Yeah, *twenty-five*." She lowers her voice. "You know I love those girls like my own, but are you *sure* that you want a ready-made family? Are you one hundred percent *sure* that you want to raise some other man's kids? Are you ready to deal with that drama for the rest of your life? Because it isn't fair to Angie or those girls if you realize after the fact that that's *not* what you want."

I know. Not like I haven't had the thought a few dozen times. Still, I'm here.

She reaches over and grabs my hand. "Baby, I just want the best for you and Angie, and I want you to really think about what you'd be giving up. Nothing is going to be new. You won't be the first walk down the aisle, the first baby daddy." She pauses a moment and smiles like she's distracted herself. "I'll never forget your father's face when the doctor held you up for him to cut the cord."

"Yeah?"

"He looked like 'What the hell do I do with this thing?' I was sure he was gonna puke." Mom grins, her eyes far away. "I want that for you."

"You want me to puke?"

"You know what I mean, smartass."

I do, but she's seeing it her way, not mine. If it were anyone else, I'd leave it be. In general, I'm not pressed about whether or not folks agree with me. But Mom's got to drop this. I don't change my mind on other people's say-so.

"Remember the Charger?" I ask her.

She snorts. "How could I forget?"

"Remember how it cost twice as much as a brand-new Challenger, and it needed a new transmission besides?"

"Yeah, and new chassis and brakes. I remember." Mom is still salty that Dad's good friend Bob Bantock sold me a piece of shit. I was never able to convince her that the car was a deal despite the work it needed. It was an '87 Shelby.

"I wanted the Charger." I give her a small smile. "I got the Charger."

She bristles in her seat, uncharmed. "Well, you might've loved that car, but you ended up selling it to buy the Ram."

"Yeah," I say softly 'cause that's my point. "Because I figure I might need a vehicle with a second row."

If I thought Mom would roll over and take the point, I wouldn't know her like I do. She crosses her arms, her thin lips spearing down. "You know that your stubbornness is no guarantee things are gonna work out with her, and another thing, you both need to be clear that she wants *you*, not a daddy for those girls or a way out of my basement."

I don't reply. I just look at her and wait. Soon enough, her better nature wins out, and she blows out a sigh, her shoulders lowering. "You know I don't say that because I don't love her. But she's struggling, and she'd be stupid not to go for a good man if he was going to rescue her with his big ol' truck and its second-row seat. If you weren't the man, I wouldn't have anything to say about it."

I'm not stupid. I know it could play out that way. It's not a good bet. There are a dozen ways it could end bad.

She frowns deeper and focuses on straightening her coupon stacks. "Tyler hasn't been over to see those girls but twice in the two months they've been here, and the second time, he brought some girl with him, and she stood there in my foyer with a sour look on her face the whole time."

I'd heard that he'd been taking Emily Mather out in public now that he and Angie are split. "Have the girls been asking after him?"

She shakes her head. "Not once."

We're both quiet for a minute. The sweet chatter from the TV in the front room mixes with the drama from Mom's court show.

Mom sighs again. "Well, I guess you think you know what you're doing."

I give her a grin. "Not really."

Before I forget, I hike up my hips, dig out my wallet, and take out some twenties. It's payday.

I lay the cash on the table and push back my chair. "Toward the groceries," I say before she can argue.

"You don't eat that much," she grumbles as she tucks the bills into her coupon pouch.

"I'll try harder. When's the barbecue gonna be ready?"

"It's ready now. I was going to hold off until Judge Judy's done to feed the girls if you can wait."

"I can wait." I drop a kiss on her fluffed and feathered hair-sprayed hair. "I'm going to say hi to the girls."

I take my beer and wander back down the narrow hall.

As a kid, I used to race from the living room to the kitchen when Mom called us for dinner. Now I've got to be careful that my shoulders don't knock into the walls.

Without peeling their eyes away from the TV, the girls make room for me, scooting to either side of the couch to clear my usual seat in the middle. I sit and sink at least a half foot down. The couch is older than me and going bald in patches, but it's comfortable as hell.

"No Orioles, Brandon," Tamblyn warns me. "Not until after our show."

"Okay. No worries. Season's over." I guess they've got my number. They relax a little, assured that I don't have designs on the remote control.

"What happened to the horse with wings?" I ask. The lady on screen is singing and dancing through some kind of ice cave now.

"Gone," Ivy answers, resettling herself with her back to the arm of the couch so that she can stick her cold feet under my legs.

Tamblyn sidles closer until she's smooshed against my side. They both smell like cereal milk and rubber tires. Mom must've taken them to the Lion's Club playground today.

I rest my head on the back cushion.

"The horse with wings is called a pegasus," Tamblyn tells me.

"Cool." I sip my beer and let the stress of the day go.

"He left Sarabelle in the crystal cavern because she's got to find the wand alone," Tamblyn explains.

"Got it." Doesn't seem like Sarabelle is looking too hard, but I guess she's got to sing about it first.

"Sarabelle is a princess," Ivy adds her two cents. "She's my favorite."

"Right."

"She lives in Aventuria, her sister is Imogen, and her mortal enemy is the Bane of Doom. The Bane is my favorite. I like bad guys," Tamblyn informs me, reaching into the crack between the couch cushions and takes out a rumpled baggie of miniature muffins. Mom doesn't allow food in the living room. That's exactly where I used to hide the wrappers from the Slim Jims I lifted from my dad's stash.

Tamblyn holds out the bag to me. It's nothing but crumbs. The couch crack is probably not the best place to hide muffins. "No thanks."

Tamblyn shrugs, sticks her finger in her mouth, and uses it to Swiffer up the muffin bits. When she's cleaned the bag, she goes on. "Her best friend is Cara Anne, and she has brown hair, and her other best friend is Farah Lee, and she has red hair."

"Nice." I hold out my hand. "I'll take that." Tamblyn passes me the bag. I fold it so the spit side is covered and tuck it in my pocket to trash it later.

"The pegasus is called Swift, and his mortal enemy is Fireball."

"Oh yeah?" As I vaguely recall, there was a night my senior year of high school when Fireball was my mortal enemy, too.

"Yeah." On screen, the rampaging bull has shown up again, and this time, he's brought friends. Unfortunately, the ice floors of the crystal cavern are slippery, and apparently, Fireball does not have all-wheel drive.

The girls fall silent. The tension in the room is so thick you could cut it with a knife. Ivy clutches my forearm, digging her grubby little fingers into my shirt. Christopher Nolan has got nothing on whoever wrote this shit.

At the very last moment, Princess Sarabelle believes in herself enough to melt the ice cave with the wand she found —also by believing in herself—and she stands on a stalagmite while the evil, red bulls are swept away on a wave of sparkling ice water.

The girls go nuts. They leap up and zip around the living room in figure eights like unknotted balloons, buzzing past the sharp corner of every piece of furniture and every breakable tchotchke like a pair of sugared-up Blue Angels.

"What's going on in there?" Mom hollers down the hall.

"Princess Sarabelle defeated the evil forces of Fireball to save all of Aventuria," I holler back. Tamblyn grins at me like I'm a genius.

"Well, then wash up for dinner," Mom calls.

The girls race for the half bath. I scan the room for the remote, but I don't see it. I consider the crack in the couch cushions for a second—it's most certainly stuck down there—but I'm not that reckless. I go ahead and push the button on the TV to turn it off.

I take a second to drain the rest of my beer before I follow the girls to the kitchen. By the time I get to the table, they're scrambling into their seats, interrupting each other in a rush to tell Mom about a cricket they saw behind the toilet. Princess Sarabelle's narrow escape is yesterday's news.

Mom listens as she brings the dishes to the table and serves up the barbecue and cuts up Ivy's sandwich so she can eat it with a fork. When I try to help, she slaps my hand and tells me, "Eat."

Each time the girls pause for a breath, Mom interjects to remind them to put their napkins on their laps and chew with their mouths closed. They take her nagging with good humor.

When Tamblyn's napkin falls to the floor, she immediately dives under the table to get it back, and when Ivy accidentally takes a bite mid-sentence, she immediately stops what she was saying to chew her food with her lips mashed together, and as soon as she swallows, she starts all the way back at the beginning of her thought.

Mom doesn't understand how I see the girls. They're not "some other man's kids." They're not baggage.

They're Angie's kids. She grew 'em. I like 'em the way I like everything she makes. They remind me of her. Of how it used to be.

When Tamblyn rambles about Princess Sarabelle and Aventuria, I remember Angie and Madison lying on their stomachs on the living room floor, feet kicked up and swinging, reciting facts about Harry and Niall and Zayn to each other in excruciating detail. I thought the two of them were such dorks, such pains in the ass. I didn't realize then that we were happy.

When Ivy burbles as she laughs, I remember how Angie used to sound exactly like that before she started to laugh behind her hand—before she stopped laughing out loud altogether and wouldn't even show her teeth when she smiled.

I remember when she stopped coming around so much. Then, before my dumb sixteen-year-old ass could figure out what to do about it, she hooked up with Tyler and never went anywhere without him.

I remember when her mom passed, and she was bent over and sobbing into her hands on the couch where I sit now to watch cartoons with her girls, and how I didn't know what to do or say. Dad sent me to go find Lisa's car since it wasn't out front of the motel room where they found her body. I found it in the back of the Family Discount parking lot on Holabird.

I remember the sneaky conversations when Angie came up pregnant and how Madison was so quick to shut her bedroom door if I happened to pass. One night, when Angie was almost due, she had stayed for dinner and was doing the dishes while Mom coaxed Dad to eat something. He was stuck in the hospital bed that hospice loaned us at that point.

The kitchen was dark except for the light over the stove. The front of Angie's shirt was soaked with sudsy water. She caught me looking at her bump, and she asked if I wanted to touch it. I remember how it felt—like a fucking miracle and a punch to the gut at the same time.

Tamblyn sneezes just like Angie. Ivy has her chin. Ivy's chin dimples just like Angie's when she cries.

How could I not be crazy about them, too?

But Mom isn't wrong. There's no guarantee that Angie is ever going to feel the way I do, and if I shoot my shot, and she says yes, it may very well be because she's in a bad place, and I look like a way out. Part of me says fuck it. A lot of women are with a lot of men because they can provide. How wrong is it? It makes me want to puke, though, thinking about being with her if that's what's in her head.

She almost married that asshole, and from my perspective, he had nothing going for him but gainful employment. And she got all the way down the aisle for him. If he hadn't fumbled the bag at the last minute, she'd be Mrs. Asshole.

If any of my buddies went after a girl in her situation, I'd tell them it was a bad bet. Just like everyone said to me when I was looking at that Charger.

It's a depressing thought, so I drop it.

After dinner, Tamblyn wants me to check the air in her bicycle tires—it's an excuse to run wild outside for a little longer—so I oblige her. Of course, then Ivy needs me to check a squeak on her tricycle. I give the axle and the pedal crank bearings a squirt of WD40 to make her happy. Mom sees what I'm up to and asks me to check her tires and oil, too, since I'm here.

For my efforts, Mom takes out an Entenmann's that she's

been hiding in the good china hutch for dessert. By the time I have seconds, it's half past nine. I could head down to the bar, but the beer here is free, and the couch is a hell of a lot more comfortable than the stools down at Donovan's.

Mom tries to put the girls to bed, but they keep sneaking back up the stairs, and finally, Mom tells them they can bring their blankets up and camp in the living room until Angie gets home. I'd be creeped out sleeping alone in a basement at their age, even if it is finished. Basements are creepy.

I settle in to play on my phone while Mom watches one of her hot firemen shows. The girls giggle for a while, but soon enough, they're sprawled on a pile of comforters on the carpet, passed out like little drunks. Mom drifts off during the local news, and I swipe the remote, switch to ESPN, and lower the volume.

I put my phone face down on the end table so I can't keep checking the time. Sometimes, I make myself nuts.

Angie's not late. Even this time of night, it takes a good thirty minutes to drive here from the hospital, and she changes out of her scrubs before she leaves. Besides not wanting to bring anything home on her clothes, I'm pretty sure she doesn't want to remind Mom of Dad's last few months. She's considerate like that.

I don't get how a woman can be so thoughtful of others and so careless with herself. It pisses me off. It makes me want to boss her around and do for her and fuck up anyone who takes advantage of her.

I've dreamed of beating the shit out of Tyler Reynolds way more than a sane man should.

My gut unknots when I hear her car pull into the drive, and my pulse picks up. She turns her key in the lock, drops her purse on the hall tree bench, and appears in the door-way. My lungs catch.

Even after working two shifts, back-to-back, she's pretty as hell.

Her hair is in a messy bun. The streaks she put in for her wedding have almost grown out, so the top knot is blonde, but the roots are her natural brown. She'd hide behind that hair if it was down, but since it's up, the faint, yellow glow from the lamp on the end table lights her face. She's beautiful.

She's made on generous lines. Her mouth is wide, her lips pink and plump. Her hips are broad, and her brown eyes are wide set and warm.

She pauses on the threshold a moment, taking in her girls conked out on the floor and Mom snoring in her recliner with her Sudoku book open on her lap. She flashes me a small smile, and my heart stutters. I nod to the seat next to me and hold my breath.

She kicks her clogs off, pads over, and sinks down beside me. I'm sitting in the middle, so she doesn't have a choice. She smells like the vanilla body spray she's been wearing for as long as I can remember.

My dick doesn't get hard—that'd be freaking weird in a room with my mom and Angie's kids—but let's say I'm aware of it.

She squints at the TV. "Watching cricket?"

She's teasing me. My stomach tightens, but in a different way from when I was waiting for her.

She sighs, stretching her legs and wiggling her toes. She does patient transport at Bayview. Her feet have got to be killing her after sixteen hours.

If she were mine, she wouldn't be pulling doubles. She wouldn't work unless she wanted to. I see all the things my mom does with the girls. Frankly, that's more than enough work for one person.

"Who's winning?" She glances up at me, shy but with a

sweet, sneaky smile teasing the corners of her shiny lips. She's wearing gloss. Looks fresh.

Did she put that on because she saw my truck out front?

"I have no idea." I smile back. Her eyes dip down to my mouth, her thick lashes brushing her cheeks.

I want to carry her down to my old bedroom, lock the door, and lay her out on the bed. I want to make her blush way worse than she is now. I want to make her struggle to catch her breath. I want her to hurt for me, like she makes me hurt for her.

Instead, I grab the remote and switch to the home improvement channel. I have no idea what she likes to watch—whenever I'm here with her, so are Mom and the kids, and apparently, they get first choice—but Madison is crazy about the house-flipping shows.

I must make the right choice. She sees a guy spreading mortar for a backsplash and settles back in her seat with a happy sigh. Her bare thigh presses against my jeans. It's the first time I've ever wished I was wearing shorts. Hers have ridden up, bunching at her hips. I pass my beer bottle to the hand closest to her leg so I don't lose my mind and touch her to see if her skin is as silky as it looks in the low light.

She blinks, surprised, as I move the bottle, and she must think I'm passing it to her. She takes it from me and sips, I think to be polite.

"Were the girls good for your mom?" she asks.

"They always are."

She snorts softly and hands the beer back. I take a swig. The mouth of the bottle tastes like petroleum jelly.

"You didn't feel like going down to Donovan's?" she asks.

"I don't always go down to Donovan's." I mean, nine times out of ten, if it's a Friday or Saturday night, I do, but not *always*.

"I guess not if there's a big cricket match on," she says. She's teasing again. My whole chest fills with...something.

"You know how it is." We're not quite whispering, but our voices are pitched low, and the room is dim and shadowy. Excitement swims in my belly, heightened by my frustration. I want to be alone with her. I want her naked and bucking underneath me. I want to figure out how to make her scream.

She holds out her hand for the bottle. I pass it. She sips.

"How was work?" I ask, cool and easy, like my brain isn't tossing up perverted thought after perverted thought.

"Good," she says. "No trips to the morgue."

"That's a good day, then."

She lets out a little sigh and slumps deeper against the back of the couch. "I've been thinking about this CNA program down at the community college. The hospital will reimburse you for the tuition if you go to work for them afterwards."

"Yeah?" I refocus. This sounds serious.

"I didn't think I'd have time to do school on top of the girls, but if I'm already pulling doubles, I might as well, you know? Once I've got enough saved for first and last month's rent on an apartment, and we're out of your mom's basement, I could do it—if I wasn't pulling doubles."

I grunt so she knows I'm listening. Every cell in my body wants to solve her problem. It'd be easy. All it would take is money, and I've got that, what with double time and sometimes triple time when operations go long.

I don't want to be that guy, though. I don't want to buy her. But I do want to take care of her. It was easier in my grandparents' day. Men paid for shit, and they just never wondered whether that was the only reason their women stayed around.

"I think I can do it this year if I don't get any surprises."

She grimaces. "The hospital will pay for you to get your RN, too. I could do that once both the girls are in school all day." She drains the rest of the beer, a look of cautious determination in her eye.

She's different than she's been for the past few years. More tired, but also calmer, somehow. Less jumpy. I'm glad for that.

I want to see her really happy. Relaxed. Naked and spread-eagled on my bed, smiling, with cum leaking from her pussy and legs that don't work.

"You're a good listener," she says to me, handing me the empty bottle. I set it on the end table.

"You think?"

"Yeah." She gives me another soft smile and fiddles with her fingers. She's nervous.

I make her nervous.

I take a breath and chew my lower lip a second before I collect myself. I'm nervous, too. If I make a move, and she's not totally cool with it, that's it. She's crashing in my mom's basement. I can't push it. It'd be, like, harassment.

But I'm not about to wait for however many more months it'll take before she ends up next to me alone on a couch again. I don't lack balls. If I've got a shot, I'm gonna take it.

I'm shaking on the inside though as I raise my arm and rest it gently around her shoulders. For a second, she tenses. My chest seizes. Then she exhales and kind of melts against my side. She rests her cheek on my chest. Her bun tickles my face.

I inhale. Her hair smells amazing.

"Is this okay?" I whisper in her ear. She shivers.

"Yeah," she whispers back.

I stroke her upper arm with my thumb and listen as her breathing gets quicker. Both of us are holding the rest of our bodies motionless like this is a game of freeze tag, and we got caught.

I want to drag her onto my lap, drive my hands into that bun, and taste her mouth. I really want my mom and the girls to be somewhere, anywhere, else.

Mom is still snoring away, though, and the girls are sprawled on their stomachs in their footie pajamas. All I can do is tug Angie a little firmer against my side.

"You feel good," I say to her.

"You do too," she says and then winces, like she's embarrassed. I chuckle and squeeze her closer. She shivers under my fingers.

"Are you warm enough?" I ask.

"Yeah."

I stroke the goosebumps appearing on her skin. I was right. She's soft as silk, even with the bumps.

We fall silent and pretend to watch TV—at least I'm pretending—and we sit there, my arm around her shoulder, the rest of our bodies stiff as sticks, as the house settles around us for the night. Eventually, her breath evens and the weight of her head on my chest increases as she falls asleep.

I flip back to cricket and watch the end of what is apparently one hell of a nail-biter between India and Australia.

I've never been higher—or more terrified of fucking up—than I am in this moment, surrounded by sleeping, snoring ladies, in my mom's living room, at closing time on a Friday night.

5

ANGIE

"So he asked you out?" Madison asks.

I've already told her the story over text, and then again on the phone, but she's making me repeat it a third time in person. We're hanging out in the kiddie pool while the girls tear around the yard like wildebeests. Miss Dawn is at pickleball. Brandon is trimming the grass sprouting by the back fence with a weedwhacker.

He's ignoring me, and I'm ignoring him.

Mostly. I've caught him looking over once or twice. And he's caught me.

"Yeah," I say. "He texted and asked me if I wanted to see a movie."

"And you said?"

"I told him I was busy with the girls." Frankly, I panicked. That night in the living room, Tamblyn woke me up at three in the morning, shaking my shoulder, and Brandon was passed out with his head resting on the back of the couch. I'd drooled through his shirt.

Luckily, he didn't wake up as I got the girls downstairs to their beds, and Tamblyn didn't ask any questions. The whole next day, I was a wreck. When he texted, I lied about being busy before I even had the chance to think it through.

"And then he asked you out again? In person?" Madison is very concerned with the order of events for someone who's heard them twice already.

"Yeah, when he dropped by after work to gas your mom's car up." Madison's dad kept her mom's car gassed up before he passed, and Brandon takes care of it now. Miss Dawn brags on that, too, and I don't blame her. He's a good guy.

"And you turned him down?" Madison cocks her head.

"I kind of mumbled, and then the girls started fussing, so I said I had to get them into the bath, and I took them and hid down in the basement."

Madison sighs and leans further back against the inflated rubber side of the pool. "Why are you dicking my brother around, Angie? If you don't want to go out with him, put him out of his misery. Are you afraid to tell him no because you're living in his mom's basement?"

"That's not it."

"You used to like him. You were always stuttering and tripping over stuff around him."

"When I was, like, thirteen." My cheeks heat. I had no chill.

"Thirteen-year-old Angie had way better taste than fourteen-year-old Angie." Madison raises her palms in the air. "Just sayin'."

Tyler and I started going out when I was fourteen, and he was sixteen. He drove, and he had the balls to ask me out. I was so unduly impressed.

"Granted." I can't argue facts.

"So why aren't you into my big brother anymore? Is it because he always smells like motor oil?"

"He doesn't always smell like motor oil." Well, he does when he comes over straight from work, but I wouldn't say *always*. When he showed up earlier, he smelled like soap and convenience store coffee.

"Is it because you hate movies?" Madison raises a thin copper eyebrow.

I snort. Madison reaches over the pool to fetch her red Solo cup. We're both on our second Orange Crush of the day. It's Saturday and sunny with blue skies for miles, so we're having a party for four.

The girls are playing Barbies, dashing back and forth between the sandbox and the swing set and the town they've set up in the grass beside us. The town is made of shoebox houses, a silver Corvette, and the Fisher Price barn that Madison and I played with when we were kids. Madison and I are soaking up the end of summer vitamin D and listening to 104.3 on her mom's old portable AM/FM radio.

I take a sip from my own red cup. "I like movies fine."

Madison sighs. "So it *is* because he smells. I mean, I can't blame you."

She's having the time of her life with this. She thinks it's hilarious. It's thrown me into three full-blown panic attacks in the past two weeks—once each time after he asked me out and a third time when I realized he wasn't going to ask again.

"Why am I such a mess?" I cringe at the self-pity in my voice, but I know Madison won't blink an eye. We can be our worst selves with each other. I've cleaned up her puke, and after I had Tamblyn, she compared my vagina stitches with pictures from the internet because I swore that it hurt so bad, they must've done them wrong.

"We're all a mess." Madison gulps from her drink and wipes her mouth with the back of her hand.

"What if I go out with Brandon, and it doesn't work out, and you have to pick sides?" I ask. Making things awkward with Madison isn't my worst fear, but it's a big one.

"Easy. I pick you."

I roll my eyes. "No, you wouldn't."

"Yes, I would. And Mom would pick him, so the sides would be even, and we'd all just go on like normal." Madison changes position, draping her legs over the sides of the pool. She's only decent because she's wearing a T-shirt that comes to her knees. I sit cross-legged in two feet of water like a lady.

"I can't go out with him."

"Why not?"

"You know why." We don't have secrets from each other.

"Humor me and explain." Her face gentles because she *does* know.

"I just got out of an eight-year relationship."

"Uh-huh." Her expression says *go on*; *we both know there's more.*

"I need to learn how to be by myself."

"It's hard, is it?" She rounds her eyes. "And yet I do it every day without even thinking about it."

Madison isn't into relationships. She'll bring a guy home once in a while to scratch an itch, but she says she doesn't want a man in her house unless he can find both the clit and the spare vacuum cleaner replacement bags without her help, and she hasn't met a man yet who could.

"I have bad judgment in men." I keep running down the list that's been cycling on repeat in my head.

"You think Tyler and Brandon are in the same league?" She wrinkles her nose like the very idea stinks.

"No." I know Brandon's on a whole different level, but he never talked to me, and Tyler did. Tyler kept coming around despite how sad my life was with my mom falling apart, and I was so young and dumb that I thought that meant he was good for me. I lower my head. "Maybe I don't deserve a guy like Brandon. And how do I even know that I really like him, and I'm not just fooling myself again because I want someone to want me?"

The question is so honest, so shameful, I can't look at Madison as I ask it. I turn my head to watch the girls over on the playset, pumping the tandem swing as high as they can get it to go.

"It's real messed up, wanting to be wanted," Madison answers. "No one that selfish deserves to go to the movies with a guy who smells like motor oil."

I splash her lightly. "You know what I mean."

Like a ninja, she covers her drink so pool water doesn't get in it. "I know that everyone deserves dinner at Olive Garden followed by a feature at the Regal 8. I don't think you have to earn that with, like, a certain level of personal development or a long enough record of successful romantic relationships. I mean, who even *has* a record of successful relationships?"

"You just want to be sisters for real." She's also supernaturally compassionate, way more than normal people.

"Girl, we already are." She raises her red plastic cup. I tap it with mine. We both sip, and when we're done, her face gets serious. My stomach clenches. She's going to bring it up. I'd give anything if she wouldn't.

I check on Brandon out of the corner of my eye. He's still by the back fence, trimming a vine that's growing over the fence from the neighbor's yard. His arm muscles flex as he raises the weedwhacker, his back arched, lunged forward on one leg. There are grass trimmings stuck in the hair on his forearms. He's the hottest man I've ever seen, in real life, on TV, or the internet.

My belly feels weird.

"Are you afraid to tell him?" she asks.

Heat rushes up my neck to my face in a wave. I tuck my

knees up under my soaked T-shirt coverup and hunch my shoulders.

"Yes," I mumble.

"It's not a big deal."

I cast her a *yeah right* look.

"It's not like you were sleeping around. That was Tyler."

"It doesn't matter."

"Everybody's got baggage," Madison says.

I wrap my arms tight around my shins and rest my chin on my wet knees. "I've got herpes."

Madison gives me her sweetest smile. "I love you and your herpes. The right man will, too."

"You love my herpes?"

"Every single last one of them." Madison's straight face holds until she gets her red cup to her lips, and then she loses it and snort-giggles. I splash her again, and she gets a mouthful. She shrieks and splutters and slaps the water in revenge. Across the yard, the girls whoop in high-spirited solidarity from the swing set. Brandon takes off his safety glasses and looks over to see what's going on.

"Uncle, uncle," I squeal.

She narrows her eyes, palm raised and ready to swing.

I keep my eyes locked on hers and stretch my legs out, sinking lower until my chin is under water like a hippo. She slowly lowers her hand.

"So how are you going to tell Brandon about your adorable lil' case of her-*pes*?" Sometimes, she likes to say herpes with a French accent, like boomer ladies pronounce Tar-*jet*.

"Oh my God," I moan. "I can't talk about this."

"You're going to have to if you want to get busy with my brother."

"No, I don't. I can be single for the rest of my life. Or I'll join one of those special dating apps."

Madison puts her feet back in the pool so she can press her soles against mine. She tries to make my legs bend, but I brace my knees.

"But you want to date Brandon," she says. "You want to go on a movie date with him and ride in his truck and let him take you for a drink at Donovan's and talk until closing time about—" She scrunches her face. "The Orioles? Diesel engines? Bass fishing?"

I curl my toes over the top of hers. "I can't do it."

"Yeah, I'd be out of there in five minutes tops, but you love pretending you like sports and acting like you're interested in what other people say."

"You know what I mean."

"It isn't going to be as bad as you've made it in your head."

"You don't know that."

"Your doctor said sixteen percent of the women in her practice test positive, and, like, virtually *everyone* used to get HPV before the shots. That's a lot of awkward conversations that must have gone fine, or you'd hear about it."

"Not necessarily." I've never told a soul except Madison.

I found out when I was almost due with Ivy. My OB/GYN did the routine tests they do right before you pop, and I came up positive. I confronted Tyler, and he tried to act like I must have cheated, but we both knew I didn't.

He was gaslighting me, and I let him. I was nineteen, my mom was gone, I had no other family, and I was about to have two babies under two.

Where was I going to go? Not to either of the foster families I had after Mom died. They were both nice enough, but it's not like we connected or anything. Definitely not to the Kaczmareks. They were still reeling from losing Mr. Mike.

A few weeks after Ivy was born, Tyler got wasted and admitted that he cheated on me with a girl from work. He swore that he'd never do it again. I was so sleep deprived that I would have forgiven him anything if he'd only watch the girls long enough for me to take a nap.

I'm not proud of it. Any of it.

I wish I'd left him then. I wish I'd had the brass balls of the people on social media who talk about disclosing to their dates like it's no big deal. But I thought no one would ever want a nineteen-year-old with herpes and two kids, so I'd better make the best of it. Even before the second baby and the diagnosis, I thought no one would want a teen mom who'd barely earned her high school diploma.

I'd better be *grateful* for Tyler Reynolds.

I don't know when that conviction began to unravel, but it was long before the wedding debacle. It was like every so often a part of me would catch a glimpse of a different future, and then the rest of me would panic and double down on Tyler.

Once, when Tamblyn was about eight months old, Tyler went hunting in Montana with his dad, and I had two whole weeks alone with no one but me and the baby to worry about, and it was fine. Better than fine. It was *nice.*

I didn't have to put dinner in serving dishes because that's how his mom does it. I left laundry in the dryer overnight and just shook the wrinkles out in the morning, and I didn't have to hear anyone bitch. It occurred to me that it could be like this all the time.

Then he came home, and I *clung* to him. I *knew* I'd been fine, but for some reason, as soon as I saw him, it was like I'd stared death in the face while he was gone. Not long afterwards, I convinced him to have Ivy. I pointed out how it'd be better to have our kids close together so that when we're done, we're done. The logic spoke to him.

In my head, I was all in, but a part of me just wouldn't fall in line. When Ivy was about three months old, I got the job at the hospital. Sometimes, when I was working the weekend and Tyler was at home with the girls, I'd stay after work to get a cappuccino from the cafeteria. I'd drink it so slow that it'd be cold before I was even halfway finished.

I'd start daydreaming word problems, calculating how much it'd cost to get a two bedroom for the girls and me, adding utilities and co-pays and a cell phone bill without Tyler's parents' family plan. Then, without fail, a cold feeling would come over me, like a ghost walking over my grave, and I'd dump the cappuccino and speed home. I'd make something nice for dinner, and later, in bed, I'd let Tyler do one of the things he liked.

Because wanting things—and going after what you want—is for people with nets under their tightropes. It's not that it's *easy* to say yes to the boy who won't take no for an answer, or to stay with the man you're with. It's that it's *smart*.

Life throws bombs. It yanks the rug out from under your feet. People disappear. One day, you have a home, and the next, you've got a bed in someone else's room, in someone else's house. If you're safe and secure, you thank your lucky stars. You hunker down, and you make it work. Especially when you have little girls who depend on you.

When Tyler stood up in front of everyone we know and said those vows, he'd run the numbers, and he figured I'd take it. He didn't misjudge. I'd shown him over and over again that I would. Deep in my innermost self, though—unbeknownst even to me—I had a limit.

In the end, he gave me an out. He set it up, and to take it, all I had to do was say *no*. One word. Just once. Yeah, I had to say it in front of all our friends and family, but after it came out of my mouth, it was done. Tyler and I were over.

Brandon isn't safe or easy. Going after what you want is a way different proposition than blowing up your life. Saying *no* when you're pushed to the edge is a cakewalk compared to saying *yes* to taking a risk. At least for me.

What if I tell him about the herpes, and he looks disgusted?

What if I tell him, and he acts like it's fine, and then he ghosts me? What if he tells people?

What if he's really nice and kind and says that he respects me for being up front, but that it's not something he can handle?

And if it doesn't go off the rails at that point, but it does later when it's not just a crush? What if we get a few months down the road, and he realizes he doesn't want a ready-made family? Since we split, Tyler has been a complete dick. What if Brandon decides he doesn't want the hassle?

"You're working yourself up into a panic attack, aren't you?" Madison asks. Apparently, she's been watching me spin out while she chews the ice from her drink.

"Yes," I squeak.

"Life is hard and scary as shit," she says as she tilts her face back to bask in the sunshine. "At least it's sunny, and we've got Orange Crushes and each other." She lifts her head, doubling her chin to give me a smile and a wink. "You're gonna be okay, girl. I've got your back."

"I've got yours, too." The pressure on my chest eases. The girls, suddenly done with the swings, come tearing over and fold themselves over the side of the pool, squealing and shrieking. Madison splashes Tamblyn, and I drag Ivy onto my lap. She curls up against my chest, sweaty and sticky from melted popsicle.

I'm lucky.

Sometimes I feel like I've lost everything, but it's not true. I have an entire kiddie pool overflowing with love. The future is terrifying, but this moment, right now? This specific Saturday afternoon on this specific day in

September, in the backyard of this particular house in this particular cul-de-sac, it's as warm and soft as I hope heaven is.

~

AFTER PLAYING A LITTLE LONGER, Ivy says she has to pee, and Madison wants a refill, so she takes both girls inside for a bathroom and snack break. I soak in the sun, listening to the weedwhacker. About when its engine cuts off, I realize that I've probably been abandoned for the TV and air conditioning.

I survey the yard to assess the damage. Dolls, accessories, and sandbox toys are strewn in a twenty-foot blast radius around the pool. I need a laundry basket and a helper. I also need to get out of here before Brandon comes over—or decides not to.

I make a start by scooping up the various plastic critters floating around me like vegetables in soup. I've almost cleared them all when a shadow falls across me. I tilt my head back and squint. Every inch of my skin wakes up.

Brandon stands over me, hands on his hips, back straight and chest broad like Superman. Tan work gloves hang from his front pocket. His damp T-shirt clings to his pecs. I feel caught like a mouse in a trap. My heart flutters as fast.

"Is the water cool?" he asks.

I nod. I don't know why, but a cheap, blue, plastic, kiddie pool holds the cold better than an Igloo cooler.

Brandon glances around and then drags a lawn chair over from the deck and places it flush against the side of the pool. "Mind if I join you?"

I shake my head. "I was just heading inside," I say, but I make no move to get up.

I don't want to now.

Brandon bends over—unlacing his boots and peeling off his socks, I guess—because when he straightens up, he's bare foot and rolling up his jeans. It's a tight fit getting the denim past his calf muscles, but he manages to fold them up above his knees. He eases his feet in the water, leans back, and exhales.

I can't see his eyes since he's traded his safety glasses for his mirrored wrap sunglasses. I hope he's got them closed. I'm already self-conscious enough.

I'm wearing a bikini under my T-shirt. It's full coverage on the bottom, but the top ties together around the neck and back. The triangles cover my areolas, but not much more. Of course he can't see that, but I'm super aware of how I'm spilling out of the spandex under my shirt, and how he could see my nipples popping through the cold, wet cotton if I didn't have my arms crossed. I must look as uptight as I feel. I can feel my heart thump against my forearm.

"Is this the same pool that you and Maddie played in back in the day?" he asks, oblivious to how I'm freaking out that I'm naked underneath my clothes.

"I don't know. Could be." Knowing Miss Dawn, it's likely. She can make a penny squeal.

Brandon was already too old for kiddie pools when Madison and I became friends. He's not much older, but he always seemed so much more mature. Maybe because Mr. Mike was big on teaching him how to be the man of the house. They always had their heads stuck under a car hood, or Brandon was holding a ladder or a toolbox while Mr. Mike messed around with something. A lot of kids would've been bored, but Brandon was so serious about it. To me, it never seemed like he was helping, but like he knew what he was doing.

"They've left you to clean everything up?" he asks.

"Looks like it."

He stretches his legs until his feet are almost an inch from mine. I can't tuck my legs any tighter to my chest, and I can't stop looking down. His feet are tanner than mine and twice as large. I can see the tendons running up from his toes. In comparison, mine are pale and soft and pruned from the water. I can tell my red nail polish is long overdue for a touch up, but I don't think a man would notice.

Brandon flexes his long toes. My cheeks flush, and my stomach goes squishy. He chuckles softly. "It's like the difference between Coco and Bailey's paws."

Coco was the Great Dane the Kaczmareks had when we were growing up. Bailey was a dachshund. It was funny because everyone kind of agreed that Coco was Miss Dawn's, and Bailey was Mr. Mike's.

My heart twinges like always when I think of them. Coco passed when I was in sixth grade, and Bailey passed the summer before eighth.

"They were good dogs," I say quietly.

"The best." Brandon's mouth softens. I bet he's feeling exactly what I am—that happy sadness. Or sad happiness.

To me, time feels split in two—before, when Coco and Bailey and my mom and his dad were around, and afterwards, when there was so much missing.

In a way, I was lucky. I was moved into foster care where I had a blank slate. In the Kaczmarek house, you were always tripping over reminders—a leash left hanging on a peg behind the mudroom door or an old plastic lighter in the places where Mr. Mike used to sneak his smokes.

"I miss them," I say.

"I do, too."

I can't be sure because of the sunglasses, but from the angle of his head, I'm pretty sure he's looking into my eyes, and in my heart, I know that underneath the everyday words, we mean the same thing.

I'm missing part of myself.

It's weird how you can only talk about loss with cliches. It's like no one wants to risk being specific enough to stir up the worst of the pain. So you stick to the generic things everyone always says. *Those were good times. He was a great guy. She'll be remembered.*

Nothing about the mole on her right cheek that she hated and that you can still place in the exact right spot on your own face which looks more like hers every year. Never how every winter, when the sky turns that particular shade of gray, you still catch the ghost scent of Marlboros and snow on a leather jacket when you step through the front door to drop the girls off.

"Remember when you and Maddie did that backyard carnival, and you used this as the duck pond?" he asks.

"Yeah. We made a roller coaster out of pushing a laundry basket down the slide."

"I almost broke my arm on that ride." Brandon's lips curve.

"You loved it."

"I did." He grins wide, showing his bright, even teeth. I can't help but smile back. Something in my stomach skitters.

He leans forward a little, and the weather between us changes, like a wispy cloud crossing the sun, not worrisome, just a change in the mood.

"Angie," he says, lowering his voice. "Go to the movies with me."

My abs clench, my blood rushes in my veins, and I have no idea if I'm excited or terrified. I can't mumble something and duck away this time. I'm sitting at his feet in a kiddie pool.

I don't know what to say. I want to go with him. And I can't.

His mouth gentles into an easy smile. "We can go as friends."

"Friends?" It comes out a breathless squeak.

"You buy your ticket, I buy mine. You buy popcorn. I buy malted milk balls. We share."

"I don't like milk balls."

"More for me, then." The corners of his lips sneak higher, cajoling, and I feel mine curve, too. "I'll even let you drive."

"Let me?" I roll my eyes. All of a sudden, I can't be still. I shift-slide on the plastic under my butt, bumpy from the grass underneath.

"Why not, Angie?" The tone of his voice has changed. It's still calm and even, but the playfulness is gone. He really wants to know. He sees me squirming and blushing, and he's not stupid, and I'm not subtle, so he wants to know why I won't say yes.

What can I say?

"It's complicated," I blurt, and with a burst of nervous energy, I stand. Water gushes down my legs, dripping from the T-shirt that clings to all the places I'd rather it didn't. I hop over the side of the pool and start picking up toys.

He stands, perfectly cool and collected, and steps onto the grass. "Tell me."

"You wouldn't understand." I know that's not fair. I should say *I don't want to explain* or *I don't want you to know*. That would be honest, at least.

He stalks off toward the deck, and my heart rockets into my throat. Is he mad? Is he giving up?

As quick as he goes, he's back with the mesh bag Miss Dawn keeps the outside toys in. He holds it open and half-smiles down at me. He's not happy, but he's not mad.

I've got two arms full of dolls, dresses, Nerf balls, and tiny pink plastic teacups. I awkwardly drop all of it in the bag.

"Here," he says and hands me the bag. I take it before I can think. My brain is moving slow and fuzzy, and I can't blame the Orange Crush. I sipped it so slow it never even went to my head.

He starts picking up toys and shooting them into the bag, basketball style.

"Two points," I say when he sinks a teapot from five feet away.

He grins. "Nothing but net."

We gather everything, and then without talking, we stand side-by-side by the pool.

"On three," he says. "One, two, three." We lift at the same time, tipping the water into the grass. He lifts higher than me, so it rushes over my bare feet.

I pick up the bag, and he grabs the hose that Madison left lying on the ground. We head for the shed.

There's a pulsing between my legs, and I can't seem to catch my breath. I feel like I'm sneaking away with him, but behind the shed is where the tub for outside toys and the hose reel are kept. We have a completely legitimate reason to be alone back here, hidden from the house.

But when I drop the toys in the tub, I linger, watching Brandon recoil the hose. When he's got only a few feet left, he turns the nozzle and rinses grass clippings off his feet.

"Your turn," he says when he's done. His lips quirk. Suggesting things. Daring me.

I stick out one foot at a time, and he rinses them, very slow and very careful, all the way up past my ankles.

My breasts grow heavy, and my nipples are hard, but I can't casually cover them while standing on one leg.

He straightens, takes a drink from the hose, and sighs, satisfied. "Tastes just like I remember."

"Like pennies?"

"Yeah, delicious." He holds the hose higher between us. "Thirsty?"

At some point, he took off his sunglasses and folded them over the collar of his shirt, so when I glance up, there's nothing between me and the full-blown effect of his bright brown eyes. Pure need punches me in the gut. Yes, I'm thirsty.

I part my lips. He raises the hose.

"Are you going to jerk it away at the last minute and spray me in the face?"

"Never."

I side-eye him like I have my doubts, but I don't really. I'm just nervous because something is pulling us closer and closer together, and I don't want it to stop, but I'm not prepared, and also, in my daydreams, I've been waiting for this moment forever.

I lean forward and sip. It does taste just like I remember.

I glance up. Brandon drops the hose. My lungs catch. He reaches for me—I don't know if he means to cup my face or plunge his fingers into my hair or what—but he misses because our lips meet first, and he tastes like cool water, like home, like *remembering*.

I fling my arms around his neck. He's one step ahead of me, lifting me, wrapping me in his arms, urging my legs around his waist, backing me against the shed.

My thighs squeeze his rock-hard sides. My heels bump the backs of his rock-hard thighs. I feel soft and delicate and light and scared and *alive*. His mouth is firm and demanding and so, so sweet.

Now his hands cup my jaw. Now his fingers tangle in my hair. He presses his hips forward and grinds his tented fly against my pussy. I whimper into his mouth. He groans deep in his throat.

"Fuck," he moans.

I tug his bottom lip with my teeth. I want to make him cuss again.

He pins me harder with his hips and fumbles at my shirt hem while rubbing his rough cheek along mine until his teeth find my earlobe. He's not content to stay anywhere longer than a second, his lips seeking out the thudding pulse point in my throat, the crook of my neck. Shivers race across my hot, bare skin.

My shirt is gone. He peeled it off, and I hardly noticed. He tossed it on the ground.

He shoves the little triangle of my bikini top aside and covers the peak of my right breast with his hot mouth, his tongue lapping my aching, tender nipple. I whine and arch my back. Peeling paint scratches my shoulder blades.

He is so strong and certain and *hungry*, but he's not putting my hand on his dick or lowering me to my feet so he can urge me onto my knees. He wants to touch me. Everywhere. He can't decide. His hands clasp my hair, stroke my thigh, splay across the small of my back, slide up my spine and grip the back of my neck. He wants to hold me as close as I want to be to him.

He smells like fresh sweat and cut grass and sunny days and aftershave.

He suckles my breast, and the ache reaches all the way down to my swelling clit. I don't want him to stop—any of it —but his mouth is as greedy as his hands. He abandons my nipple to cover my cheeks with kisses and then takes my mouth and my breath and my sense. Every touch is a shock, like ice cubes on sunbaked skin, and as good and sweet and *right* as the memory of drinking straight from the hose.

This must be what it feels like to belong. To be where you're supposed to be.

His fingers slip past the elastic of my bottoms and stroke between my slick pussy lips.

He's touching my pussy.

Panic blares in my brain. *No. Dirty. Don't. Stop. Too much, too fast, too far.*

My stomach heaves, jarring me from my delirium.

I snatch his hand and drag it away, digging my nails into his wrist, and without conscious intent, my entire body bucks and twists. My hips jerk back. I drive a shoulder forward into his chest and dive to the side. I'm fighting to get loose, and if he doesn't want my hip to pop out of the socket, he has no choice but to let go.

"What the fuck?" he says.

I tumble onto my ass and pop straight back up, stumble a step, and sway to a stop.

I gape at him, wide-eyed and gasping with my boobs hanging out, nipples swollen, rosy with rashes from his stubble. I snatch the bikini cups and yank them back into place. The humiliation is one hundred percent complete.

I hardly remember my dad at all, but my body has never forgotten what to do when a man gets angry.

Brandon's shoulders go back and chest goes up. The veins on his forearms pop. His face sharpens, and his eyes darken.

I hold my breath. I keep myself very, very still.

"What was that, Angie?" he asks, his voice leashed.

I don't know.

My legs are jelly, and I've lost the ability to explain myself.

His nostrils flare, and somehow, he grows taller. "I wasn't attacking you."

I know that, I do, but my throat won't work, so I can't tell him. I wrap my arms around my chest.

"You could just have said *no*. I'm not a fucking creep. Damn." He glowers, waiting for me to say something. Like what? I'm sorry? I am, but I'm getting mad, too.

It wasn't a graceful dismount, but I've stopped going along with things I don't want to be doing, and I'm not going back to being that person, not even for Brandon Kaczmarek.

He scrubs the back of his neck. I've never seen him like this before. He's always been calm, assured, and even-tempered, but it's like someone spun him around, tipped him over, and spilled him out. My brain isn't scared of him, but the rest of me is ready to bolt.

He cranes his head back to glare up at the sky, exhales, and shakes out his arms. Then he levels me with a hard, cold gaze. My stomach knots. I didn't mean to ruin things.

"I'm not Tyler, you know," he says.

"I know," I whisper even though I don't understand what he's getting at.

"He's a dick, and you didn't say shit about it for *years*."

My chin wobbles. I never would have expected for Brandon to be an asshole about something like this. "So that means I don't have the right to say no to you?"

He expels breath like hot air from a steam engine at that and stalks a few feet away before he turns, plants his feet, fists his hands on his hips, and clenches his teeth.

"That's not what I meant," he bites out.

"So what do you mean?"

He closes his eyes, like he's collecting himself, and then levels me with his gaze, and there's hurt and confusion in it, and I'm not prepared. Tyler is Teflon. I've never been the one to hurt someone.

"Goddamn it, Angie, you almost married him. You were at the altar. You were going through with it."

How are we talking about the wedding? I don't know how we got from A to Z, and I'm not sure exactly what he's mad about, and whether or not I should be mad, too. All of this has gotten away from me.

"Didn't you *ever* see me there, Angie?" he asks. "I was always there. *Goddamn*."

He throws his shoulders back and stomps off again to walk it off. He gets a whole five feet before he turns back around. "*I* would never do anything on purpose to hurt you."

And I understand perfectly well what he means now. *He* wouldn't, but Tyler did, and I let him, over and over, for years. Even though everyone except Madison was too polite to say anything, they all saw, and they heard. The jokes. The names. The put-upon pissing and moaning when I was in his way or too loud or not quick enough or asking for something.

And Brandon blames me for it. Like I blame myself.

My head drops.

Moments pass. We're silent. Finally, he sighs. "Just forget it, okay?"

"I don't know why you think you can be mad at me," I mumble at the wet blades of grass stuck to my bare feet. I shiver. It's cool in the shed's shadow, and my bones are cold inside me.

Because I do understand what's happening here. He wants me.

Now.

Before he knows everything. But if I let this go one step further, what happens then? I have to tell him what's going on with me, and what if he's disgusted that I just let him touch me down there, and I didn't even warn him?

It's easy, right? I just tell him, and he's either cool with it, or he's not. It's no big deal. People have this conversation all the time.

And he might not freak out. Tyler did when I told him, but he was gaslighting me. It was an act, and he wanted me to be ashamed so I didn't ask any questions. Brandon isn't like Tyler at all. He could very well be cool with it, and who knows what might happen then?

Maybe we fall in love and make a home together. Maybe we become a family—him and me and the girls—and we live happily ever after, and I have everything I've ever wanted.

I just have to sit him down and have a conversation. It's no big deal. If we don't have sex during a breakout and use a condom, he might not catch it, and I haven't had a breakout in a couple years. And if he wants kids, we can talk about it. It's a conversation. People who want to be in relationships have conversations about harder stuff than this.

He'll be cool, or he won't, and either way, I'll handle it. I know how to deal.

I just can't breathe, that's all. He's mad at me, and the stakes feel so fucking high, and I don't have a grip.

"Talk to me, Angie," he says.

I stare into his deep brown eyes, and even though it feels so raw that my stomach goes sour, I still search for help there, for a miraculous burst of understanding, for the right words to say or the courage to say them, I'm not sure which, but he can't read my mind, and I'm fumbling this moment in excruciating slow motion.

He shutters his face and tightens his jaw.

"Fine," he says, and I can hear the *fuck this, I'm done*. He turns and walks away, calm and cool and collected. *Fine*.

I'm left alone behind the shed. There's a daytime moon like a smudge in the blue sky, and a stuffed elephant in a doll's dress forgotten by the swing set.

For a second, I ball my fists. I see myself beating them against the shed, pounding until the meat of my palms are bruised, screaming so the birds in all the trees in the entire neighborhood take flight and the ground opens up and swallows me whole.

Instead, I bend over and pick up the hose. I turn off the water and coil it neatly on the reel.

I go pick up the elephant, and I walk calmly back into the house because I am grown, and I have two little girls.

I have to be fine.

6

ANGIE

I'M CAREFUL TO KEEP MY FACE RIGHT WHEN I GO INSIDE AND join Madison and the girls in a cuddle puddle on the couch. Tamblyn asks me where Brandon went. I say he had to go home. Madison raises an eyebrow, but she doesn't say anything. We finish our party with pizza and a hike up to the gas station snowball stand on Bayshore.

When Miss Dawn gets home, Madison leaves to get ready to go out to Donovan's, and I make a late dinner of BLTs and the last of the watermelon I cut up for lunch. As soon as I've done the dishes, I take the girls to the basement so that Miss Dawn can have some downtime. She never makes us feel unwelcome, but it's got to be a lot to go from an empty nest to a full house with kids again. Sometimes, she must just want to kick her feet up and watch grisly murder shows in peace.

At nine o'clock, Ivy is already conked out on the carpet in front of the TV, so I have to wake her up to brush her teeth and put her jammies on. She's never handled being woken up gracefully, so she sobs her way through the nighttime routine, and she's still hiccupping when she drifts off again in the middle of our bedtime book.

Tamblyn stays awake until the end, and she climbs into the top bunk with none of her usual stall tactics. The sun has worn them both out. I'm exhausted, too. I throw a load of laundry in the washer and go to my narrow room. I vividly remember when Mr. Mike built it for Brandon when Miss Dawn needed his room upstairs for her daycare kids.

Madison and I messed around and watched the construction, dancing in our socks on the concrete floor and generally being annoying, while Mr. Mike did all the framing and drywall and paneling with Brandon's help. This was a few years before he laid down carpet and put in the bar and the woodstove.

The room is hardly wide enough for a single bed and a nightstand. There's a dresser at the far end, and that's it. There's no window, and you can hear everything through the walls, but at least I can close the door and change my clothes in private. And honestly, it's handy to be able to hear the dryer buzz.

I put on a clean T-shirt to sleep in, click the overhead light off, and climb into bed. It's a weird, cheap thrill to think that the bed used to be Brandon's. When Miss Dawn let us move in, she said it only made sense to use the furniture already down here, so my clothes are in his old drawers, and since I didn't come with any twin sheets, I'm tucked under his old, plaid, flannel sheets.

I feel like I've gone back in time, and I'm thirteen again with the world's most painful crush. I don't know why people are cute about crushes. In my experience, it was one of the most agonizing, embarrassing experiences in my life, and I almost married Tyler Reynolds.

I remember sniffing Brandon's letterman jacket when I hung my coat up next to it on the hall tree. His room doesn't smell like him anymore—the basement musk has taken over—but I can call it to mind perfectly. It's ridiculous. I don't think we've ever had a conversation longer than five or ten minutes, and nothing that wasn't casual, but behind the shed, I was kissing him like he'd come back from war.

I have to get us out of here before I lose my last scrap of dignity.

I pull up my banking app on my phone and check the balance. It's the same as when I checked yesterday and the day before. Not enough.

Omari, my partner on day shift, is doing the radiology tech program at the community college, and he has a family, too. That's a two-year program, though, and he has a wife who watches the kids at night.

I think I'd like being a tech. It would be weird to say out loud, but what I like about my job now is helping people who are in a bad way. A lot of the time, they're scared or hurt, and if they're pissy, it's usually because they're in pain and out of their comfort zone.

I like being kind and calm for them, making their shitty day a little better, showing them understanding in whatever small way I can. I've had plenty of bad days, and I know how a hand on your shoulder or a kind word can be enough to keep you going.

I can see myself doing mammograms or something where people are freaked out and need an understanding, capable touch. I have that in me, but it never really occurred to me before. I think Tyler used up all my capacity in that area when we were together. I was always having to be understanding and capable while he was throwing temper tantrums and going deadweight whenever life got even slightly inconvenient.

Why did I put up with it for so long? Is it that once you eat enough shit, the taste doesn't bother you anymore?

I don't know why I did it, and that might be what bothers me the most about it all now.

If I think too long about it, I give myself acid reflux, so I distract myself by scrolling social media. I'm not really focusing on anything when a text pops up on my screen.

R u up?

It's from Brandon. He's never texted me before. I don't think I've ever seen him text. He calls people like a boomer.

What do I say?

I haven't gotten a late night "are you up" text since high school, and it was always Tyler, drunk and wanting to see if he could sneak into my room to get laid and crash until he'd sobered up enough to go home.

This can't be a booty call. Not with how we left it. And where I'm living right now.

Does he want to talk?

Do I?

I turn onto my side and curl into a shrimp. On the one hand, no, I don't. I'd rather pluck my eyeballs out. But on the other hand—I'll probably explode if I don't find out what he wants.

My stomach clenches and careens at the same time, and even before my thumbs tap "yeah" of their own accord, I know it's inevitable. If someone shows an interest, I respond.

I'm expecting to see dots appear, but instead, the phone rings. For some reason, the volume is turned up loud, and I fumble it. I have to lean all the way over the bed to fish it out from under the night table. When I click the green button, I'm breathless.

"Hi?"

"Angie." Brandon's voice is low. Stern. Now my stomach feels like I'm in trouble.

"Yeah?" I say, suddenly defensive.

"I've got something to say, okay?"

"Okay."

He sounds so serious. Is he dumping me? He can't. We're not going out. Oh Lord, he's not calling to let me down easy, is he? No normal guy would, not after a single make-out session, but no other guy I know would be making a whole-ass phone call when he could text, either.

He clears his throat. "I'm sorry. I went too far, and I know that. I didn't mean to go that far, but I did, and I accept responsibility for that. I knew Maddie would keep the kids inside, but you didn't see her wink at me, so you didn't know that, and you put a stop to things, and rightfully so, and I was an asshole." He stops for a breath.

My brain whirls, trying to process. Maddie knew he was making a move?

He plunges on. "I shouldn't have said those things, but I want to be clear—I am always going to be up-front with you, and I want you to feel like you can be honest with me, too. I fucking hated that you were with Tyler, but I'm an adult, and that wasn't my choice or my business. I didn't need to talk to you like I did today. I only ever want to treat you with respect, and I didn't, and I apologize."

He falls quiet. What do I say? Is he reading this? It sounds way too smooth to be something he's coming up with in the moment. "And just to be clear," he adds. "I'm not sorry it happened, only that I pushed it too far."

I wait a few seconds to make sure he's done, and then I can't help but ask. "Did you write that out?"

"Yeah," he says without missing a beat. He's not the least embarrassed.

"On paper?"

"In my notes app." He's not bothered at all that I'm asking. I've never met a man less touchy about his pride than Brandon Kaczmarek. "There's more."

I'm already having a hot flash from embarrassment

under his old flannel sheet. I don't think I can handle more. "Listen. It's fine. Don't worry about it."

"Angie, it obviously wasn't fine with you," he says.

"It's fine, really. But thank you. For saying." Tyler would *never*, not in a million years.

"It's nothing." It obviously isn't, but I get what he means from his tone. It doesn't bother him to say sorry.

I want more than anything for this conversation to end, but also, I don't want to hang up. Except for the glow of the phone, it's dark in the room, and lonely. "Let's just sweep it under the rug, okay?"

He chuckles from the back of his throat, and I shiver. "Sweep it under the rug?"

"Yeah. You know what I mean."

"Yeah." He draws in a breath, and the phone is pressed so close to my ear, it's like a whisper. "We can do—or not do—whatever you want."

I bite my bottom lip until it stings. "I let things get carried away, too."

"Yeah, you got carried away," he says, a touch of smugness in his voice. "I did, too," he adds.

"So you said. A few times."

"Let me read the rest of what I wrote," he asks, almost playfully.

I don't want to let him. Whatever he says, I'm going to have to respond somehow, and I just want to be in this moment a little longer, listening to him breathe in the dark, my whole body tingling and warm. I want things to be new with him, not complicated and probably doomed.

"Did you know I'm staying in your old room?" I change the subject.

"How's it treating you?" He goes along without missing a beat.

"It's fine."

"Everything's fine," he says, and it's a little dig, but he doesn't say it like a dick.

"Do you remember when you and your dad built it out?"

"Yeah." He chuckles. "I was so excited. I had this idea that I was getting, like, a sweet bachelor pad. I was gonna have a big-ass TV and beanbag chairs and a mini fridge, and I was gonna invite you down to play *Mario Kart*. And then it turned out to be the size of Mom's minivan."

"You never played Mario," I say.

He was into shooter games like every other boy, and he got sullen the few times Madison made him get off so we could play.

"But you didn't like anything except Mario."

He's right. I still don't even though it's been years since I played a video game.

"Why did you want to play with me?" I ask, my stomach fizzling. I know why, but I want him to say.

"Because you were pretty," he says, and if any other man said it, it'd be a line, an ick, but the way he talks—the way he's always talked—he's just saying what he thinks. Simple as that. "Still are."

My face flushes so bright, there's no way he can't hear it in my voice. I try to play it off. "Miss Dawn never would've allowed it."

He laughs. "I guess not. I would've had to wait until Dad was in charge."

"I don't think he would've gone for it, either." Despite the ponytail, Mr. Mike was an old-fashioned kind of guy. He was the one who wouldn't let Madison wear lipstick or get her ears pierced until she was thirteen, and he was always lecturing us to stick together when he dropped us off at football games and stuff at the school.

"Nah. He trusted me."

It's true. Mr. Mike never treated Brandon like a kid. He

didn't call him "bud" or "buddy" like most dads. He called him "partner," like a cowboy from a western. Maybe that's how you raise good kids—you treat them like they're already what you want them to be. I need to think about that more later.

"Would you have come and played Mario with me?" he asks, his voice a little lower, a little huskier.

"If Madison could have come, too." That's just the truth. I was shy back then. Still am. The only reason I went out with Tyler in the first place was because he showed up at my front door, and my mom was high and hollering "Who's that knocking at my fucking door," so it was less embarrassing to go with him than tell him no.

Why is saying *no* my kryptonite?

Why is saying *yes* just as hard?

All of a sudden, I'm so damn tired of being stuck between them, being afraid of them both. I wasn't always like this. There was a time when I ran for the ice cream truck and stuck my hand out for candy and raced to the pool and cannonballed in, as free as every other kid, and I was so young then, but I can remember what it felt like to be fearless and bold because the sun was shining and the sugar was sweet.

I break my back so the girls will know that feeling. Do I really have to live the rest of my life without any sweetness for myself?

I don't want to.

"Angie? You still there?" Brandon asks, his voice gruff.

"Yeah." I take a deep breath. "You know, I liked what we were doing earlier. I didn't mean to fight you off like you did something wrong. You didn't. That was me, getting in my head."

"I liked it, too." The gravel in his voice uncurls something in my belly. "Let me read the rest of what I wrote?"

"Okay." I stretch my legs all the way to my toes. For some reason, I'm not so worried now about what he's going to say.

He clears his throat again, but this time, it's not nerves. He's playing around. "I know that you're not ready yet, and I respect that. But I'm going to ask you out again. Or you can ask me out. I'll say yes." He pauses a second. "I will always say yes to you, Angie."

"Why? 'Cause I'm so pretty?" I wince. I'm playing, but I don't ever act bigheaded, not even joking around. It makes me feel exposed, like I need to throw up a wall, some kind of defense, because my entire body is Jell-O now, squishy, wobbly, tender, defenseless Jell-O.

"Yeah, that." He pauses a second and then says, "That and how you make me feel."

"How do I make you feel?" I felt like I was at the edge of a high ledge, and now it feels like my toes are curled over the edge.

"Like I've got reasons."

"For what?"

"Everything."

Oh, hell, what do I say to that, especially with my heart stuck in my throat?

I wish he was here.

I wish I'd already told him what I need to tell him, and we were past it, and it all turned out fine. If I had his confidence, I'd know now whether we have a chance.

But I'm a coward, albeit less of one than I was a few months ago. I summon up those small, tender shoots of courage. "I do want you to ask me out again. In a few months."

"Yeah?" His voice goes so warm, it could melt marshmallows. "You'll let me buy you dinner?"

"Sure. I'll order the lobster."

"You like lobster?"

"I've never had it. Have you?"

"Oh yeah. Lobster rolls. Lobster tails. Lobster mac and cheese. You've been missing out."

"Do you wear the bib?"

"Of course. Got to protect the fine threads."

"Fine threads, eh?" I've never seen him in anything but T-shirts and flannels and the lone blue denim shirt he wore on away-game days back in high school.

"If I'm wearing it, it looks fine."

The conversation wanders away from there. We talk about restaurants and the jobs we had after school—I worked fast food, and he crabbed—and the times I went with his family to the ocean and Tamblyn's first time at the beach. We talk for hours, and my eyelids droop. We both start drifting off and losing our trains of thought, but I don't suggest hanging up and neither does he.

His voice makes the room safe and cozy, quieting my ever-present background worries like magic, as familiar as the lines on my palm and exciting and new at the same time.

I'm yanked back from the brink of sleep when he says, "Angie, you've got to hang up and put the phone on the charger for tomorrow."

I'm too tired to reply with anything but a mumble.

"Goodnight, beautiful," he says.

I pass out before I can answer him back.

That night, I dream.

I'm in this same pitch-black bedroom, but it's like a stage, an empty stage in an empty theater, and I can't see anything besides Brandon, standing at the foot of the bed. He's wearing his work clothes—a neon reflective vest and jeans. All I'm wearing is an oversized T-shirt. No bra. No panties.

I'm propped on my elbows, my knees pressed tightly together.

"Show me," he says, his voice rough and demanding.

My heart pounds in my chest. "I can't."

"Why not?"

"You're Madison's brother," I say.

"She's not here," he says. "No one's here. Show me."

I want to. It aches. Throbs. He won't touch me down there unless I show him, and it should be a simple thing to ease my legs apart, but I'm frozen, and he won't come any closer. I rub my thighs together, desperate for the friction.

"Let me see, Angie," he growls.

"No," I whine.

"Do you want me to make you? Is that what you want?" His hand goes to his belt. He unbuckles it and yanks the strap free from its loops. I whimper. My ass clenches. He winds the belt around his hand once. The rest dangles.

"Please." I want him to make me, but he just stands there, broad-shouldered, straight-spined, confident and in control, while I squirm on the bed, hot and needy.

"Why won't you show me? Are you scared?"

"Yes," I whimper.

He growls. "Show me." This time, it's an order that I don't dare ignore. This is Brandon, but not my friend's brother. He's the man who makes the house's ceiling lower and the hallways narrower when he steps inside. He's bigger and stronger and tougher than me.

"Show me, or you're not gonna like what I do."

Suddenly, dream me isn't scared anymore. She wants to see what he'll do, and she knows he's going to drop the belt before he does. His fist unfurls. The strap slithers through his fingers. The buckle thumps against the ground.

He flicks open the button of his jeans. Unzips the zipper. Draws himself out. My belly spasms.

I let my knees fall to the sides.

"You're not going to hurt me," I pant.

"*You* hurt *me*," he says, his hand working his cock, his eyes burning. "Now you've got to make it right. Touch yourself. Touch that pretty pussy."

"I can't," I moan. "You won't want me."

"I'm here," he says. "I'm here right now. Come for me."

The orgasm tears through me, jerking me awake. My heart pounds. I gasp for air, sweaty, with sticky fingers in the dark.

I look at my phone for the time. The call is still going.

"Brandon?" I whisper, my whole body catching fire.

There's no answer.

I've never tapped *end* so fast, so hard, so many times.

7

BRANDON

It's Saturday night, I'm at the gym, and Angie's going out, but not with me.

I had to hear it from Maddie. They're going into the city to the Power Plant. Girl's night.

It's fine. I have no right to be pissed. We're taking it slow. Sometimes she sends me memes. I think about calling her all the time. We talk when I come over to the house. Nothing heavy. She tells me about work and the girls, and I listen.

The weights clank as I let go too soon. Shane says, "Whoa." Everybody looks over. I wince. This isn't that kind of gym.

I take a deep breath. A night out at the bars is no big deal. Angie's not cruising for dick.

I'm not fucking everything up again by giving her time.

The day after the shed debacle, I figured she'd get skittish if I gave her space, so I showed up the next morning with pea gravel to level up the driveway. Mom had been talking about doing it for a while.

I got Tamblyn to help, and Ivy's at the age where rocks are the best, so Angie had to sit out on the front porch and watch us work. She wasn't obvious about it, but she was as fascinated by my arms as Ivy was by the rocks.

I thought I was good, and I was gonna ask her out again for this weekend. Then Maddie called me, and from how reluctantly she was breaking it to me, I thought she was gonna tell me Aunt Sylvester out in Ohio finally died, but she said Angie asked to go with her out to the bars. She wants to "have fun."

I'm fucking fun.

I slide ten more pounds on the bar and start a new set, lifting fast, paying no attention to form.

I guess I understand. While the rest of us were out making bad choices—including Tyler, who I saw down at Donovan's more weekends than not—Angie was at home raising her babies. She deserves a night out, especially since, as best I can tell, Tyler's still at the bar on the weekend, and she's still home with the kids.

I finish my set and re-rack the bar. Shane is supposed to be spotting me, but he's scrolling on his phone. In fairness, we've been here for almost three hours at this point, and he tapped out a half hour ago. I've still got too much energy.

"You can hit the showers if you want," I offer, hopping up from the bench. "I'm gonna get on the cable machine for a while. I'll meet you down at Donovan's."

"Dude, you drove," he says.

"Oh, yeah." My head isn't exactly screwed on straight. I keep picturing Angie in a dress and high heels with her hair done. Before the wedding, I hadn't seen her dressed up since homecoming senior year. She was too far along with Tamblyn to go to prom.

At homecoming, her dress was baby blue and sparkly, and her hair was up with curls hanging down. She smiled and blushed all night. You could tell she felt pretty.

She's gonna be smiling like that tonight, and some

asshole's going to mistake it for flirting. Or maybe she will be flirting. Fuck.

"Gimme another twenty minutes," I say to Shane. He wanders off to the back of the gym to sit at the circuit's bicep curl machine and play on his phone. No one's gonna bother him there. I'm probably good for another forty-five minutes.

Angie doesn't flirt. She's too surprised that someone's paying attention to her. Her parents did a number on her. That's why Tyler got in so quick and easy, and why she stuck with him. Because she's grateful.

Maddie calls it "co-dependent," and I guess that's bad—I don't really follow therapy shit—but I don't think it's totally fair to be down on her for it. Tyler is the asshole. She tried to make it work with the father of her children. I didn't like it —hated it, in fact—but what would people say if she didn't? They'd say she took his kids from him. They'd call her a bitch.

I don't want her hard-hearted. I like her how she is. I'm not a raging dick like some, but I am a man, and hard times are inevitable. I don't want her tough. I want her clingy.

I guess you're not supposed to want that these days, but I still like vinyl records and manual transmission, too. What gets you hard, gets you hard.

I want to talk to her about this shit, but I don't know how to start, and whenever I get her to myself for a minute and ask how she's doing, she goes off on something like Tamblyn can "read" her elephant and piggie book—not really, she memorized it, but that's still impressive for her age in my opinion—and she's just so happy and chatty that I don't want to mess up the mood. Happy Angie is hot.

So I just walk around with a semi and a bunch of pent-up feelings, and spend too much time at the gym, and piss off my friends, and make up every excuse I can think of to go over to my mom's house.

For *months* at this point. And I've gotten so far that she's going out downtown without me. I'm doing this wrong.

"Dude, you almost done?" Shane leans over the railing that separates the machines from the free weights. He hit the showers. His hair is wet, and he smells like he spilled his cologne on himself. "I told Hannah and Ashley we'd be down there by nine."

I blink and glance around. It's so late on a Saturday night that we're the only guys under thirty left in the place.

"Why'd you tell Ashley I'd be there?" We had a brief, casual thing a few years ago, and every so often, she texts. I don't know what to do, so I reply with a thumbs up.

Shane shrugs. "She asked. You have something against getting laid?" He thinks that since I haven't nailed Angie down, I'm free.

"I don't know if I'm actually up to go out tonight," I say, stretching my traps. "I could use a hot shower."

Shane rolls his eyes. "Sure. A hot shower."

"What? I'm tight." I stretch an arm across my body. It's true. I've been spending more hours with the weights than usual. I'm also bulking up since I'm eating more of Mom's cooking, and to her, butter is a food group.

Shane snorts. "You mean you're a simp."

"I don't know what you're talking about, man." I grab my keys and water bottle off the floor.

"You gonna head over to your mom's after that cold shower?" Shane watches me from the corner of his eyes, smirking.

I don't give him the satisfaction of a reply. Instead, I slap his back a little harder than is friendly and say, "Come on. I'll drop you off."

And yeah, after I leave him at Donovan's, I consider going around to Mom's, but I think better of it.

If I'm there when she gets home, Angie will know I'm

checking up on her. And if she comes home late—or not at all—I'll lose my shit. I can control myself well enough not to let it show, but I don't want that energy around the girls, even if they're tucked in bed.

What the fuck is she doing?

She likes me. I'm not stupid. It's obvious. She likes it when I touch her.

I've gotten ridiculously handsy lately. I rest a hand on her lower back when she passes through a door ahead of me, and she glances up at me and blushes. I inch my chair real close to hers at dinner, and she doesn't scoot away. She lets her thighs relax so her leg rests against mine. She wants this, too, but something's holding her back.

Does she think she's got to prove her independence or sow her wild oats or some such shit?

I wouldn't think she's the wild oats type, but Maddie is, and she's in her ear all the time. I rub my chest. I'm hungry, and I've got indigestion at the same time. And I'm only twenty-five years old. Goddamn.

When I get home, I do take a cold shower. I turn the TV on and ignore it to scroll my phone without really paying attention to anything. It's midnight. Is she home yet?

Maddie usually doesn't roll home until past closing time, but Angie's a mother. She's probably too worn out to close down the bar. Unless she met someone. She wouldn't go anywhere with a stranger, though, and besides, Maddie wouldn't let her.

I can breathe normally. There's no reason to stress.

I toss my phone on the couch and go see what's in the fridge. Same shit as the last time I checked. I eat a few cold wings from yesterday's carry out, and about a minute after I lick my fingers, I regret it.

If I drove past Mom's, I wouldn't even know if Angie's back or not. They took a ride share so they could drink.

I should not have eaten those fucking wings. I brush my teeth, but it doesn't help. Now I've got minty-flavored heartburn.

I'm considering lying down in bed and staring at the ceiling when my phone rings from the other room. I sprint for it and get it before the third ring.

"Brandon?" It's Maddie, shouting to be heard over raised voices in the background. Men's voices.

My heart thrusts into my throat like a fist. "What's wrong?"

"Brandon?"

"Yeah, Maddie, what's going on?" I put her on speaker so I can shove my feet into my boots. I don't spare the time for socks.

"Can you come get us?" She sounds pissed, not scared, thank God.

"Yeah, what happened?"

"I forgot my purse. I'll tell you about it when you get here."

"Are you and Angie okay?"

"Yeah, we're fine. We're at the Power Plant. At Piano Man. We'll be out front."

"Wait inside."

She laughs. "No can do."

"You're not waiting in the street with a bunch of drunks, Maddie." I yank my laces tight. Besides, it's cold. Fall came late this year, but it's here now.

"It's the Power Plant. There are Segway cops everywhere."

"You can wait inside." It's not even one in the morning, and I can make it there in thirty minutes. Maybe twenty-five.

She laughs. "No, we seriously cannot. I'll tell you about it when you get here. Just bring your wallet."

By the time she hangs up, I'm hopping into the truck. It

would be a fifteen-minute drive if it was a straight shot, but I live on a peninsula, and most times, I love how it feels like the country even though we're less than a mile to the city line. Tonight, though, I'm crawling out of my skin, crowded forward in my seat, forcing myself to stay close to the speed limit.

It won't do any good if I plow into a deer on my way, and as far as I can tell, the bastards spend their nights wandering back and forth across North Point Road, taking occasional breaks to hang out on the yellow line and gape at oncoming headlights. When I get to Peninsula Expressway, I hit the gas. It's two lanes in both directions, and I'm fairly sure I can slalom around any deer who tries its luck.

I slow down again when I get into the city. The roads are mostly empty in this part of town. I stop at a red light with no cars in sight in any direction, and I sit there, sweating, for what feels like an eternity before it changes to green.

This part of town is lonely at night—the cranes in the distance, the office buildings with the lights on like jack-o'-lanterns, the men huddled and shuffling in front of the gas station convenience stores, passing time, waiting for morning. You can't find parking around here during the day, but at this hour, there's no one but folks working the midnight shift or left behind. Like a ghost town.

When I get a few blocks further, closer to midtown, the vibe changes. Everyone is still awake here. I drive past groups of folks stumbling to their rides and vaping in front of the pizza and burger joints as bright and crowded as if it's two in the afternoon, not two in the morning.

I've been to the Power Plant—everyone has—but not often. It's for corporate bros and college kids. I prefer Donovan's or The Fort where I've already made a drunk ass out of myself in front of everybody and a domestic beer doesn't cost as much as a venti mocha Frappuccino.

By some luck, I find street parking two blocks down from Piano Man. My nerves are strung tight, but I'm breathing a little easier now that I'm here. I don't need to jog. They're okay. Maddie said so, and she's a shitty liar.

I see them before they see me. They're both sitting on a planter in front of the club. Maddie's arm is around Angie's waist, and Angie's head is resting on Maddie's shoulder. Maddie is running her mouth, and by her face, I can tell she's trying to coax Angie into smiling. I've done the same myself, more than a few times. It sounds messed up, but getting Angie to smile is like getting a dog to roll over for belly rubs. It feels the same, like you somehow got God's stamp of approval.

Something's upset her tonight. Her shoulders are slumped, and her mascara is smudged. She's still beautiful, of course, in a pink dress with bare legs and those Han Solo boots. No coat, just a thin white sweater. She must be freezing.

All of a sudden, my temper flares. I don't care that we haven't officially gone out yet. In my heart, she feels like mine, and here she is, dressed up for someone else and sad. Again.

I glare down the sidewalk. They haven't seen me yet. Maddie says something, and Angie fakes a weak smile. I feel a jerk as the hook sets in my chest. The flare of temper fades. She's mine, all right. Time to get her.

I approach slowly. Maddie notices me first. She pops to her feet and shrieks, "Finally!"

Angie blinks, confused. Her eyes are bleary. She's buzzed.

So is Maddie. She zigzags to meet me, and the rum fumes hit me well before she does.

"I need your credit card." She holds out her open palm.

Behind her, Angie hangs her head. I reach for my wallet.

"I forgot my purse, which we thought was fine because we had Angie's bank card, but when we closed out the tab, it got declined because—you're never going to believe this—" She pauses to snatch my card from my fingers.

Behind her, Angie shrinks in her thin sweater.

Maddie rants on, ever more belligerent. "Tyler cleared her out. *While* we were here. He took himself on a shopping spree at Thom's Cycle." Maddie shakes her head, and the motion makes her tip from side to side. I know better than to steady her. If she goes down, she'll take me with her.

Maddie clutches my arm. "He literally picked the girls up, saw that Angie was going out, and went straight to Thom's Cycle and just cleared out their checking account. You know how much he left?"

"Go pay the tab," I say quietly. Over on the planter, Angie looks like she's leaking air by the second.

"Sixty-seven cents. He's like the freaking Grinch. He Whoville-d her. He even took the roast beast." Maddie's voice has climbed so high that she has no choice but to drop it. "What kind of person does that?"

An asshole, but I don't know why any of us should act surprised. "Maddie, it's almost closing time. You better go settle up."

"And then that bartender, he said we better go find some money, or we're getting banned, and he took our picture with his phone—without permission—and he said he'd be passing it around to all the other places here, and no one will serve us."

At "he took our picture," my blood rushes to my brain. My vision telescopes, and my hands fist. Immediately, I hear my dad's voice. *Whoa, son. Think.*

Maddie watches me carefully, a spark in her eye. It takes a lot for me to lose my shit, but this might do it. She loves trying to wind me up and aim me at someone. Most times, I'm too smart.

But Angie's shivering, and she's wilting every second that ticks by. She's not having fun, and I know I was mad about it a minute ago, but now I just want to get her in my truck and blast the heat.

"Go pay him," I tell Maddie. "Make him show you while he deletes the pictures. If he doesn't, take a picture of him and send it to me."

"You're not coming in?"

"Do you need me to?" She doesn't. Maddie is like my mom—vicious when provoked. Like a hippopotamus.

She huffs, pissed that I won't lose my temper on her behalf. Besides Dad, that's probably what taught me how to control myself growing up—the satisfaction of not letting her push my buttons.

"Watch Angie," she barks at me as she twirls and flounces back into the bar, remarkably confident for someone almost falling off her high heels every few steps. It's like watching a clown on stilts.

My body is ready to fight, but I don't want to give a beat-down to a dickish bartender doing his job; I want to break Tyler Reynold's face. I want to smash his bones into tiny pieces until he's a heap on the floor, and he can never strut around like a big man again, lifting himself up by stepping on the woman in front of me.

I'm angry—at him, and her—but I also need to be next to her.

I close the distance between us with slow steps, giving her time to finish scrubbing her eyes with the cuffs of her sweater. She glances up at me with a forced, watery smile, and I'm pierced through the chest.

Even with a clown face of smudged makeup, she's pretty as hell.

"Can I sit?" I ask, nodding to the planter beside her.

She sniffs, which I take to mean that it's cool. I check my pockets for a handkerchief, but all I've got is my wallet and the mostly empty plastic container of nicotine lozenges I carry around in a break-glass-in-case-of-emergency kind of way. A tissue wouldn't really help at this point. The damage is already done to her sweater sleeves.

She sees me noticing and tries to tuck her hands far enough into her sleeves to fist the cuffs and hide the mascara stains, but it doesn't quite work. All of a sudden, I'm mad, *and* I want to pull her onto my lap, press her face into the crook of my neck, and mumble sweet shit in her ear until she forgets anything that's ever made her sad.

But obviously, I can't. She'd fight me off again, and I'd get pepper-sprayed by one of these chicks walking by. So instead, I say, "Rough night?"

She summons up another half-smile. "Could be worse. You heard Madison. I've still got sixty-seven cents."

"Hey, that'll buy you a stamp."

"Not anymore."

I raise an eyebrow. Now I'm mad and ridiculously pleased that she's going along with my dumbass joke.

"They raised the price to sixty-eight cents," she says.

I widen my eyes. "Highway robbery."

Her smile kind of finds its feet. "We're being had."

"They dipping stamps in gold these days?"

"Must be." She's quiet for a minute. Folks stumble past, laughing and loud. "Thanks for coming."

"Yeah."

"I'll pay you back."

My instinct is to argue, but I refrain. I don't want her to feel indebted. I want her to feel like she doesn't need to go looking for fun. My temper simmers, and I try not to look like I'm breathing in her vanilla perfume.

I nod and change the subject. "So were you having a good time before shit went south?"

She sighs. "I tipped the piano guy my last twenty, and he didn't play my song."

I've been dragged to Piano Man a few times. Their schtick is a grand piano in the middle of the place. You jot down what song you want on a scrap of paper with a golf pencil and drop it in a big glass bowl along with some cash. They've got guys who can play and sing and do a little crowd work. It's fine if you don't mind hearing "Sweet Caroline" at least three times in one night.

"What song did you ask for?" I ask.

"'Stand By Me.'"

"Good choice."

"You think so?"

"I don't say what I don't mean." I watch her consider that and conclude that, yeah, I'm telling the truth. I am. I'm very good at keeping my mouth shut if I don't have something nice to say. There's a lot of shit I'm not saying right now.

She glances up at me, her eyes shiny. I see the moment when she decides she's too tired to keep up the front. "It's the first time Tyler's taken the girls for a weekend."

I nod like I'm totally following the direction the conversation has taken.

"I just didn't want to miss them all night."

I nod again. I get that. And now I feel like an asshole for being mad that she went out.

"But I ended up missing them at a bar instead of from the comfort of home." Her eyes lock on mine while the rest of her mask falls away.

Pain and worry are etched on her face, and still, somehow, she looks years younger than she did a minute ago. My lungs freeze. She's talking to me. Really talking. This is what I wanted. In a way, it feels like scoring a touchdown in overtime, but at the same time, her sadness, and my inability to fix it, claws at my heart.

She sighs. "I wanted to get dressed up and feel confident, you know? Go dancing and be in my twenties for once, but all I did was stand around and go to the bathroom and sit in the stall and look at pictures of the girls on my phone."

I have no real concept of what she's feeling. I've got no similar experience, and even if I was a single dad, I don't think it would hit quite the same. It doesn't seem to be the same for the guys I know who are split from their kids' moms. It's ugly for them, too, but it wears different. At least it seems that way from the outside.

I don't know what to say, so I bump her with my elbow. "Show me?"

"The pics?"

I nod. She smiles, surprised, but also like that's exactly what she wanted to be asked. Score. Two points. I feel seven feet tall, even though I'm sitting down.

She pulls out her phone from where she tucked it in her bra, and her fingers fly.

"This is down the ocean last year." She shows me a picture of her with the girls, all lined up, one behind the other. She's furthest back, her legs spread in a V. Tamblyn sits crisscross-applesauce in front of her, leaning back against her mama's chest. Angie's arms are wrapped snug around her.

Ivy is lying on her belly, her chin propped on her hands and her feet kicked up, inches from nailing Tamblyn in the face. All three of them look dipped and rolled in sand, their wet hair in matted tangles, smiling their matching, orange slice smiles.

It softens my insides, but at the same time, jealousy grips my chest. "Who took the picture?" I ask.

"A lady on the blanket next to ours." Angie looks up

from the screen, a shadow crossing her face. "Tyler bailed. At the last minute, he got free tickets for seats right behind the dugout." Her expression hardens. "I know he was no good."

She says it like I'm about to tell her that, and she wants to head me off. She's not picking up that I'm jealous if she thinks I'm trying to point out how her ex is an asshole. It's not news. We all know that.

I want to know who made her smile like that, so I can torture myself. Would it make a difference if she knew? How would I even tell her?

"I know I should have had higher standards," she adds. I don't know who she's defending herself against—probably Maddie and Mom and every other decent person who knows her or has ever met Tyler Reynolds—but I don't want her to think she has to do that with me.

"I don't give a shit where Tyler was. I just don't like you smiling at guys."

Her eyes go wide. I guess that's how I'd tell her. Smooth.

"You've got to stop beating yourself up about him. You did what was best at the time." Her brow furrows, and she searches my face. To see if I'm serious? Or if I'm just trying to make her feel better? I am, but it's the truth, at least how I see it.

She's got two whole humans she's responsible for keeping fed and clothed and clean and happy. There have been several times at mom's when I've wondered "Where's Tamblyn?" or "Where's Ivy?" because I suddenly realized I hadn't seen or heard them in a while. Thank goodness they were always in the basement or the daycare kids' room, but if I can lose track of them in a rancher, what's it like to make sure they're safe and accounted for every single moment of the day?

"I did do my best," she says, looking up at me, fierce and

defensive, like I hadn't just said it myself, but also like the idea is new to her. "I wanted the girls to have a real family."

"I get that."

She exhales and glances down at the sidewalk. "*I* wanted a real family," she says like she's confessing to a shameful thing.

My brain shuffles as quick as it can through possible replies. I suck at this. I'm a man, and I've never had a serious relationship, at least none that required me to talk much beyond compliments and showing an interest, and I need to get this right.

There's nothing bad about wanting a family—I want one, too, most people do—but I don't want to be like "there's nothing wrong with that" when it's clear from the way she said it that *she* thinks there is.

She shivers and hunches a little further over. Shit. What do I say? Well, I guess if she can be real, I can, too.

"I do, too. I want a real family," I say.

She glances over, surprised. "Yeah?"

My brain kicks into panic mode, hollering at me to make it a joke. Back away with my hands in the air. I'm too exposed. I need to say something about having a woman to put dinner on the table, something about home-cooked meals.

Why does my panicked brain sound like Randy when he's trying to piss off his wife?

The throwaway words are on the tip of my tongue, like they've been written out for me, but I can also picture exactly what happens when I say them—she whacks me playfully, rolls her eyes, and collects herself to leave, pretending to be offended, but actually disappointed that she was real with me, and I didn't have the balls to be real with her.

I am operating light-years beyond my capabilities as a

man. I have no choice. I let go and let God. "I wish there was someone who looked at me like the girls to you," I say. "I'd like to know what it feels like to matter like that."

She peers up at me like she can't quite believe what she's hearing. I smile at her. She cocks her head. I shrug. I'd never have been so honest if I weren't at a loss for what to say, but I said it, and I own it.

Her chin dips, coy and shy, and her lips curve. For the first time tonight, a spark returns to her eyes. I'm only noticing how brown they are—relieved that I somehow said the right thing—when I begin to fall into them. I lean closer. My breath hitches. Her ripe pink lips part. A soft sigh of expectation escapes.

She smells like rum and mint gum and vanilla body spray and whatever she puts in her hair. If my lungs worked, I'd inhale the scent so deep I'd never forget it, not in a hundred years.

I'm crazy for her.

I'd do anything if it meant she would look at me all the time like she's looking at me now—like I'm too good to be true.

I've never felt more real, more out of my depth and out of my league. I'm skating on pure dumb luck, and I know it. What do I say next? Do I kiss her? Even though she's drunk and sad, and to be honest, I'm still pissed that she came out tonight?

I didn't know you could be mad at a woman and love her this hard at the same time. I mean, I've heard of a hate fuck, but I'm not talking about anything like that. This is delicate. Like defusing a bomb.

Angie kind of tilts her head, waiting, patient and trusting and so goddamn lovely that my chest aches.

What do I say so that she never stops looking at me like this?

I dig deep. I send up a prayer. Once more, I let Jesus take the wheel, and I ask, "Do you want tacos?"

She smiles, the biggest, realest, best smile. "Hell yeah, I do."

"Tacos?" Maddie stumbles over to us, a receipt and my credit card clutched in her fist. "Let's go."

"He give you trouble?" I pry my card from her hand.

She pouts. "He asked for my number."

"Bold choice," I say.

She nods in agreement, her drunk bobblehead making me dizzy. "I told him if he wanted a shot, he should've covered our tab."

"Right on." I hold up my palm for a high five. She aims, swings, and misses. I snort. It's my favorite game to play with blitzed Maddie. You don't even need to move your hand away.

Beside me, Angie snickers.

"Traitor." Maddie pouts at her. "You like him better than me now."

"He said we'd go get tacos," Angie stage-whispers to Maddie as she wraps her arm around Maddie's waist and guides her in the direction of my truck. I follow a few feet behind so Maddie can't take me out if she falls off her heels onto her ass.

"You can't like him better. He's boring," Maddie stage-whispers back. "He randomly smells like fish. He only passed English because Mom rewrote all his essays. He keeps worms in the butter compartment in his refrigerator."

Screw her. The fish smell isn't random. I just smell that way when I haven't had the chance to change my clothes yet after I come back from the creek.

"Don't ask me for any more favors, Maddie," I call up to her.

"Hah," she says. "If I say I'm with Angie, you know you'll come running."

My face heats, but I'm past acting like I don't care. "I would," I say quietly.

Angie darts a glance back at me over her shoulder. She knows I'm talking to her. Her cheeks flush, her eyes sparkle, and while Maddie wobbles more with each step, Angie walks taller.

She keeps her eyes straight ahead. When we get to my truck, Maddie lurches for the door, hauls herself into the second row, and sprawls across the entire bench before Angie has a chance to make a move.

I swing the passenger door open. Angie ducks her head and uses the grab handle to pull herself up.

"Buckle up," I tell Maddie as I settle myself in.

I like a spacious cab, but at this moment, I'm wishing there wasn't so much space between Angie and me. She's nestled on her side, and there's no casual way to brush her arm or grab her hand. She looks nervous.

I am, too. Nervous and alive and awake. I'm not mad anymore. I feel like somehow, I won.

"Turn the radio on," Maddie whines from the back. I flip on the country station out of spite like I always do.

"Anything but that!" Maddie hollers.

Angie glances over.

"You choose," I offer.

She changes it to a Top 40 station, and we're quiet while I drive us out of the dark city, silent and still except for steam rising from grates and blinking yellow lights.

First, Maddie's head slumps against the window. Then it droops until her chin rests on her chest, and she starts snoring.

Angie and I grin at each other. She rests her forearm on

her side of the center console. I wait a few minutes and rest mine next to hers.

She's staring at her lap, but her lips turn up at the corners.

I move my forearm over so that it brushes against hers. My heart beats quicker. It feels like fishing when you've been waiting all day, that fraction of time between when your bobber first disappears under the surface and the next bite that tugs it under. That moment of uncertainty and hopefulness when you've got to be ready, but you don't dare act.

She glances into the rearview to check on Maddie, and then she curls her pinkie around mine.

Now I'm forcing myself not to grin like an idiot and to keep my eyes on the road while my pinkie is hooked around a girl's like I'm sixteen again, and I could fly, I could fight a bear, I could drive like this forever.

We get to the restaurant too soon, but also just in time. The drive-through is open, but it closes in ten minutes.

"Hey, Maddie. Want tacos?" I call back to be polite. She keeps snoring. "How many can you eat?" I ask Angie.

"Oh, I-I don't know. Two?"

That's a bold-faced lie. I've been around on taco night. I order the crunchy taco combo, the burrito box, two orders of nachos, and the cinnamon rolls.

"You want the orange or blue Slushie," I ask.

She sputters a second like she's going to argue or bring up money, but thankfully, she ends up just saying, "Blue."

I squeeze her pinkie with mine. I know her pride stings.

"We're never going to be able to eat all this," she says when they pass the bags through the window.

"You can take the leftovers home for the girls." It's something to see those two eat tacos. Lettuce ends up scattered under the table. Shredded cheese gets stuck in their hair.

Sauce splurts everywhere. Makes 'em happy as clams, though, and God did invent brooms.

For a second, I consider parking in the lot to eat, but then a better idea strikes me.

"Mind going up the road a bit?" I ask Angie.

"Sure." She's holding the bag in her lap now instead of my hand.

I drive us down to the next light and turn into the neighborhood. Down a few streets, there's a park by the water with a boat launch where I used to play tee-ball. Every neighborhood on the peninsula has a community park just like it with a pier and a playground and a baseball diamond, all of it the worse for wear, but hanging in there. A lot like the town itself.

In the parking lot, I do a three-point turn and back into a space near the boat ramp. I jump out to open Angie's door and take the bag from her.

"Last chance, Maddie," I call, but she's dead to the world.

I lower the tailgate and swing Angie up to sit on it. She squeaks and clutches my shoulders. I'm standing between her knees, and all I want to do is drag her hips closer, wind my arms around her, and lose myself in her like I did behind the shed. But that didn't end well, did it? I've got to play this smarter.

I satisfy myself with brushing my fingers along the sides of her thighs while I step back. "Comfortable?" I ask her.

She wiggles her butt. "Totally."

I vault up to sit beside her and move the bag so it's not between us. "Taco or burrito?" I ask.

"Taco."

I pass her one and grab another for myself.

We sit and eat, shoulder to shoulder, our legs dangling. The water laps at the bank below us. The taco shells crunch. Angie giggles and groans as lettuce and cheese fall down her front. Tamblyn and Ivy come by their messiness honestly.

I dig a napkin out and offer it to her. She tucks it in the neck of her dress.

"Dignified, eh?" she says, her cheeks shadowing in the moonlight. There are no working lights on this side of the parking lot, but the moon is full, and the streetlamps along the expressway cast their reflections on the far side of the creek. Cars shush in the distance, but they're few and far between at this hour.

Angie always has a vulnerable look to her, but not here, alone in the dark with me. Her eyes are like the woods that the man described in the poem, the only thing I remember from English class. His name was Robert Frost. He said the woods were "lovely, dark, and deep."

She keeps darting glances at me, her need and her nerves as clear on her face as mine must be. Blood rushes to my dick.

"Beautiful," I say, brushing a stray hair behind her ear.

She ducks her head and smiles. I pass her another taco.

When she finishes, she crumples up her napkin and wrappers, tosses them in the bag, and tucks her hands into the cuffs of her sweater. Neither of us makes a move to leave.

"Cold?" I ask when she shivers.

"A little."

I shrug off my jacket and settle it on her shoulders. It's my work jacket. Hope she doesn't mind that it smells like a container ship. I wish I'd thought to wear a clean hoodie.

She slips her arms into the sleeves, huddling in the bulky canvas, tucking her nose in the collar. She must not mind.

The sight pleases a part of me that I didn't know I had, satisfying me in a way I didn't know I could be satisfied. Angie is sitting on the tailgate of my truck, wearing my jacket, her belly full of the food I bought her. I have no idea why that makes me hard as hell, but I thank the Lord that I'm wearing lined jeans and an untucked shirt or else I'd be indecent. And thank the Lord, as well, that Maddie will sleep through the end of the world once she passes out drunk.

Angie sighs and snuggles a little closer to my side. It's everything and not enough. I want to hold her. Touch her. I want to feel how our bodies fit together again.

We're sitting on a tailgate, though, and my truck bed is in decent shape, but I wouldn't lay her down on it, not without putting down a tarp or something first, and I don't keep anything like that in my vehicle. I could kiss her. She's watching the water, drifting off, but I could take her chin and turn her head and kiss her mouth. I think she's with me.

I thought that behind the shed, too. I'm not a pussy, but her fighting me off was the worst feeling of my life, and I'm not going in overconfident with her again. But I'm not going to ask if I can kiss her, either. I know that's what you're supposed to do these days. Ms. Roscoe drilled that into our heads in eighth grade health class.

She made us watch this video about going on a bike ride with a girl, and the bike ride was supposed to represent consent, but it got really elaborate. The video started talking about the girl wanting to quit mid-ride 'cause she got too hot, and thirteen-year-old me didn't know if that meant the guy was going too hard or too long, and I was confused because I thought you were supposed to go as long as you could.

Back then, I figured I'd go with what my dad said, which was if you make a move, and she says no, stop what you're doing and go get dinner or something instead. His advice hasn't led me wrong until behind the shed with Angie, when it really fucking counted.

How do I get this girl in my arms? Horizontal would be amazing, but I'd take vertical and closer if I could figure it out. Ask her if she wants to take a walk?

I don't want to leave Maddie alone in the truck, even to go a short way. I need to hear her if she yaks, so I can get her out of the cab before she exorcists all over it. She did that once when I gave her a ride home from a kegger last year. I had to get the platinum-level detailing at the carwash, and she said she'd pay me back, but she never did.

The sky over the far bank of the creek is fading to gray. It's getting late. I'll need to take them home soon, and I can't bear the thought. I don't want to let Angie go anywhere without me.

She's not going out on any more girl's nights. I have no way to stop her—and no right—but all the same, if she wants to dress up and go dancing, I'll take her.

Oh, shit. That's an idea.

Can I carry it off? I'm not smooth. I can buy flowers and open doors and text good morning, but beyond that, I've got no game. I've got no pride with this woman, though. I will happily make an ass out of myself.

I fish my phone out of my pocket. She glances over at me, distracted by what I'm doing more than curious. I open the music app, tap, and scroll. I hit play. Bare notes from an electric guitar ring out.

Recognition dawns and her broad smile breaks across her face. My body comes alive.

I got it right.

I spring to my feet and offer her my hands. She takes them. I pull her to standing.

Tracy Chapman sings a song by Ben E. King, and I draw Angie into my arms, willing her to understand that the words are from me to her. I'd stand at her side forever, no matter what.

She winds her arms around my neck and sinks against me, softening, exhaling. I gather her to my chest.

We sway in the bed of my truck, the song on repeat, the sun rising over the water stretching from Bullneck to Bear Creek to the bay. In the distance, gradually as the sky lightens, the outline of the bridge appears and then the cranes at the terminal.

The daylight also shows the blonde streaks in Angie's hair, and the smudged makeup under her lower lashes as she gazes up at me, our eyes caught on each other. Her breath warms my cold chest through my flannel shirt. The toes of her boots bump mine. Neither of us have much rhythm.

My hands smooth down her back, inside my jacket. Her hips shift forward. She can definitely feel my hard-on. Her dress is lightweight.

Her breasts rise and fall quicker. Her fingers trail up my neck to play with my hair. I swallow a groan.

I want her so fucking bad, but we're in a truck bed in a public park, and any second now, an old lady with binoculars is going to look out her window at the birds, see us, and call the cops. Odds are good I'll know whoever they send, but that's not the vibe.

I can't let her go, though. Not for a million dollars.

I step on her foot by accident. She giggles. I lift her up and set her down so her feet are on top of mine, like I do with the girls.

"I'm gonna crush your feet," she whispers, shifting her weight.

"They're steel-toe boots." I hold her tighter.

She relaxes. I cup her ass. She tenses, her butt cheeks clenching. Okay. Message received. I slide my hands back up to the small of her back, and she softens again, nuzzling her cheek against my chest. Her fingers play with my top button, and it comes undone. Her lips graze the skin she's exposed.

I rock side-to-side in time to the plucking of the guitar.

In all the world, there is only us. Angie and me. We're warm together, in the early morning chill.

I've wanted to hold her like this since before I can remember, since before I even understood what it was that I wanted from her. This is even better than I imagined.

Without warning, she gasps.

My head spins. What is it? Where? Every single muscle in my body tenses, ready to fight. I swing her behind me, blocking her body while I squint where she's pointing.

"Great blue heron!" she squeals. "It's huge!"

Damn. So it is. The bird is wading in the shallows, less than a yard away, staring calmly into the distance, and it is enormous. It's almost as tall as Tamblyn.

Angie takes her phone out and begins to take pictures. She doesn't even need to zoom in.

Most blue herons aren't actually blue—they're more of a dingy gray with a bluish tint—but maybe because of the way the sun hits the water, this one looks as blue as a robin's egg.

"Your mom won't believe it," she says, breathless.

Yup. There goes the mood. Mom does love herons, though. She's got the upstairs bathroom decorated with them.

Since Angie's distracted, I take the opportunity to readjust my deflating dick.

We watch the heron for a while, Angie snapping pictures, totally absorbed, until for some reason, her wide doofy grin fades into a shy smile. She blinks up at me. She wants something. My abs clench.

"Um. Can we—um..." She turns her back to the heron and tentatively reaches out her hand to me. "Selfie?"

I don't take selfies. Where do I stand?

I let her take my hand and pull me against her side. She holds the phone as high as she can. "Smile."

I do, but I think I'm a second too late. She seems happy, though, when she scrolls. Somehow, she took, like, twenty pictures in no time at all. They all look the same to me, but she deletes most of them until she's happy with what's left.

Then she goes back to watching the heron until he finally spreads his wings and takes off for greener pastures.

"Whoa," Angie exhales in awe. It is a sight to see. Big fella's got the wingspan of a pterodactyl. "So beautiful."

I watch her face as she tracks his flight down the creek towards the bay. She squints, her nose wrinkling. The daylight shows dried tear tracks in the makeup on her cheeks. Her lip liner is still there, but the filler color is gone.

"Yeah," I agree. "Beautiful."

She turns her head and smiles up at me.

So beautiful.

So perfect.

I stand behind her, wrap her in my arms, and rest my chin on the top of her head. Together, we watch the sun finish rising, listening to each other breathe.

She yawns.

"About time to get going," I say. She murmurs in agreement, but I don't let her go, and she doesn't move, either.

"Next time you want to go out, I take you," I tell her. I'm not sure where that came from. Maybe knowing I'll have to let go of her eventually, and how some animal part of me is considering just not ever doing that.

"You're not the boss of me," she says, angling her head so it rests in the crook of my neck. Her lips brush the underside of my jaw as she speaks.

"You do what I say." I squeeze her tighter. Our words are teasing. Our bodies aren't.

"I'm a free agent."

"You belong to me."

"I didn't agree to anything." She presses a soft kiss to the spot under my ear so I know she's still sweet. She's playing sassy, and I love it.

"Squatter's rights," I say, and because if I don't do it now I never will, I lift her up and gently lower her down from the truck bed. Before I let go, she looks up at me, her arms looped around my neck, smiling.

This is the picture I'd take.

Her happy face.

Her sparkling eyes.

Holding onto me with all her heart.

8

ANGIE

After the amazing time with Brandon and the heron, the rest of the weekend sucks. On Saturday, after a few hours of sweaty sleep, I shower and call Tyler about the money.

He says he's busy with *his* girls, and besides, he won't fight with me in front of them, so I need to call back after they're in bed. I spend the day nursing a hangover and trying not to freak out about whether the girls are okay and what's going on with Brandon and me. I call Tyler back that night at eleven, and the girls are still up.

They hear my voice and clamor to talk to me, and I'm gutted like a fish. They want me, and I'm not there, and my arms have never, ever been so empty, and there is nothing I can do except keep my voice calm and sweet.

Tyler passes them the phone for a minute. Tamblyn asks if Chickie is okay. She forgot it here, and Tyler wouldn't come by to get it because Chickie's gross, and she's too old for a blankie.

Chickie does get gross between washings, but not as gross as Tyler's dirty socks, and he leaves them wherever he takes them off—in the living room, under the kitchen table, behind the bathroom door, wherever. And Tamblyn *always* knows where Chickie is. Can't say the same about Tyler and his socks.

Saturday night, I sleep with Chickie, and I don't care that it's grubby. Inhaling its weird graham cracker smell keeps me from losing it.

Tyler doesn't answer my calls or texts on Sunday morning. The only way I can stop myself from racing over to the house, frantic, is reminding myself over and over that this has always been his M.O.

When he's in the wrong, he works himself up into thinking he's been so misused and misunderstood that whatever he's done is completely justified, and no one is owed an explanation. As a matter of fact, *he* deserves an apology, *and* he'll be damned if he doesn't deserve that apology *to his face*. So he doesn't answer his phone.

I do a load of laundry, vacuum the stairs, and annoy Miss Dawn by scrubbing her tub before she has the chance to shower. She thinks it's somehow wasteful to clean right before a shower—like you get more *clean* out of a scrubbing if you maximize the time between cleaning it and using it.

I think that since she's too stubborn to get those grippy stickers, the less soap scum there is when she's in there, the better, especially since her knees have the habit of buckling on her.

Eventually, she tells me I've done enough and shoos me downstairs, and I wait for six o'clock drop-off time, curled up on the futon in the basement, sipping my cold morning coffee and staring blindly at the TV. Miss Dawn leaves me to wallow in peace.

At noon, there's a sharp rap at the front door. Instantly, my brain blares. *Police! Accident! Sorry to inform you, ma'am, but—*

I sprint up the stairs, two at a time. I should have gone over to Tyler's. I should have never let the girls go with him.

This is punishment. This is what happens. People leave, and I never see them again.

I throw the front door open just as Miss Dawn hollers from the kitchen, "Who's that knocking?"

Oh, thank God, thank God. It's Tyler's mom, Carol.

Carol is in her church clothes. She's got Tamblyn and Ivy by the hand. The girls are wearing matching dresses that I've never seen before, new sparkly backpack purses, and frilly white dress socks with their dirty sneakers. They look desperate to bolt into the house, but they know better. They stand at Carol's heels like sad, chastened dogs.

I want to rip my girls away from her, but I'm so happy it's not the police, and they're safe and home early.

"Hi, Carol." I step back so everyone can come inside.

She frees the girls' hands. They surge forward toward me. She coughs. They stop in their tracks.

"Now, do what I told you, girls," she says. "Go change into your play clothes, fold the dresses, and bring them back to me to put in the wash."

They surge toward me again. She coughs, sharper.

"Yes, ma'am," they say in unison and then throw themselves forward the last foot into my arms.

I scoop them up and smoosh them together, gathering bony elbows and knobby knees and sweet-and-sour, grubby skin. My little girls. Love bleeds through me like spilled ink.

Ivy grabs a fist of my hair. Tamblyn monkeys her legs around my waist so tight that it hurts my hip bones. It takes all my strength to hold us upright and together, but I do.

"Oh, I missed you, babies," I whisper. They're trembling, and I would be, too, but I'm the mama. This is the way it is now. I need to maintain the fiction—everything will be okay, we'll all get used to it soon, and it's not bad, it's just different. I need to sell it. Make it true. This was my choice, after all.

I steel my muscles and gently lower my girls to their feet. "Chickie's on your bed," I tell Tamblyn. The girls understand that we can't hug too long—Carol is looming—and once I gently unpeel their fingers, they flee down to the basement. My leashed heart leaps after them.

Carol stands with her back almost touching the storm door, her arms folded. If she were the type of woman to roll her eyes, they'd have fallen out of the sockets and onto the floor.

"That was quite the demonstration," she says, her thin lips pursed. She drums her long, acrylic nails against her thin upper arm.

I've literally never done anything Carol approved of. Long ago, I figured out the best I can do was keep it moving with her. I still haven't figured out how to not let her remarks sting, but maybe one day. I'm growing as a person. I got all my paperwork in on time, so I'm in the next CNA cohort that starts after the holidays. And I don't cry in the shower anymore.

"Thanks for bringing the girls home," I say. Bob and weave. That's what I do with Carol Reynolds.

She sniffs, looks down her nose into the living room, and then turns her nose up at whatever she sees in there. "Tyler went with his dad down to the property in Virginia for the day. He needs a break once in a while, too."

She took what I said like I was questioning why Tyler didn't bring them home. That's what she does—she sees things in the worst possible light. Except Tyler.

"Should I get the girls' bags from the car?" I ask.

That throws her, but not for long. "Can't the bags stay there? Aren't they going to need their things on the weekends? I don't see why you had to take everything with you."

She presses her lips together like she's preventing herself from saying what she really thinks.

"It's fine if you forgot." And it's not going to be every weekend.

Early on, Tyler said, "I guess you want to do that every-other-weekend shit," and I didn't disagree. Madison thought he'd want fifty-fifty so he wouldn't have to pay support, and he'd end up dumping the girls on his mom. But I know Tyler. He figures I won't put him on support, that I wouldn't risk him getting primary physical custody by some fluke. And he's right. I won't.

I'd been making do with the hundred and fifty dollars he's always had deposited from his check into our joint checking account for groceries, but I guess that gravy train is over if he's going to be spending that money out of spite at Thom's Cycle.

"I didn't forget. I just think that things need to be fair. For the girls." Carol folds her arms tighter, really making those boney elbows pop, and lifts her chin higher. She totally forgot. She'd rather pick a fight than admit she made a mistake, though. Like mother, like son.

"It's fine," I say again. I never fight if I can avoid it.

In the kitchen, a chair creaks. Miss Dawn must be losing her mind. I bet it's killing her not to storm out here and give Carol a piece of her mind. They were actually friends back in high school, but as Miss Dawn puts it "as you get older, at some point it's not class, it's a stick up your ass."

Carol's shoulders fall a fraction of an inch. "Well, they didn't have anything suitable for church. I had to run them up to Target yesterday."

I know it's criticism, but I'll take it as an out. "Thank you," I say. "The dresses and the backpacks are cute."

"I was going to take them to Denny's afterwards—they'll probably tell you that I said I would—but they were just all over the pew. Slipping down in their seats, trying to reach over my lap, touching the hymnals." She blows out a long breath. "They really need to be going to church every week if they're going to learn how to behave."

You couldn't pay me to go to St. Pius X. It smells like burnt bacon from the social hall in the basement, and I don't need weekly confirmation that I'm a dirty sinner on the wrong path.

Carol reads my face and summons up her catch-more-flies-with-honey smile. "I'd be happy to take them Sundays when they're with you." She rounds her eyes. The whites are stark, outlined by her blackest-black, spider-legs lashes. "It's no trouble. You can use the time for yourself." She scans me from my rumpled T-shirt to my baggy sweats. "Get your hair done. And your nails."

Before I can answer, the girls trudge up the stairs, bearing their dresses and wadded-up fancy white socks. Tamblyn has made an effort at folding hers. Ivy has rolled hers into a ball.

They approach Carol, as solemn as prisoners, and offer her their bundles. Carol sighs, plucks out the socks and hands them to me, and then snaps the dresses out, laying them over her forearm. It really is *quite the demonstration.* There's no need for all the fuss. The cotton is a blend; it won't wrinkle.

"So shall I come for the girls next Sunday, then?" She levels her cold gaze down at them. "Perhaps if we don't fidget so much, we can go to Denny's afterwards, eh? Wouldn't that be nice, girls?"

The girls deflate, their shoulders shrinking, their chins dropping.

It's not church they hate. They love St. Rita's. We go with Miss Dawn sometimes.

St. Rita's has a children's liturgy. A nun leads the little

ones out to the annex where they have AA and Bible study, and she plays guitar. The kids sit around her on the floor and sing. Then they try to help her pull up cartoons about Jesus on her iPad until she throws her hands up and plays more songs and lets them get into the rubber tub of musical instruments that she keeps under her metal folding chair.

I went with the girls a few times to make sure it was okay. It was anarchy. Noisy, happy anarchy.

Mom didn't take me to church, but I have vague memories of going with my grandparents to St. Pius X. I don't remember much besides the charred bacon smell and helplessly sliding off the curved wood pews.

The irony is that if I were still with Tyler, I'd have certainly said yes, but Carol wouldn't have dared to ask.

When I was with Tyler, I always said yes to her. If I didn't, Tyler would hear about it from her, and he'd be unbearable to live with until I "got his mother off of his ass." But she never would have brought it up. Tyler hates church like he hates the Steelers and bike lanes, like they did something to him personally. He really must have needed a break to let the girls go with her this morning.

"Thank you for taking them today," I say, and I mean it. The only way I've been able to breathe—let alone sleep—is knowing she's close by, and Tyler would never be shy about calling her if he needed help.

"So, next Sunday then?" She frowns at the dresses, and I watch her wrestle with the idea of handing them over to me, the woman who washes everything together on cold.

Both girls slump at the same time. They know how I am with Grandma. They assume it's a done deal.

Ivy stares longingly into the living room at the TV. They're tired and done. I can smell the impending meltdown.

Neither of them makes a move, though. Because they

want to be close to me or because Carol hasn't dismissed them yet? Whatever, they aren't budging. They stand in front of me, dejected in high water pants and mismatched tops that show a little too much belly.

Because they're defending me.

That's why they're shoulder-to-shoulder, keeping their skinny little bodies between me and their grandma, when their comfy blankets with unicorn hoods and mermaid tails are waiting for them in a basket next to the couch. A memory flashes in my mind—Brandon throwing me behind him in the instant before he realized I was excited about a heron.

And then another memory—Tyler making fun of me in the kitchen while I fried potatoes for him and his friends. They were teasing him about whether he was ever going to propose to me. He was pinching the chub above the waistband of my jeans, joking that if he wifed me up, I'd chunk up until I wouldn't be able to fit in any of my pants.

I'd slapped his hands, laughing because getting mad would have been worse. Tamblyn crawled down from her chair and demanded that I pick her up. She'd wrapped her legs around my waist so Tyler couldn't pinch me anymore.

It didn't occur to me then that I wasn't the only one hurt.

But doesn't it hurt when someone you love is sad?

Of course it does.

How was I able to know that as a fact *and* hide it from myself at the same time?

I'm so damn used to going along. It's like God himself made me to cause no trouble and eat shit. And there's always a good reason to go with the flow, isn't there?

In that kitchen, I didn't want to make a scene. And here and now, well, Carol is their grandmother, and I *want* them to have a good relationship. I want my girls to have as many people in their corner who love them as humanly possible.

But church with Grandma doesn't look or feel like love.

Why is this so hard?

Marry the father of your children—that's the right thing to do. Send your kids to church with their grandma—that's right. These are no-brainers. You don't have to think. You just have to cling like hell to what you're *supposed* to have—the ring, the man, the house, family, church on Sunday—and you'll be safe.

It's so *hard* because it's not *true.*

There's no safe.

I'm on my own.

It's my call.

No one but me can decide what's right, and I have no idea.

I look at my stressed-out little girls, side by side, their bodies between me and their disapproving Grandma, their allegiance crystal clear.

I clear my throat. "No," I say to Carol. "I don't think we can make that happen."

"Well, the Sunday after then," she says, leaning over the girls' head to dump the dresses into my arms.

"No. That's not possible."

The girls turn their heads and crane their necks to stare up at me over their shoulders, kind of like herons.

"Girls, how about you say goodbye and thank you to Grandma and go see what Miss Dawn is doing?" It takes them a second, but eventually they mumble their thank you's to Carol and head off toward the kitchen, their steps lightening as they go.

Carol still hasn't stepped much past the doorway, and she's refolded her arms tight to her chest. She stares me down, and it's clear on her face—if I keep going, we're enemies.

"You're welcome to take them when they're with Tyler, if he's cool with that."

She glares at me, and my body reacts like there's a bear in the hallway—my heart bangs, my blood rushes, and my head rings. It's ridiculous, but at the same time, in a way, this might only be the second or third time in my entire life that I've stood up for myself.

"You're heading down the wrong path, Angie." Carol sniffs. "I hope you know what you're doing. I wouldn't be so quick to turn up my nose at a helping hand if I were you. It's not easy being a single mother."

She watches me very closely to see her shots land. I know my face is an open book. She'll see exactly how overwhelmed and uncertain I am.

"The girls need *values*, a strong sense of right and wrong. Maybe if you'd had that kind of positive influence in your life—" She lets the second half of her sentence hang, and I can read her face, too. She knows my business, or at least, she *thinks* she knows.

What exactly did Tyler tell her?

I'm going to puke.

"Don't you want that for them?" she finishes.

No.

Actually, no. I don't.

I want them to be happy. I want them to be able to stand up for themselves and think through things for themselves. I don't want them to have other people's loud voices in their heads, drowning out their own good sense. I want them to believe, without a doubt, that they're worthy of love, no matter what.

I step forward. Carol has no choice but to step aside. I swing the door open for her.

"I'll see you later, Carol," I say.

She glares at me. I can't help it. My gaze drops, but I push the door open wider.

She huffs and strides off toward her town car, her head thrown back and her dignity in full sail.

"Did you tell her *no*, Mama?" Tamblyn's little voice pipes from behind me.

She appears to my left, followed by Ivy to my right. They wind their arms around my thighs and watch Grandma reverse down the driveway much quicker than she usually does.

"I did." I rest my hands on top of their heads.

"Good job, Mama," Tamblyn says. "Let's go to the park."

"Okay," I agree.

There's plenty of day left and fresh air is exactly what we need.

WE CALL Miss Dawn's neighborhood park "Turtle Park" because it has a big, green, plastic turtle to climb on as well as the usual slide, swings, ladders, and poles. Turtle Park runs up against land owned by the port, so beyond a patchy soccer field, a row of huge metal cranes rise beyond a dense patch of woods.

Most of the leaves have turned red and yellow, and there are plenty on the ground for us to bulldoze into piles. Tamblyn and Ivy ignore the playground equipment and go wild with the leaves, piling and jumping and making angels like wild women. They race through the leaves, kicking them into flurries and throwing them like confetti over their heads. They shout and screech and holler my name, even though I'm right here, and there's no one else around.

The sky is watercolor blue, and the air is cool, but not

cold enough to need a jacket once you get warmed up from running around.

Every exposed inch of my skin feels raw. My bones feel exposed. Now that I have my girls back with me, I don't have to fight back the panic and fear and desperate need to make sure they're okay, but the feelings don't fade away. They settle and eat away at my peace like acid.

Is it going to feel like this every weekend they go with Tyler?

It has to get better, and honestly, I have my doubts that he's going to stick with it very long. He had no time for the girls when we lived together. My dad was the same before he bailed, but I remember being so excited to see him. He'd flip me in the air or toss me over his head, and I'd squeal, and then he'd put me down to argue with Mom. I was always surprised that Tyler didn't horseplay like that. He doesn't even try to charm the girls, and they don't pay him much mind.

It's sad, but if he does a gradual ghost, it's probably for the best. It's weird—I wanted more than anything for my girls to have a dad who loves them, for them to know that security, and turn out how I might have if I'd had the support. And I one-hundred-and-fifty percent picked the wrong man for the job.

Picked him and stuck with him and gave him a second go at bat. *Begged* him for a second go at bat. I wanted Ivy so bad. So Tamblyn would never be alone like I was. I set this whole situation up, and if he walks out of their lives, in a way, I set that up, too, by choosing so badly. Of course, if I hadn't, I wouldn't have the girls, so I guess I'd make those same bad decisions again every time.

I exhale and drop back into a pile of leaves. The sky is so damn blue. The girls' shouts fade and grow louder in curlicues as they buzz closer and race away. The sun is warm on my face. Why do I need to beat myself up when it's such a beautiful day?

How is it that I'm so powerful that everything is my fault, but so powerless that I can't do anything to fix it?

I wish Brandon was here, lying beside me in the leaves, quiet and sure. I wish I could tell him all the crap in my head. He'd listen, and I don't know if he'd understand, or what he'd say, but I don't think he'd be mean. He's a rough guy, but he's gentle with me.

He wants me. I want him.

There are a hundred—a *thousand*—ways for it to go wrong. I let him in, and he realizes what a total doormat I was with Tyler and loses all respect for me. He gets sick of dealing with baby daddy drama. We get together, and he realizes he actually can't be a dad to the girls. He decides he doesn't want a ready-made family.

I fall utterly, madly, insanely in love with him, and he breaks it off for no other reason than people break up all the time, and I'm so crushed that I can't hide it, and everyone pities me. Even more than they do now.

I tell him I've got herpes, and before he can mask his reaction, his mouth twists like he smells something bad. And then he's kind. He really cares about me. He does. And it's not because of the herpes. He's just not ready for a relationship right now.

The first thing they tell you when you get herpes is that it's not the end of the world, but also, yes, it is.

I was naked from the waist down, on my back, feet in stirrups.

Dr. Kidd was in a hurry like always. She was the top doctor in the practice, and on the few occasions I had to see one of the other OBs in the office, they always assured me that she was the best. I was in good hands.

At the beginning, when I was pregnant with Tamblyn, I

saw her name as a good luck sign, but by the time I was expecting Ivy, it made me think of the pirate Captain Kidd instead of children. She was about sixty and built like a marathoner. Her hair was real, but it looked like a wig—steel gray, thick, and styled. She was intimidating, but business-like, and I figured I was doing as good as possible because the place was called Kidd and Associates.

I was nineteen. I had an infant at home. My mom was gone. My best friend was still reeling from losing her dad. My baby daddy was always busy.

I was vaguely aware that Dr. Kidd disapproved of me. She probably thought I was too young to be a mother of one, let alone two, and the few times Tyler came with me to appointments, he managed to get in her way. I figured she was like a teacher, though. They might not like you, but if you didn't cause trouble, they wouldn't go out of their way to hassle you. Or bother to humiliate you.

That day, she checked my cervix first.

She presses hard, and it hurts. I whimper.

"Breathe," she says and pokes harder. My eyes water.

She grunts, and when she's done, she stands between my spread legs, snapping off her blue rubber gloves, her lips pinched. The paper sheet that had been draped over my knees has been pushed up over my bump.

She sighs and makes eye contact. "Your labs from last week came back. You tested positive for HSV-2. That's genital herpes."

She looks at me expectantly. My vagina is still out. I try to squeeze my thighs shut, but my heels are in the stirrups, and if I slip them free, my entire bottom half is going to fall off the end of the table. My stomach has no abs anymore. It's an enormous inflated pudding sack.

"Do you understand what I'm telling you?" There's impatience in her voice.

I nod. I want to sit up. Am I allowed to sit up now?

"Genital herpes is sexually transmitted. You get it from having sex." She says that like I don't know. Of course I know. Everyone knows. "There is treatment, but no cure, and I cannot emphasize enough—it is highly contagious."

I tuck my butt, struggling to get higher on the exam table. I need to sit up.

"Do you know when you were first exposed?" she asks.

I shake my head.

"There might have been small bumps or blisters on your labia or anus, maybe ulcers, painful urination, itching, discharge, fever?"

"No." I've been having discharge, but she tested it and said it was normal. No amniotic fluid. Wouldn't that test have shown if it was from herpes?

"It's very important that you remember, Angie. If you became infected recently, there is an increased risk of passing the virus on to the baby. Do you remember developing any sores or lesions, either on your genitals or anus, maybe accompanied by flu-like symptoms?"

Her eyebrows raise, and time reverses. I've been called on in class again, and I'm clueless. I can't even guess. My gaze scrambles around the room like the answer is on a bulletin board, but there's no help from the black-speckled white ceiling tiles or the white walls or the white cabinets.

"Angie, this is important."

Oh, God. I know. "I don't remember anything like that."

She stares at me for a few more seconds, waiting for me to confess, but I have no idea when it happened.

Finally, she blinks and says, "Well, most people are asymptomatic."

What does that mean? Most people don't know they have it? Could Tyler have had it all along? No, they did this test with Tamblyn, too, and it was fine.

"You don't appear to be having an active breakout at the

moment, but this is very serious for the baby. You will need to go on antivirals immediately, and if you're showing signs of a breakout when you approach your due date, we will need to schedule a C-section. This is very, very serious." She's lecturing me. Because I've done something wrong. I hurt my baby.

I can't breathe. My bump is crushing my lungs. How did I get herpes?

Tyler. That's the only way, right?

Tyler gave it to me. He cheated. He's probably cheating right now. He said he had to help Duck haul stuff to the dump today. Is he with some girl? Is it Emily? She's been hanging out with the boys since she dropped out of Salisbury and came back to town. That was last year.

Last spring, I had a UTI. I chugged cranberry juice and took some over-the-counter pills, and it went away. Was that herpes? I can't say anything to the doctor now, not after I said I don't remember. She'll think I'm a liar.

I have to sit up. There's nothing to grab. A plastic bin on the counter with cotton balls and alcohol packets. A diagram of the female reproductive system with the corner curled up. A stool on wheels. A blood pressure monitor on wheels. Nothing stable. Nothing that won't slide away.

"Are you following me?" Dr. Kidd asks.

"Yes," I say because that's the right answer.

"You must *use a condom when having sex between now and delivery,* every *time with* every *partner, and of course, I would recommend condom use moving forward, too, in addition to a hormonal form of birth control or IUD. You're an excellent candidate for an IUD, but we can discuss that later. For now, condom use is non-negotiable. Do you understand?"*

What is an IUD again? The one that looks like an anchor?

"Angie?" Dr. Kidd says sharply.

I nod. "Yes."

Dr. Kidd frowns, unconvinced. "Among other things, genital herpes increases the risk of HIV infection. I cannot overstate how serious this is. You must use condoms every *time you are intimate with a partner. Without exception."*

She's talking like I'm arguing, but I'm not—I'm turtled on my back, and my vagina is out, and if she thinks I'm careless because of Tamblyn, I did *use a condom. It broke. And Ivy was planned.*

I want to argue that it's not my fault—I've never been with anyone but Tyler—but I'm alone and nineteen and unmarried and dirty. I put my baby at risk. Oh, God. My hands fly to my belly. She's bumping into the walls in there, almost out of space. My eyes burn.

"Is my baby going to be okay?"

Dr. Kidd straightens herself. "That will largely depend on you, Angie. You must take your medication exactly as prescribed, and you must inform the office immediately if there is any sign of a breakout between now and delivery. And you need to be prepared for the possibility of a C-section."

How do you prepare for a C-section? What do you need to do differently? I've read a thousand posts on the pregnancy boards. What did they say about preparing for a C-section?

Is Tyler in love with Emily? Is he going to leave me? He can't, please God, he can't.

I can't take care of two babies alone with stomach stitches. I broke my ankle at the skating rink when I was ten. A bone came through the skin, and I got six stitches. I wasn't allowed to put weight on it for a long time. They gave me a scooter, and I wasn't allowed to take a shower for a long time. I could hardly take care of myself, even with Mom there to help. How can I take care of Tamblyn and a newborn all by myself?

"Angie? Are you listening?"

"Yes."

"Do you have any questions?"

Yes. How was I supposed to know? What do I do now? How do I make this okay? I'll do anything.

"No," I mumble.

"Right. Get dressed. We'll see you again in—let's say—two weeks." She strides to the wall and hits the lever on the hand sanitizer. Ca-chunk, ca-chunk. She's done with me.

The door snicks shut. I can hear the air circulating. It sounds like a seashell.

Tyler cheated. I'm in shock, but I'm not surprised. My brain says sounds about right.

He's going to deny it, but we'll both know he's lying, and I'll have to pretend I believe him because right now, I can't even bend over to tie my own shoes and carrying Tamblyn is so hard.

Or maybe he won't bother to deny it. Maybe he'll raise an eyebrow like he does when he jokes at my expense, daring me to draw a line, knowing I won't.

How did I get here?

No matter, I sure can't stay here, crying on my back with no pants on. I drop my feet out of the stirrups, and then I swing my right arm and leg, using the momentum to get myself onto my side. The paper liner on the table crumples. I push myself upright, and the blood rushes from my head.

I'm shaking.

I'm all alone.

I work my way to the end of the table and find the footrest with my toes. I can't see past my stomach, and I can't afford to miss it. The floor is too far down. My legs can't buckle. I can't fall now.

Because I'm not *alone, am I? Tamblyn is waiting for me at Miss Dawn's, and the new baby, who I call Ivy in my head, needs me, too. I can't lose my shit now.*

I cradle my bump, and I lower myself very, very carefully, holding onto the edge of the table as I step down to the floor. I pad slowly to the chair with my clothes folded on the seat so there's no chance that I slip on the stark white tiles.

I get my underwear from where I hid it between the folds of my pants. It's insane. That woman in her white coat can poke her fingers inside me, and she can use her medical words to call me slutty, diseased, contaminated, dirty, stupid, and careless.

She can say anything without saying it—I'm a bad mother. I'm a danger to my own child through my sluttiness and poor judgment. I shouldn't be allowed to have babies. "You're an excellent candidate for an IUD."

She can say and do all that, but God forbid she sees my peach over-the-belly maternity undies.

I dress myself and shove my swollen feet into my clogs. On my way out, I check with the front desk to schedule my next appointment. The receptionist smiles at me, and I smile back.

I don't cry until I'm in the car, bent over the steering wheel so no one can see my face, the radio blasting so no one walking by can hear.

Later that evening, after I lost my temper and accused Tyler of cheating, somehow my stuff ended up on the front lawn. Mr. Neudecker from next door helped me pick everything up. He was mostly silent, but after we finished, before he left, he said, "When you're finally done, don't worry about the stuff. Just take the babies and go."

I didn't cry then, either. Not until I was back inside, and no one could see me except Tamblyn who was too young to understand or worry.

In the here and now, Tamblyn shouts, "Mama!" Forty pounds of cold-nosed, rosy-cheeked little girl lands on my chest. Red and yellow leaves go flying.

"Oh, no! Stinker attack!" I hoist Tamblyn above me by her waist, and she squeals, her legs kicking, her fingers scrabbling for leaves to throw on me. She's almost too heavy to lift, but my biceps are strong from lifting patients at work.

"Ay-ay-ay!" Ivy throws herself onto the pile.

I can't defend against the two of them at once. Tamblyn wriggles loose, and they both go to town, piling leaves on my head, tossing leaves in the air to make it rain, shrieking and climbing over me and each other, tickling and flailing with utter disregard for where the hard soles of their sneakers land. Eventually, by some silent agreement, we all fall on our backs to catch our breath from laughing and hollering.

Leaf litter makes my eyes water. I pick a stem from Tamblyn's hair and pretend to stick it up her nose. She shrieks and thrashes, and Ivy joins in until the pile's a mess, and we're a mess, giggling and grinning at each other.

My girls are beautiful. They have my brown eyes and my brown hair, but while I always thought of the color as common, it's clear in the late afternoon light that it's the prettiest shade on God's green earth. Nothing is as lovely as their happy eyes and knotty hair.

Ivy snuggles close to my side, pops her thumb in her mouth, and rests her other tiny hand on my stomach. Their hands look like mine did when I was little, the stubby fingers, the dimples for each knuckle. Looking at them is like seeing the past in 3D. I love them so much.

"Getting tired?" I ask.

"Not yet, Mama," Tamblyn says. "Let's play a little longer." She snuggles closer, too. I wrap my arms around them. Tamblyn takes a little squishy bear out of her pocket and parades it across my middle. Immediately, Ivy jumps in, giving the bear a squeaky voice and an urgent problem, and it becomes a game.

I half listen to the bear drama with my eyes closed, bathing my cold face in the warm sunshine. I feel full and awake and alive.

And because it's such a good moment, I'm hardly startled when a man clears his throat. I blink and squint up. It's Brandon. I kind of already knew it was him from the sound of his cough, and because it's a perfect afternoon, so of course he's here. My heart beats faster. The jigsaw is finished. We've popped in that last missing piece.

He's got his hands shoved in his jean pockets, and he's wearing a thick gray hoodie and his usual baseball cap. His eyes are narrowed against the sun, and there are crinkles in the corners. He smiles sheepishly. Butterflies erupt in my belly.

"Princess Sarabelle." He nods to Ivy. "Bane of Doom." He nods at Tamblyn, and her smile breaks so wide that I can see her back teeth. "Sorry to interrupt, ladies."

"Brandon!" Tamblyn and Ivy are already scrambling out of our leaf nest to crowd him. They crane their necks to grin up at him and simultaneously deliver the news of the day at the top of their lungs.

"We made a leaf pile!" Ivy announces.

"And we jumped in it, but Mommy didn't because she's too big!"

Thank you very much for that, Tamblyn.

"I found this! What is it?" Ivy sticks a rusty piece of metal in his face. I didn't even see her pick it up.

Thankfully, he takes it from her, soberly examining both sides. "This is a small pry bar."

"What's it for?"

"Prying."

"Oh." Ivy doesn't complain when he slips it in his pocket. "Why are you here?"

His cheeks darken and his gaze flicks to me. "I was at the hardware store, and they had lawn debris bags on sale. I brought them over."

"What's debris?" Tamblyn asks, accepting his answer at face value.

"It's uh...um...it's like crap." He stares at me over the girls' heads like he's checking to see if he got the answer right. I'd probably have said the same thing.

I've pushed myself up on my elbows, so I'm lounging in the leaves. His gaze can't settle. It darts from my hair to my lips to my chest and my legs. I squeeze my thighs together. My limbs are numb and rubbery from the cold, but inside, warmth spreads through my belly. I like him looking at me like this, trying to be subtle and failing. Like he can't help it.

I *really* like it.

"Angie," he says, kind of gruff, and offers a hand. I grab it. He yanks me to my feet.

The girls blink up at us, round eyed and big-eared, like we're a TV show come to life. Brandon plucks a leaf out of my hair.

"Thanks," I say.

He shrugs and shoves his hands back in his pockets. "Mom said you were down here. I thought I'd walk you home."

He holds my gaze. He's not playing it cool at all. He wanted to see me, so he came to find me. He's not trying to hide it. I don't know what to do with a guy who acts like he likes me. All I can do is blush like crazy.

Brandon jerks his chin in the direction of the house and lifts a shoulder. I nod. We begin to walk, side by side. Tamblyn and Ivy wriggle between us.

"One-two-three-whee?" Tamblyn asks, grabbing my hand and elbowing her sister aside to grab Brandon's. Ivy shrieks an objection, but she circles to my other side.

Brandon scrunches his brow.

"You know," I say. "One-two-three-*whee*!" I lift Tamblyn, and she's holding onto Brandon's hand tightly enough that she gets air when she swings her legs.

The girls are used to doing this with Madison and me, and they must figure since his sister is down, Brandon will be, too. They're right. He catches on immediately.

The girls and I don't do one-two-three-*whee* with Tyler.

If we go on a family outing, we still take the stroller. He has no patience for carrying a whining kid, especially now that they're heavier.

Tamblyn and Ivy count softly to twenty as we walk. That's the rules—three *whees* with twenty seconds between for Mommy to recover. Then the girls switch. Brandon doesn't seem to need prompting. He swings right on time.

The girls know that they each get a turn and that's it, but when Ivy's done, Tamblyn grabs my hand again and grins up at me with every ounce of gap-toothed charm she can muster.

"One more turn each," she says. "It's a special day."

It does feel like it.

We walk in the gravel on the shoulder, Brandon closest to the road, but there aren't any cars to worry about. We're far from any through street, and the folks who live around here are the type to sit down early to Sunday dinner. The sun has disappeared behind the houses to the west, but the daylight lingers, fading too slow to notice from minute to minute. There's woodstove in the air.

If we kept walking a half mile and turned right, we'd reach the house I grew up in. The couple who bought it keep it up better than my mother did. They're retired with grandkids, and they've put up an Amish-built playset in the side yard. The girls always ask to drive past, and they always say, "The swing set wasn't there when you were little, right, Mommy?"

I always say right, it wasn't, but they still ask, every time. I think they do it because they want the answer to change. They want my backstory to have been happier.

Me, too.

I didn't want to be the foster kid with the junkie mom who got knocked up at seventeen by her loser boyfriend. I wanted to be the girl who married my high school sweetheart and lived happy ever after with her beautiful girls. I wanted it so hard that I could bend reality. Tyler wasn't mean. He was funny, and I was overly sensitive. He didn't have one foot out the door. He was waiting until he got the raise, until he got the down payment for the truck, until he could afford the ring. He didn't hate me. He just had a hard time showing his emotions.

Dr. Kidd did me one favor that day. She made it impossible to lie to myself anymore. Tyler was never going to be the person I was pretending he was.

Reading between her words, I figured out something else, too—I was damaged goods. No one else was ever going to want me. A single mom of two with herpes? It would be a miracle. The longest of long shots. I'd better hold tight to what I had. If I lost Tyler, the girls and I would be alone forever. We'd never be a family like the kind I'd always wanted.

But there's something in the late afternoon sunshine today, something in the crystal clarity of the air and the starkness of the branches and the crunch of the gravel. Something about the sharpness of our breath in the stillness —Brandon's, Tamblyn's, Ivy's, and mine.

The world keeps turning no matter what some uptight lady in a white, windowless room says. The seasons keep changing, and we're still made of the same stuff we always were—heart and guts and muscle, fear and love and hope. Everything is a small thing next to this—we're above ground, and it's beautiful outside, and even if not everything is possible, we cannot possibly be sure what *is* and what *isn't* until we try.

I catch Brandon's eye. His mouth curves, and his brown eyes glitter.

I want to seize the day.

He sees something in my face that makes his smile widen.

"One, two, three, *whee*!" Tamblyn shrieks and swings herself as high as she can.

"Easy now, Bane of Doom," Brandon says. "Your mama needs that arm attached to her shoulder."

Tamblyn grins up at him. "Mama is strong. Her arm will never fall off."

We reach Miss Dawn's house, and I tell the girls to run ahead and wash up for dinner. They hug Brandon's legs, surprising him, and before he can decide what to do with his hands, they race inside. I linger behind.

Brandon and I slow to a stop halfway up the driveway and face each other, shifting side to side, glancing at our feet and then up at each other, hiding our smiles like idiots.

"Coming in for dinner?" I ask.

"I told Shane I'd meet him down at Donovan's to watch the game."

I squint to where the sun has sunk past the horizon. "You're gonna miss kickoff."

"It's all right." His hands are shoved in his pockets, and mine are tucked in my long sleeves for warmth, but we're standing close, closer than friends stand. "What's Mom making?" he asks.

"I put a roast in the slow cooker this morning."

"Yeah?" The corner of his lips quirk, and his gaze finds mine and stays. I feel it low in my stomach. And between my legs. I'm nervous, but I'm not scared. It *is* a special day, and the look in his eyes is urging me on. It's telling me to say *yes*.

"Brandon?"

"Uh huh."

I didn't see him move, but he's closer now, his head bent.

I try to take a deep breath, but my lungs are tight, so to give myself courage, I squeeze my hands into fists in my sleeves and make myself look him in the eyes. "Do you want to go out with me sometime?"

"Yes." He doesn't make me wait, not even a split second. "Where do you want to go?"

My stomach is being weird, relaxing and bursting and fluttering, all at the same time. "I don't know." I didn't think that far ahead.

"How about Broyce Junior's?"

"Okay." Broyce Junior's is a new steakhouse chain. Everybody says they're great, but not as good as the original in Pennsylvania.

"How about next Saturday?"

I can't ask Miss Dawn to watch the girls on the weekend, too, and Madison has a social life. "How about the Saturday after? Tyler will have the girls."

This time, it takes him a beat to say, "Okay."

I don't want to wait two weeks, either. I don't want to lose my courage. "Okay," I repeat. I don't know what to say now.

I'm still searching for words when he cradles the back of my head, pulls me to him, and kisses me. Like he hadn't been allowed, and all of a sudden, someone told him he could.

My body floods with heat. My brain screeches to a halt. He nips my lip with his teeth. My mouth parts. His tongue plunges inside, stroking along mine. My pussy melts.

I gasp for air and grab the front of his hoodie like he's got lapels. He groans. I slide my tongue along his. His teeth are hard, and his lips are soft, but firm. He tastes faintly like toothpaste.

He kisses like if he doesn't hurry, I'm gonna run out. I sink against him, lost, sunk. My heart lifts like I've been let out of school early, unexpectedly.

Behind us, a door opens. His mouth is gone. He's already

stepped back. I blink up. His hat's askew. My fingers are still curled in his hoodie. He grins.

"What are you guys doing out here?" Miss Dawn hollers at us from the porch. "The girls are asking."

"Just saying goodbye," Brandon calls, his voice as calm and even as always.

My knees are wobbling.

"Goodbye," he whispers, his eyes twinkling, and he straightens his hat, smoothing the bill. He fairly struts to his truck.

Miss Dawn snorts. "About time," she mutters, and then she says louder, "Folks are getting hungry in here, Angie Miller."

Miss Dawn and I don't look at each other when I pass her to go inside. I think it's the only way either of us keep a straight face.

9

ANGIE

FOR THE NEXT TWO WEEKS, BRANDON TEXTS ME EVERY DAY.

is steak good or would you rather get crab

the guys say broyce has crabs.

did you hear that thunder last night

were gonna go all the way this year if the defense can get their heads out of their ass

That was after Thursday night football. I still don't quite know how conversation between us works, so I reply with GIFs. Homer Simpson chowing down on a huge steak. A cartoon sheep giving two thumbs up. A prairie dog hiding in his hole. The donkey from *Shrek*, grinning.

I'm not a big talker. Madison can go for hours, but I run out of things to say, and it's hard for me to get started. It was never a problem with Tyler. He liked having an audience, even if it was just me, but Brandon isn't like that. Every day at work, I rack my brain for something to text him, but he always beats me to the punch.

what are you and the girls up to this weekend

this ship is killing me

did i say im going to drive next saturday?
i am

respectfully

I think and think, and eventually, I give up and send a GIF. That takes me forever, too. Then, the day before our date, inspiration hits. I send him a GIF that says "good morning" with the sun smiling and drinking a cup of coffee. Literally three seconds after I send it, my phone rings.

"Hello?"

"Good morning," he says. It's hard to hear him over the noise in the background. It sounds like he's on a factory floor.

"Where are you?"

"Working a ship."

"This early?"

"We had a six-thirty start."

"That sucks." It's eight-fifteen, and I'm sitting in the parking garage at work. I like my job, but not enough to walk in early.

I wait for him to say why he called, my stomach knotting. He's canceling. When I sent the GIF, he knew I was up, so he could call and let me know. My heart sinks toward the car floor.

In the background of the call, a loud horn blares and a walkie-talkie bleeps. "I can't talk," he says. "I just wanted to say that I can't wait for tomorrow."

In an instant, gravity reverses. All my insides float like the soda bubbles in Charlie's chocolate factory.

"Me, too," I say, softly.

"Pick you up at seven?"

"Yeah." We'd already sorted that out by text.

"Okay."

He's not hanging up. Neither am I.

"I better go," he finally says.

"All right." I hit end, my cheeks flaming, and drop my head back against the headrest.

My heart pounds like I just rode a roller coaster, and I'm grinning like an idiot, sitting alone in a dank underground garage that smells like gasoline and pee. I pull myself together, but all day long, there's a spring in my step, and all my patients end up getting where they're going just a little bit faster than they usually would.

TYLER WAS SUPPOSED to get the girls yesterday evening, but he called a half hour after he was supposed to pick them up and said he has to work today. He asked if he could get them at six today instead.

Since Tyler was promoted to store manager, he's never worked a Saturday shift, but I wasn't about to argue. Each visitation weekend gets a little easier, but it still sucks.

I try to talk it up with the girls and act like it's no big deal, but they're always asking if next weekend is a daddy weekend, and how many days until daddy weekend, and is Daddy still coming or did he call? The closer it gets to Friday, the more they cling. They're anxious, not excited. But then, when Tyler shows up, they run to him, giddy and hyper, and that sucks in a different way.

I had plans to spend Saturday afternoon treating myself to a mani, pedi, and eyebrow wax at the nail salon, but I have to cancel, so the girls and I do our nails together.

Around four, I start a movie for them and hole up in the bathroom to take care of business.

First, I exfoliate and shave in the shower. Afterwards, I almost break my spine by twisting my torso in front of the full-length mirror to make sure I got all the hair behind my knees.

I shave my bush with an electric razor. After the diagnosis, I never got another Brazilian. You're allowed to get one if you don't have an active outbreak, but they say waxing can trigger a flare-up, and I haven't had one since a few months after Ivy was born. I'm not courting trouble. Besides—I wouldn't be comfortable with it.

When I'm as hairless as a Sphynx cat, I poke my head into the basement to make sure the girls are still absorbed in the movie. They've got their stuffies arranged around their blanket pile, and they're in heaven, kneeling side by side, clutching their favorite animals, saucer-eyed with their mouths open.

I quietly close the door and run a bath with the water as hot as I can stand, adding a generous splash of the English pear and freesia bath oil that Madison bought me for my birthday.

The first few years after the positive test, I never felt *really* clean, not like I did before, but it's better now. I don't really remember how I felt in my body back then. I've got a new normal.

It probably helped that so much about me changed from my pregnancies. I still have the brown freckles that showed up on my nipples with Tamblyn. When I stand for a long time, my left thigh goes numb now. And then there are the white stretch marks on my hips, and how my shoe size is still a half size bigger than it was before. Tyler didn't like any of it, but I learned how to tune out his opinion. I can apply the skill to my own thoughts, too—most of the time.

I sink into the water slowly. The porcelain is cool against my shoulders. I'm so excited and nervous that my body is basically vibrating. My belly feels like I swallowed a beehive.

I don't know if I can do any of this.

Dinner should be fine. We can talk about the food, and if it comes down to it, I can talk about the Ravens. I don't have opinions about them, but Tyler sure did, so I know enough to keep a conversation going if I've had a beer or two.

Should I order drinks?

Definitely not beer. I don't want beer breath. Will he think it's stupid if I order an Orange Crush? That's what girls drank in high school, and I never got to have a clubbing phase, so my order never evolved.

It's Brandon. He's not going to care what I drink. I don't need to be this nervous. I know him.

But not like this.

What if after dinner, he wants to have sex? He probably will.

I do.

Do I?

I lower myself in the water. The steam makes my face sweat. I wiggle my hot pink toes. It's such a childish color. I did let the girls pick.

How do I tell him my status? When? Before he kisses me? When he's heading to second base? Third?

After the diagnosis, I didn't want to have sex for a really long time. At first, I was postpartum, so Tyler couldn't say anything, but eventually, he started to complain and make life hard.

I was so damn tired at the time. Ivy was not a good sleeper, and her ears were a problem almost from the beginning. I couldn't deal with him *and* the girls, so I switched something off in my head. I don't know how. If he wanted sex, that was fine, as long as he was quick enough to finish before I got so dry that it hurt. If he went too long, I'd finish him with my hand.

I know that's messed up, and I've thought and thought about what I *should* have done instead, but all I can remember is being so exhausted that I'd break down into hysterics at the drop of a hat—in the car at the grocery store, in the laundry room, bent over and trying to fish a sock out from between the washer and dryer. Honestly, if I had national secrets, I'd have given them up for a nap, so a quickie was nothing.

I've beat myself up for being such a pushover for so long, not only after the wedding that didn't happen, but before, every day, in the middle of being pushed over. I would be jerking Tyler off, disgusted with myself for giving in just to shut him up.

I'm tired of beating myself up. Criminals get sentences, and sentences end, and nothing I did was a crime.

I'm tired of being ashamed. I want to go out with Brandon, and I want him to gaze at me over a candlelit table the way he does now that he isn't fixing his face around me anymore. He looks at me like I've never dirtied my hands a day in my life, never settled for crumbs, like my pretty feet have never actually touched the ground.

I want to let him convince me to go to his place. Kiss him until I forget I have anything to be worried about.

And then?

I have to *disclose my status* to him. That's how it's phrased. *Disclose your status*. Like it's very official.

There's a guy on social media who calls himself a herpes coach—he posts a video every day about how to tell someone you have HSV-2, which is wild. I try as hard as I can to forget that I've got it.

The guy talks about how common it is, and how since

the standard STD panel generally doesn't test for it, even folks who think they've got a clean bill of health might have it, so you could very well be disclosing to someone who's also infected but doesn't know.

He acts like people who react badly are just uneducated, and if they knew the facts, they'd be cool, but that's not true. Even Tyler looked at me differently after I tested positive, and he gave it to me.

I follow a woman with herpes on the same app. She's gorgeous, and she talks about dating and how some guys are cool with it, and some aren't. The people in her comment section are brutal, though. It's funny—the guy's comments are filled with women saying how brave he is to speak up. Hers are a bunch of trolls calling her a disgusting slut who got what she deserved.

I know Brandon won't call me names. He might not even reject me right away. He might try to make it work before he decides he can't get over it. That would be worse. The hope and then the crushing.

I let my limbs float in the water, my stomach so tight that it's cramping.

I'm not calling this date off. I'm not going to dread telling him the whole time. I'm going to have fun and order an Orange Crush and the steak-and-cake entrée like I'm a hot date and there's nothing wrong with me. I'm going to fake it 'til I make it.

There's a soft knock and the door creaks open an inch.

"Mama, Ivy sat on the remote, and the movie stopped!" Tamblyn hollers through the crack. Her mouth is pressed right up against it, but she's technically following our privacy rules. She didn't burst in like Kramer from *Seinfeld*, which is what she used to do before I laid down the law. We're living in close quarters down here, and we need boundaries. *I* need boundaries.

"Okay, give me a minute." I'm not too disappointed to cut the bath short. I wasn't relaxing, anyway. I was just freaking myself out. I don't need to tell Brandon anything tonight if I don't want to. I never have to tell him if we don't take this any further.

The thought makes my whole chest hurt. I'm already a goner for him.

An ugly voice in my head says *Oh, yeah? Like you were a goner for Tyler? Six months ago, you were marrying him, but now you can't live without Brandon? Cling much? You know what you call a woman who can't live without a man? Weak.*

I stand in the tub, wringing my hair dry like I wish I could wring that voice's neck until it shuts up. I'm not doing this to myself anymore.

I'm not weak. For years, I lived with a man who might as well not have been there. Who took care of the girls? Who cooked? Who cleaned? Who mowed the lawn and took out the trash, and called the HVAC guy when the heater went up, and the roofer when that storm took those shingles off? Who got the squirrels out of the attic?

Nobody calls a man weak if he ends one relationship and gets into another.

Breaking up with Tyler was like opening the windows during spring cleaning and letting the wind blow out all the stale air. I could *breathe* again. My eyesight sharpened, and I looked up, and I saw Brandon. It felt like when you see an old picture from when you're a kid, and you see a toy that you'd forgotten, and you remember all of a sudden how much it meant to you. It felt exactly like that sweet rush, that delight and comfort.

What if I lose that? Ruin it with my own mouth? I disclose my status, disgust flashes across his face, and then I get to be haunted by that look for the rest of my life?

My stomach churns. I grab a towel, dry off, wrap myself,

and go figure out what Ivy did to the TV with her butt. Once the girls are settled again, I go back to the bathroom to do my face and blowout my hair.

My excitement is all gone, but the dread remains. I put on a matching pale pink bra and underwear, and a cute turtleneck knit dress in oatmeal that hits above the knee and clings to my boobs and hips in exactly the right way, but I don't feel pretty. I feel like I'm getting ready for a job interview. Or court.

I finish well before Tyler is supposed to get here, and I make sure the girls are brushed and scrubbed and squeaky clean. He's never done their hair, but he'll have something to say if it's tangled. Luckily, neither girl gets her feelings hurt easily. They think "rat's nest" is hilarious.

At five-thirty, I herd them upstairs. Miss Dawn is already at the Seahorse Inn. They're doing a bingo tonight where every MLM girlie donates a basket of product. Miss Dawn went down early to scout out the prizes. She's hyped.

I'm too nervous to sit on the couch, so I take the girls out front and let them run around the yard while we wait. Dusk is falling fast, but the lights on the porch and the garage are strong enough for them to see where they're going. They're wearing their matching baby backpack purses that Grandma Carol bought them. If she sees them this weekend, I hope she takes it as a peace offering.

Six o'clock comes and goes. I'm not too worried. Tyler's always a little late. Then, it's six-fifteen.

Six thirty.

Six forty-five.

The sun has fully set, and it's steadily growing colder. I didn't put a jacket on, and I'm shivering, but I don't want to bundle the girls back into the house just for Tyler to pull into the driveway.

I really don't want Tyler and Brandon to cross paths. The

girls were supposed to be gone by now. They know I'm going out tonight, but by some miracle, they didn't ask where or who with, so I didn't say. It's a much bigger deal to them that it's a daddy weekend.

I won't lie to them, but I also don't want them to feel bad or weird around Brandon if things don't work out. I have no idea how they'll react. They seem to take Tyler's love life in stride. They talk about his girlfriend, and I was confused until I realized they're talking about Emily Mather and at least one other woman. To them, "girlfriend" is like "date."

How does Tyler disclose his status? Does he? If he does, I bet he says I gave it to him. It's exactly the kind of thing he'd do.

Just as my stomach gets queasy again, Tyler's truck rumbles up. He pulls over in front of the house, driving half up onto Miss Dawn's lawn, and honks. The girls run for the truck, their little sparkly backpacks bouncing, and leap for the door handle. I grab the reusable grocery bag that I'm using until I can get their overnight bag back and follow.

The girls climb into the backseat, chattering happily. Tyler rolls down the passenger window, gives me a once-over, and snorts. "Don't need to ask what you're doing tonight."

The back of my neck heats, and my skin crawls.

"Here are their things." I hold up the grocery bag. He raises an eyebrow like I've asked him to do something literally impossible. He can't be expected to reach over and take his daughters' stuff.

I hoist myself onto the running board to drop it through the window, and then I inch to the back to say goodbye to the girls.

"Some free advice, Ang," he says over his shoulder. "If you think your tits distract from that roll of flubber around your middle, they don't. I'd change if I were you. Unless the dude's a chubby chaser." He smirks, and as Tamblyn's eyes find mine through the back window, the truck jerks forward, like his foot slipped off the clutch.

Startled, I jump down, barely sticking the landing. The heels of my low boots sink into the lawn. It's been rainy.

"Oops. My bad," he says. "Wave bye to Mommy."

Tamblyn's mouth rounds, and Tyler roars off. I stare after his tail lights, fists clenched, my pink nails digging into my palms.

I could get in my car right now and catch up with him. He's going to the house. He won't take them out if he's the one who has to watch them. I could take them back. They're mine. I grew them in my body. I love them more than he does. More than he's *capable* of.

I force myself to breathe, the cold air making my teeth ache, and recite all the reasons I can't go after them in my head.

He's their father. They have a right to know him. I don't want them to grow up feeling unworthy. I don't want them so desperate for affection that they'll mistake any small kindness or scrap of attention for love. The lawyer said I had to let him take his parenting time.

I stand by the curb, stare down the empty street, and it claws at my chest—the indecision and regret, the emptiness, the fury and hurt and loneliness.

Miss Dawn fronted me the money to talk to a lawyer a few months ago. The lady said that she saw no reason a judge wouldn't award Tyler visitation, and that he could make a strong argument for fifty-fifty custody, or even primary physical custody, since he had a house and an involved extended family, and I didn't. She said the state was moving away from the every-other-weekend-for-dads default.

And I know if I fight him or make a scene, he'll go scorched earth. He always does.

This is the way things have to be right now. I have a plan. The CNA classes begin in six weeks. I just need to pull myself together. Pop my heels out of the dirt. Scrape the mud off on the sidewalk. Go sit on the front porch and don't think about the chub around my middle or Tamblyn's face through the window or absent fathers or the hundred horrible things that can happen to children if you don't watch them like a hawk.

I'm staring into the middle distance, having a silent, frozen meltdown, when Brandon turns into the driveway. He parks all the way up by the garage.

My eyes burn. I am not bursting into tears. He didn't do anything to deserve this.

He hops right out of the cab and strolls over. I firm my chin, straighten my spine, and suck in my stomach.

He's wearing a blue plaid button-up shirt and a dark pair of sturdy pants, the kind that could be for hunting or a nice dinner out, depending on if they're clean or not. He's hatless for once, and he's got his right hand hidden behind his back.

His smile fades when he sees my face. "Hi," he says softly.

"I'm not going to cry," I say. Tears leak down my cheeks.

"I see that," he says. He takes a handkerchief from his pocket with his free hand and sits next to me on the top step. He keeps his other hand behind his back.

"Tyler came for the girls, and it's just hard," I explain, wiping my nose. The tears have already stopped. They just wanted me to know that I'm not the boss of them.

"I get that," he says. He knocks his knee against mine. "Want to do a rain check?"

"No. I'm good. I promise." Now that he's here, I can breathe again. He feels like a rush of oxygen, like surfacing in the pool when you've tried to stay under as long as you can.

He smiles, and it's so bright and wide and *relieved* that it bowls me over. Something inside me tumbles ass over teakettle. He likes me.

"Here," he says. He takes the hand from behind his back. He's got a single red rose in a plastic tube for a vase.

"Oh." I take it and give it a sniff since that's what you're supposed to do. It kind of smells like burnt coffee.

"I got it from the gas station," he says.

"Yeah?"

"I wasn't gonna tell you that. I was going to throw that plastic shit away, but I forgot, so I figured the jig was up, you know?"

Is Brandon Kaczmarek running off at the mouth? I'd never thought I'd see the day. Even his voice is weirdly gravelly. He's nervous.

"It smells like coffee." I don't know what I'm saying. He's looking at me, and I'm looking at him, and there's only inches between us. I don't know what's happening in my body. I feel like a shaken snow globe.

"Yeah, I had to pay a premium for that."

"You did?"

"They get you coming and going down at the Gas-n-Go."

"That they do." We smile together at our dumb joke, and the pieces flying around inside me feel less frantic. His eyes are so pretty. They're not girly in the least—he's got the crinkles that all the men do around here who work outside—but still, pretty is the only word for them.

"Can I take you to Broyce's and buy you a wagyu filet with a lobster tail?"

"What's wagyu?"

"The most expensive thing on their menu."

"Are you trying to make me forget that you brought me a

gas station rose?" I hold it to my nose and bat my eyes. His crinkles deepen.

"You better press that rose in your diary when you get home tonight," he says.

"I don't have a diary."

"You better get one." His eyes dance. I drop the rose to my lap. He leans closer. Tires peel. Someone takes the turn into the cul-de-sac real fast.

I startle. Tyler's truck roars up the street, screeching to a halt in front of the house. The driver's door slams. I jump to my feet. Tyler storms around the bed and throws open the back door. The girls are crying. I run.

"Jesus fucking Christ!" Tyler's shouting. "Out! Out!"

Tamblyn tumbles out, crying, Ivy following after. I crouch, and they fling themselves into my arms. Tyler pitches one sparkly backpack purse onto the lawn after the other. He's got the light on in the cab, and he's cursing a blue streak.

"What happened?" I ask the girls. Tamblyn's crying too hard to answer, and Ivy's buried her face in my armpit.

"I'll tell you what happened," Tyler booms from the truck's second row, a microfiber rag in his hand. "The juice you gave them exploded all over the fucking backseat! It's seeping into the floor mats. Is it fucking *fruit punch*? Goddamn it, Angie!"

He throws a silver foil packet at me. It lands in the grass at my feet.

"That's enough." Brandon steps in front of us.

It's like someone hit Tyler's pause button. He stops cursing, his jaw drops, and the hand with the rag falls to his side. He didn't expect Brandon.

I watch the realization sweep over him. He notices what Brandon's wearing. He glances over our heads and sees the rose on the step where we were sitting. His lip peels back in a sneer, and his pale blue eyes narrow.

Something inside me that's been trained like a dog cowers. I feel dirty and small and pathetic. I don't want Brandon to see this play out. Or the girls. I want to throw myself on this nasty, sneering man like a hero on a live grenade—to save us all.

I don't want his nastiness to touch any of them.

I don't want Brandon to see what he dishes out with perfect entitlement because I've taken it for years. I don't want the girls to see it yet again.

"This isn't your business, Kaczmarek," Tyler says.

It isn't. It's mine. My fault. My responsibility. I climb back to my feet, hiking Ivy onto my hip. Brandon seems reluctant, but he steps aside so he's standing next to me rather than blocking us. He makes me feel safe and ashamed. Like I'm not alone for once. But also, I've got a real man now to witness how beatdown I am.

"Are you gonna pay for the detailing, Angie?" Tyler asks like Brandon isn't even here. "Because this shit isn't coming out of the mats."

"I didn't give them juice."

"So it just appeared out of nowhere?"

I can *feel* Brandon's muscles tensing tighter by the second. Except for an occasional sniffle from Tamblyn, the girls have gone quiet. I have to diffuse this before it gets even uglier.

"I'm sorry," I say.

I'm not. It's not my fault. His mother buys those juice packs. I can't afford them. I bet it was in one of their backpacks from when they went to church with her.

I'm not sorry at all, but that's what I say when he's angry, and I'm stuck in another stupid standoff, and sorry never works, but maybe it will this time, and what else can I do that won't make it worse?

"Is 'sorry' gonna clean this interior?" Tyler shoots back.

Brandon catches my eye. His jaw is clenched so hard that there's a muscle popped that I've never seen before. He's furious. The back of my neck prickles. What is he going to do? I can't manage them both.

I stroke Tamblyn's head. She's plastered it to my side.

Brandon's nostrils flare. His chest rises. I hold my breath. He exhales. The muscle at the hinge of his jaw relaxes. He's never looked grimmer.

"What do you want to do?" he asks me, holding my gaze as firmly as Ivy's got her arms wound around my neck.

What do I want to do? Disappear. Reverse time. Cry. Shut Tyler's mouth with my fist. Torch that stupid truck, mats, interior, and all. Wave a wand so my girls never heard or saw it. *Any* of it.

These are not choices I have, so I do the only thing I can. "I'm taking the girls inside," I tell him.

This has probably ruined everything between us, but I know, without question, Brandon will have my back for now. This time, Tyler hasn't got me totally trapped.

I turn and head for the house, Ivy in my arms and Tamblyn plastered to my leg.

"Hey!" Tyler snarls. "Get back here!"

Brandon says something, but it's so deep and quiet, I can't make it out.

I get the girls inside and shut the door. They stand in the foyer, blinking up at me. Tamblyn is beet red, and there's a sheen of snot from her nose to her chin.

"Come here," I say and wipe her face with my sleeve. "It's okay. It was an accident."

"It just came out the straw. I didn't even squeeze," she wails, her face crumbling as she dissolves into tears again.

"I know." I desperately smooth her hair. "Those pouches do that all the time. It's not your fault."

"It is!" she cries.

I drop to my knees and grab her arms. "No, it isn't. It was an accident. It could happen to anyone. You didn't do it on purpose."

She looks me straight in the eye, her hair wild like mine was when I was little, her nose a miniature version of mine, the same exact shape, her wide mouth, identical to mine, trembling, and she says, "But *you* said sorry."

Oh, God.

I did.

I've apologized for hundreds of things I didn't do. And she's watched me.

"I take it back," I say, urgency making my voice shake. "I'm not sorry."

"There's no eating or drinking in the truck," she says quietly, watchfully.

"Yes, but there's no throwing things or cussing, either."

She narrows her puffy eyes. We both know that's not actually true.

"I'm sorry I spilled, Mama," she finally says. "I'm sorry to *you*."

"Thank you," I say, the knot in my stomach loosening the smallest bit. "Let's go to the living room and take a minute to calm down."

"Kitty videos?" Ivy suggests.

"Definitely," I say.

The girls shuffle off like sad little zombies, and before I follow, I peek out the narrow window beside the door.

Tyler has gotten down from the truck, and he's standing face-to-face with Brandon. He's running his mouth, but I can't hear anything through the glass. Brandon has his back to me, so I can't see his expression. He's tense, but his arms are at his sides. He must not be speaking because Tyler isn't pausing for a breath.

There's a rock in my stomach. I didn't mean to leave Brandon to fight my battle for me. Should I go back out? I should.

I reach for the knob and Tyler finishes whatever he's saying. He spits on the ground, smug self-satisfaction giving his face that piggy look.

Brandon's fist swings so fast that I don't see it. All I see is Tyler sail backward and land on his ass in the soggy grass. Tyler's hand flies up to his jaw. For a moment, he just blinks up at Brandon in absolute shock. He's not from the same neighborhood as Brandon and me. He's from one of the nice houses on the waterfront. He scraps, but only when his boys are there to back him up.

He's running his mouth again by the time he picks himself up off the ground, gesturing wildly with his left hand as he cradles his cheek with his right. His face is so red and mottled it looks seconds from exploding into meaty bits. He doesn't take a single step toward Brandon, though.

Brandon calmly raises his arms to his sides, offering Tyler a clear shot, and holds them there like he's got all the time in the world.

Tyler says something else and spits on the asphalt again. It's clearly meant to show contempt and save face, but it doesn't work. Tyler looks like a feral possum that got whacked by a broom as he skirts Brandon and scurries back toward his truck, talking shit the whole time. Brandon just stands there with his arms open, daring Tyler to take a shot.

I can't tell whether Brandon's saying anything back, but I bet he's not. He wouldn't waste his breath. They might as well be two different species—a hissing possum and a tough old bear who doesn't need to make himself feel big. That's how Brandon hit Tyler, like a bear swiping with his paw, like you'd swat a gnat.

I wish I was strong like him. What does it make me if I run scared of a raggedy possum?

The shame burns, but it doesn't stop me from replaying the moment when Tyler lands on his ass, over and over, a small, mean seed of satisfaction warming my belly. And then I look over to the girls huddled together on the couch. They haven't even bothered to turn the TV on.

Why aren't I strong enough to be a mama bear for them? I'd die for them. Why can't I raise my voice to their father?

I turn away from the window. Tyler's truck roars off. What do I do now? Play kittens on my phone for the girls and slap a Band-Aid over it like usual? *Daddy's just mad. Let him cool off. He loves you. Everything's going to be fine.* How many times have I said it? How many times did I hear my mama say the same thing before she didn't bother covering up for him anymore?

Why is life a fucking carousel?

I'm not riding this shit around one more time.

"Come on, girls." I tug my dress straight. We're not moping around the house. We're not letting a single minute more of our lives get ruined if we have a choice, and we do.

The girls crawl off the couch and trudge over. Their eyes are dull, and their faces are tear streaked. They've been through the wringer. They blink up at me, waiting for me to say the thing that'll let us all keep going like everything's okay. Guilt is a worm in my chest.

There's a soft knock at the door. Tamblyn tenses. Ivy peers through the sidelight. "It's Brandon," she says, darting forward to let him in.

He steps tentatively across the threshold, a question in his eyes, his right hand shoved in his pocket. I bet the knuckles are swollen.

"Hey," he says to the girls. "You want these, or should I make them disappear?" He holds up the sparkly backpacks with his free hand.

Tamblyn immediately reaches for hers. Ivy furrows her forehead. "How would you make them disappear?"

"Shove 'em in the back of the coat closet, I guess," he says.

Ivy's head bobs as she considers. "No, I'll take it." She holds out her hand. He hands the bag over with his trademark seriousness.

The girls gaze up at him, and I realize they're waiting for him now. They trust him. They *know* him. And all of a sudden, it isn't me and my girls and him, it's the four of us, crowded into the foyer, unsure and off-kilter but *together*.

Brandon clears his throat. "Well, I, for one, am hungry. Who wants endless soup, salad, and breadsticks?"

Who would've guessed those were the magic words? The girls whoop. Then Tamblyn needs the bathroom. Then Ivy does. Then they need to change their outfits, and I figure I might as well put jeans on, too, and when we come back upstairs, Brandon's put the game on, and we let him watch the last five minutes of the quarter while the girls have me French braid their hair.

It's almost eight when we pile into my car since it's got the car seats. Brandon insists on driving. Tamblyn insists on picking the radio station. It's fifteen minutes to the restaurant, and the entire ride is filled with chatter and singing and giggling from the backseat.

After a few miles, Brandon's tension eases, and he rests his right hand on the console between us. His knuckles are swollen and red. He sees me noticing and frowns. He flexes the hand and moves it to his thigh and then to the steering wheel, eyes on the road, his face somber while his cheeks color.

I take the hand and move it to my lap, gently covering his knuckles with my palm, keeping my eyes straight ahead, too.

In the back, the girls sing along to a Taylor Swift song at the top of their lungs. Tamblyn knows some of the words and makes up the rest. Ivy repeats what Tamblyn sings on a two-second delay, and the end result is somehow both gibberish and sweet as peaches at the same time.

Brandon's lips soften. He's nearly too big for the seat. He has to hunch his shoulders so his hair doesn't get mussed by the headliner. His seat is as far back as it goes, but his knees are still bent at a ninety-degree angle. He looks like someone origami-ed him up in order to make him fit. He looks happy.

He wants to be here. With us.

It's a mess—this day, this situation, this life. It's the one we've got, though.

It might all end in disaster and heartbreak. Lord knows it has before. But not tonight.

By some happy accident, Tamblyn and Ivy belt, "Ooo, oh, whoa" in unison before once again devolving into their individual, incomprehensible variations of the song they're drowning out.

Brandon looks over at me and grins. His eyes crinkle. My heart soars.

It feels terrifying and new.

And at the same time, it feels like in another world, it's the way it's been all along.

10

BRANDON

SOMEHOW, I FUCKED UP BETWEEN LAST SATURDAY AND tonight, and I have no idea what I did.

Last week, Angie sat beside me in a booth and laughed her ass off with the kids while I sucked up spaghetti, pretending to be a vacuum cleaner. Because I'm an idiot who will do anything to make those three smile. At the end of the evening, she sent the kids inside to put the leftovers in the fridge, and she whimpered into my mouth when I yanked her to me and kissed her on the porch.

Tonight, she's sitting across the table at Broyce's like she expects me to leap over the table and attack her. I can't get her to say shit, and she won't meet my eyes, but every time I look away, she sneaks glances at me with this expression I can't quite make out. It's like a mixture of gloom and panic and desperation, and it's not good. It's not what you want to see on your woman's face.

If she's thinking about bailing on me now, I'm gonna throw her over my shoulder and—I don't know what. But it ain't happening.

"So what do you think Maddie and the girls are up to right now?" I ask to break the silence.

She blinks and stiffens in her chair like the teacher caught daydreaming in class. Exactly the vibe I'm going for this evening.

"Um. Uh. Probably watching TV?"

"Yeah, they sure do love TV." It's not the *dumbest* thing I've said in my life, but it's up there. My toes curl in my boots.

Hurt flashes in Angie's eyes. Shit. She thinks I'm criticizing their screen time.

"I do, too," I rush to add. "I fucking love TV."

Now she's looking at me like I'm an idiot. Fair. Very fair. What do I say now?

I'm running out of topics. I've brought up the girls, Madison, Mom, her work, my work, Christmas, the restaurant, its décor, my food, her food, other restaurants, football. I'm not good at this. I'm not saying I'm proud of it, but I'm used to women leading the conversation on dates. Until it was all on me, I had no idea how much that sucks.

"So, uh, you think it's gonna snow this year?" I ask. Inside, I wince. I can't believe I've resorted to talking about the weather.

Angie pushes the fifty-five-dollar steak around her plate. "Yeah. Maybe." She eyes the king crab legs that I pushed her to get. Is that why she's mad? Because I was pushy?

My shoulders bunch so tight that my neck aches. I'm sweating. I can't stop tapping my foot, and despite the excruciating awkwardness, I've got a semi. At least she's not wearing the dress from last week that clung to everything—her tits, her ass, the cute little lower belly pudge she got after Tamblyn that never quite went away. I want to nibble it and blow kisses on it and watch it jiggle while she rides me.

Shit. No. I can't pop wood right now, full mast, in the middle of a crowded restaurant. We're seated smack-dab in the center of the dining room, and every table is full.

Is that why she's on edge? She doesn't like attention, and people *are* looking at her. Her outfit isn't as hot as last week's —she's wearing a skirt and the kind of thin, soft sweater that doesn't show any cleavage but still gives you plenty to look at—but she's the prettiest woman here. I assume. I haven't looked around.

"Gonna take the kids sledding at the community college?" They've got a great steep hill.

"Yeah. If it snows enough," she says. It hasn't snowed much the past few years, and it's sad. I remember making tunnels and forts with walls higher than my head. Maddie and Angie would play house in there for hours while I stockpiled snowballs, and in my head, I'd pretend Angie was a princess, and I was a World War II soldier defending her. The girls aren't going to have any memories but snowballs and Mom's snow cream.

"We should go up to the mountains when it gets colder. You ever been skiing?" I haven't, but it can't be that different from water skiing, right?

She shakes her head and frowns at her crab leg. It was a dumb question. Neither of us had ski money coming up, and Tyler sure wasn't spending his time off taking his family on ski trips during prime hunting season.

"We could go up to Whitetail and take a lesson. Can't be too hard."

She gives me a weak smile that says "yeah, never." Then she picks up the crab leg and cracks it, launching a piece of meat that lands on the back of my hand.

I pop it into my mouth and grin. "You gotta say 'incoming' before you shoot it at me."

She should grin back. She's Angie. I'm Brandon. We've eaten together a hundred times over the years. We've both made messes out of many a bushel of crabs. She's heard me get yelled at for eating like a pig. I've watched her dribble basically everything down her front—cornbread crumbs, pasta sauce, taco meat, and very memorably, melted vanilla ice cream.

She doesn't crack even the slightest smile. She flushes and looks even more miserable than she did before.

My brain races. What is happening? Second thoughts?

My stomach twists into a tight knot, and I set my fork down. A vise tightens on my chest. How do I figure this out when my throat is choking my air off? I chug the rest of my ice water. It doesn't help.

I thought things were going good. She took my hand in the car last week. She made that sound when I kissed her. She blushes as much looking at me as I do looking at her. I can *feel* that she's as excited as I am.

Except right now, she's not.

An alarm that I've been ignoring since that day behind the shed wails a little louder in the back of my mind.

She was excited at the kiddie pool, but behind the shed, all of a sudden, she got scared and basically fought me off. And then when we were dancing in the truck bed and I grabbed her ass, she tensed up until I moved my hand.

She gets excited, and then when we're touching, something happens, and she pulls away.

A sour taste floods my mouth, and a sick feeling creeps over me.

Is it about sex? Is that why she's so uptight—because she thinks I expect something to happen tonight?

Did Tyler do something to her?

Under the white linen tablecloth, my hands ball into fists.

I shouldn't jump to conclusions. I should ask.

How the fuck do I ask her something like that?

Behind the shed, she really freaked out. Why didn't it

occur to me then that something might have happened to her?

Because I didn't want to think that. Because the idea makes me want to puke and hyperventilate and pummel someone.

Was it Tyler?

I'll fucking kill him.

Across the table, Angie has gotten really still. Her eyes are trained on my face, and they've grown really, really wide. I need to relax. Breathe. I don't know anything except she's not having a good time.

"Are you done?" I ask. My voice comes out gruffer than I intend.

She nods, and her eyes get shiny. She's fiddling with something in her lap. Her napkin, probably.

"Do you want dessert?"

"No. Thank you." She looks miserable.

I can't get her to talk about whatever the problem is here, in the middle of a packed restaurant. What if she cries? I don't know why, but I don't want anyone else to see that. I mean, *I* don't want to see it either, but I can't stand the idea of her breaking down where people can see. It'd be like leaving her in the freezing cold with no coat.

We can go somewhere private, and I'll figure out how to ask, and I'll listen to what she says, and I won't lose my shit. Whatever it is, I'll handle it. Whatever's wrong, I can fix it.

Unless she tells me she's not feeling it, but if she does, it'll be a lie, and we'll talk it out. I'm not being cocky. I've been working on a gang since I was eighteen, and before that, I played football and lacrosse. I know what it feels like to play on a team, and Angie and I are a team. We're new in these particular positions, but we can talk just by looking at each other—or not looking—and if I think about it that way, we've been having a conversation all night. She's freaking out about something, and she doesn't want to tell me.

When I think about it that way, my job is easy. I make it okay. That starts with getting us away from center stage. I catch the waiter's eye and mouth 'check.' Angie is completely out of it as I pull out her chair like a gentleman, help her with her jacket, and lead her between the tables.

After the hot, crowded restaurant, the cool air hits hard, clearing my head. It's a crisp, clear night. Venus is visible, and so are the navigation lights of a few planes heading toward the airport. Our shoes are loud on the blacktop. I want to pull her close. The impulse feels so natural I have to focus on leaving my arms at my sides.

I hand her up into the truck, get in my side, and then I fuck around. I take my jacket off and toss it into the back. I fiddle with the seat warmers. I let the engine run awhile as if a V8 can't handle a cold start. I don't want to take her home. And it's not just that I've been imagining tonight in pornographic details for days. Years, really, if I'm being honest.

I can't walk away when she's unhappy. I've done that enough. I'd rather pick a fight. If I have to take her home and drive away, I'd rather do it angry, but that's not a choice I have. I'm not a child to throw a tantrum because someone doesn't want to play with me. I can take 'no' for an answer. It doesn't feel like it right now, but it's not going to kill me.

I need to ask her what's wrong, but what if she says nothing? She probably will. She keeps herself to herself. Always has. Then what do I say? I *know* something's wrong? What if she tells me to mind my business and take her home?

I don't want to do that. I *can't*. I *won't*.

But I don't have a fucking choice. I'm easily five times stronger than she is physically, and there is not a damn thing I can do to keep her except say the right thing. *Talk*. It's like God's joke on the working man.

I blow out a slow breath, grip the steering wheel, glare straight through the windshield, and steel myself. "Where to?" I ask.

For the three seconds it takes her to answer, nothing in my body beats or flows or blinks.

"Your place," she finally says, softly, like we're on the edge of the Grand Canyon, and I'm about to floor it while we grab each other's hands and sail into the blue sky. In my entire life, a woman has never shown such a complete lack of enthusiasm to go home with me. I do not have a semi anymore.

I'm not relieved. This is a stay of execution, and I don't know how I earned it, or what to do now, so I just try not to make any sudden moves. I keep my mouth shut. She wouldn't want to go all the way to my place to tell me it's over, right?

But she might to tell me someone hurt her, and she's not ready to be with me.

Fuck.

I need a cigarette.

I drive the speed limit all the way to my townhouse. I bought it two years ago when Randy said rates were only going up, and 'if you don't want to get priced out of home ownership by Wall Street fat cats who have no better place to park their cash than Chateau de Shit Factory' then I better use my container royalty check for a down payment. Chateau de Shit Factory isn't quite fair. The waste treatment plant hasn't been operational since the '90s. They pump it all south of the city, now.

Anyway, it's nice. Three bedrooms, two baths, and a deck I built myself. It's not exactly decorated, but I keep it clean. It's an investment. When I have kids, I want a single-family home with a big yard, a two-car garage, and a good tree for a treehouse. The girls would love a treehouse. Or a playhouse. They'd go nuts over that.

A heavy weight settles on my shoulders. I need to figure out what's happening. I don't want this to be over. For me, it never will be.

My throat is too tight to talk as I park in my spot, open her door, and walk her inside. She's never been to my place before. She never had a reason.

I had this idea that it'd be cool to watch her check it out tonight, like she'd be really impressed with my leather sofa set and the fruit bowl on the breakfast bar that I bought yesterday and filled with the expensive apples. That's not how it's going to go.

I untie my boots and kick them off in the foyer. It's habit. I work ships. If I wear shoes in the house, the carpets are getting ruined. Angie seems surprised, but then she unlaces hers and slips her feet out. She's wearing thin little socks that barely cover her toes. I crank the thermostat up as I pass. The hardwood is going to be cold.

Angie wanders in behind me, lingering in the space between the living room and kitchen. The first floor is open concept. She doesn't seem to take notice of anything.

"Can I get your coat?" I ask.

She blinks. "Oh, yeah." She wrestles it off before I can get there to help. Her cheeks are pink, and worry lines her face.

What the hell is wrong?

"The bathroom's there if you need it." I point toward the half bath under the stairs.

"Okay."

I hold my hand out for her coat, but she doesn't seem to register what I'm doing. She folds it over her own arm instead. Her purse hangs across her chest. It doesn't look like she's planning to get comfortable.

Do I ask her what's up now? While we're standing here in the middle of my silent house, staring at each other like strangers?

I cough to clear my throat. "You want to sit? We can watch a movie?"

"Okay."

"Do you want popcorn?" I ask.

"Yeah, all right."

"The remote is on the coffee table. You pick something. I've got all the streaming services."

"All of them?" she asks, a vague smile flashing across her face.

My chest eases the slightest bit. She's tense, and there's something going on, but she's still Angie. I head into the kitchen.

"Want a beer?" I ask over my shoulder.

"Sure."

I stretch to check the highest cabinet, praying I still have a bag of microwave popcorn left. Score. I have a whole unopened box. I check the expiration date. It's from two years ago. Popcorn doesn't go bad, right? Who's ever seen spoiled popcorn?

I'll just taste it first and make sure it's good.

While I nuke the bag, I wash my hands. Immediately after I dry them, my palms begin to sweat again. I hope Maddie is right about women being into men's pheromones because I started the evening fresh and clean, but at this point, I smell like I'm at the end of an eight-hour shift.

I'm so focused on not scalding myself with steam as I dump the popcorn into a bowl, and then scrounging up little baggies of salt from carryout orders since my shaker has been empty for a while, and then grabbing two beers, that I don't fully register that I haven't heard Angie sit down and turn the TV on.

When I come out of the kitchen area, she's still standing there with her coat and purse. Her face looks stricken. There's no other way to describe it.

"What's wrong?" I ask. My body tenses, getting ready to fight whoever made her feel like this, but I'm also in my stocking feet, my hands full with a bowl of popcorn and two bottles of beer.

"I-I have to tell you something," she starts.

My guts seize. Please don't let her say someone hurt her. Please, God. Let her dump me. Tell me she's not really into me, that she's not ready for something serious, fucking anything but someone hurt her.

She keeps talking without meeting my eyes. "I-I can go after if you want. I can leave. It's no problem."

I drove. She's not leaving. If she does, I'll take her. But that's not what I need to say right now. I need to be calm, cool, and collected. I nod, my face sweating from popcorn steam.

"I'm sorry," she says. "I have herpes."

"What?"

"I have herpes." Tears spring to her eyes.

Immediately, Mrs. Roscoe's eighth grade health class pops into my head. Which one was herpes?

Shit. All I can remember is that fucking cartoon about consent with the bike, and that bike doesn't help me one bit now.

The tears are now falling down her cheeks in a sheet.

What do I say?

I'm frozen in place, my brain offering up useless shit from sex ed—abstinence is the only one hundred percent effective method of birth control; when you sleep with someone, you sleep with everyone they've ever slept with, too; there's no such thing as safe sex, only *safer* sex.

Angie looks up at me, her arms wrapped tight across her chest and her chin wobbling, like I'm about to hit her.

And in my entire life, I have never felt so big—like Godzilla—or so hopelessly, utterly unprepared.

11

ANGIE

I DIDN'T WANT TO TELL HIM LIKE THIS, AND I SURE AS HELL didn't want to cry, but the past few hours have been torture. He looks so handsome and nervous, and he smells like a combination of three different soaps, colognes, *and* aftershaves. It should be too much, but it's perfect. He's perfect. He tried so hard to keep the conversation going, and I was no help at all.

The whole time during dinner, I kept worrying about what happens when he kisses me. He'll want to take it further, and I'll have to tell him and ruin everything. I had an idea that when we got to his place, I'd sit him down and tell him, but the dread was too much. I couldn't take it anymore. I blurted it out. I didn't even let him put the popcorn down first.

The little bit of steak that I was able to choke down is a lead weight in my stomach. He stands in front of me like he got slapped in the face out of nowhere. My throat convulses. I'd puke, but the only thing in my stomach is that lead weight, and it's not going anywhere.

I should run.

I'm not wearing shoes. They're next to his boots in the

foyer, and they're lace up, so I can't just slip them on and bolt. I could grab them and just carry them.

I don't have my car. Why did I let him drive? Why did I say I wanted to come here? I should have had him drive me home. I could have told him in the truck and bailed. What was I thinking?

My gaze lurches from the front door down the hallway to the stairs, desperately searching for an escape from this moment, but there's no way out. I said it, and now I have to live through what he does now. At least I don't have to worry about breaking into tears anymore. I'm already crying.

I was going to be calm and business-like, but my face is crumpling like a baby about to melt down.

I keep my eyes on him and brace myself.

He looks confused.

He clears his throat.

This is it.

My hands ball into fists.

He takes a step forward and holds out the popcorn bowl. What does he want me to do?

He holds it out a little further. I take it.

"Here. Sit," he says and guides me back toward the coffee table. My calves bump the wood ledge, and I lower my butt. It's a sturdy piece from the '70s with storage cabinets in the middle. My grandmother had the same one.

I wrap my arms around the bowl. He sinks down next to me, reaching across my lap to set a beer down by my other side. Then he takes a long swig from his own bottle.

My shoulders hunch forward and rise toward my ears like I can protect myself now that it's all out in the open. A tear splatters into the bowl, shriveling a piece of popcorn. Brandon exhales and sets his beer down with a clunk.

"Herpes is the one you can't get rid of, right?" he asks.

"Yeah." Everything inside me sinks, and every inch of my skin burns.

"But you can't die from it, right?" His voice is really gruff, like it used to be. Sometime over the past few months, it had gotten warmer. Not less deep, but less curt, and I didn't even notice until now when it's harsh again.

"No. There's medicine that I take. I don't really get breakouts anymore, but I can still give it to people." I stare at the popcorn. I heard the microwave beep earlier. He must've dumped a bag in the bowl, but the bowl is huge. It looks like we already ate most of it.

He reaches in and grabs a few pieces. I startle, and he bumps my thigh with his. It's a reassurance—*don't freak, it's just me.*

I glance over. He has his phone out, and he's scrolling with his thumb. With his other hand, he reaches for more popcorn.

His screen is a bunch of search results. In the box at the top, he typed: *is herpes fatal*?

I guess he's not taking my word for it. "You can ask me what you want to know," I say. "I know everything about it."

At first, I didn't. I didn't want to think about it. A few weeks after Ivy was born, though, I got really paranoid that I'd give it to the girls without knowing—like if we used the same towel or something—so I read *everything* I could find online. You can't get it from towels or toilet seats or soap or silverware.

"You're shook," he says. "Drink your beer and eat some popcorn. You hardly ate anything at dinner."

I couldn't possibly swallow anything with the lump in my throat, so I watch him search.

does herpes hurt?

what is it called when you have a disease and it causes something else really bad to happen?

The top search result for that question is *sepsis*.

"Herpes doesn't cause sepsis," I tell him. "You want the word *complications*."

He grunts and types *herpes complications* into the bar, and his face goes gray.

"I don't have any of those things," I say.

He grunts again and keeps searching.

is herpes dangerous?

"Did you have it when you were pregnant?" he asks.

"Yeah. I found out when I was almost due with Ivy."

His teeth clench, and that bump on his jaw pops. I can see him adding two and two in his head, and not coming up surprised. He types some more.

herpes symptoms

"Does it hurt?" he asks.

"Yeah. It used to, but I haven't had an outbreak in a long time."

He hums and taps.

sex with herpes

He goes down a rabbit hole with that one. My face burns, but it's a different kind of burn than a few minutes ago. More prickly, less scalding.

At one point, he mutters, "What the fuck is a dental dam?"

He taps and skims, intent on his screen, occasionally grabbing more popcorn with his free hand and washing it down with a long swig of beer.

Like Madison and me, Brandon was not the best at school. Unlike us, he wouldn't do his homework unless Miss Dawn sat on him.

When we were young, there were many times when I was over for dinner, and Brandon had to stay at the table afterwards until he finished his missing work. He hated it, and he'd glare at the worksheet as if it had done him wrong, the same way I stare at my car's engine when it won't start, like I know it's the problem, but damned if I know how to fix it. That's how he looks now, frowning as he scrolls on his phone.

Is he figuring out whether or not this is a deal breaker, right now at this very minute, based on what he's reading on the internet?

While he eats popcorn?

Oh, fuck that. I don't want to be here when he decides.

I stand, forgetting about the bowl. It flips off my lap and onto the floor. Popcorn spills on the carpet. Brandon blinks up at me, surprised.

"Shit," I say, my lower lip wobbling.

"Shit," he somberly agrees.

"I've got to go."

He quickly stands, too, dropping the hand with his phone to his side. "Why?"

There goes my chin. Now it's wobbling, too. "B-Because I don't wanna hold your popcorn while you decide if I'm too gross to fuck or not, Brandon."

My vision blurs. I'm tired of crying.

Where's my purse?

I squint all over the fuzzy room before I remember that I'm still wearing it.

"Hey," Brandon says from inches away. He closed the space between us while I was distracted. "No. Don't."

He tilts my chin up, holding my head in place as he awkwardly blots at my eyes with the cuff of his shirt. His face comes into focus. His deeply serious brown eyes. His firm jaw. His stern mouth. So familiar, but also a total mystery, like a boarded-up building you pass every day for years but you have never once seen inside.

Now he smells like beer, melted butter, and cologne, and underneath, he smells like *Brandon*, like the past, the good times, the long, happy hours when we were young. I want to dig my fingers into his biceps and *make* him feel like I do—like there's nothing that could make me let go—but I'm the mess here, so all I can do is breathe him in, and hold him close that way, but I've been crying, so my lungs shudder.

"That's not what I'm doing," he says and grabs me by the upper arms so I'll look him in the eye. He gazes down, as serious as I've ever seen him. "Fuck, Angie. I'd take a bullet for you, and this ain't a bullet."

It's not a line, not the way he says it. It's a fact. Like Cummins makes the best engine, Pittsburgh sucks, and he'd take a bullet for me.

He leans down and presses his lips to my forehead, tender and awkward, as he cups the sides of my neck. "Don't cry now," he says against my skin. "This is nothing. This is just life. We'll deal with it."

I sniffle. He drops another kiss.

"You don't have to be the good guy," I mutter into his shirt. "I get it. If this is too much, I won't blame you or tell anyone." I don't know why I'm saying all this. It's not like I want to run him off. I want to stay right here, huddled against his chest, tucked under his chin. Forever.

He wraps his arms around me and holds me tight. For some reason, we rock in place, slowly, side to side.

"Shut up, Angie," he says softly. "It's not too much."

"It might be...after you've had time to think about it. You might change your mind." I can't stop. I have to recite all my fears.

"You know me to be one to do that?" he asks, somehow gathering me closer.

I crane my neck, trying to meet his eyes, but all I can see is the five o'clock shadow under his jaw.

"No," I say to his Adam's apple. He has always seemed to

know what he's doing and what he thinks. Drives Madison nuts.

The muscles in his neck tighten as he smiles. "That's right. Stop worrying. We're good."

My arms are folded and squished between our bodies. One of my socks is slipping down my heel. My eye sockets are swollen, and my sinuses ache.

"I can't ever stop worrying."

"I know." He smiles gently. "I'm just sayin'—it'd be okay if you took a break for now. We could watch a movie. Afterwards, we could talk about it some more. Or not."

He strokes my back soothingly. I've never felt this close to a person before.

Every breath he takes, his chest rises against mine, and I feel the same thing I felt watching Tamblyn and Ivy sleep when they were babies and every inhalation meant the world. Like I'm not floating alone in space anymore.

"So what do you say? Want to watch some shit blow up?" he asks, his low, teasing voice sending shivers down my neck.

"Does that mean you're done with the internet?"

He growls, bends, and puts his shoulder into my stomach, hoisting me up and over until my front is dangling down his back. I shriek, but I don't dare struggle lest he drop me on my head. He slaps my ass and strolls toward the couch.

"Put me down! You can't carry me!"

"I just did," he puffs, lowering me to the cushions, more quick than careful. Then he grins down, a little out of breath and pleased with himself.

He takes in my mussed-up hair and twisted skirt, and his lips curve higher at the corners. His brown eyes somehow darken and sparkle at the same time. My stomach flips, my cheeks heat, and I drop my gaze. I don't mean to look, but his fly is poking up. It's not a whole tent pole, or anything, but it's definitely not an air pocket.

"Just ignore that," he says, flopping down next to me and kicking his feet up on the coffee table. He's got the remote in his hand.

"The popcorn is still on the floor," I point out.

"I'll get it after we pick something." He clicks on a streaming service and scrolls.

He's bent the knee closest to me, so I can't see his hard-on anymore, but it was there. He told me to ignore it. That means he's not permanently turned off. I lean forward, snag my beer, and sink back into the leather.

"Now we're talking," he says, swipes up his own drink, and clinks our bottles. "You want to watch Jason Statham blow shit up or John Wick or what?"

"Do we have to watch an action movie?" I begin to feel like I'm on steadier ground. I've argued with Brandon over the TV many times before, although usually, it was Madison arguing while I hold the remote in a death grip so Brandon wouldn't take it.

"So what are you feeling like, then?" He squints to read off the screen. "Here, we've got 'Award-Winning Directors?' Or how about 'Gems for You.'"

"They won't be gems for *me*," I say.

"Me, neither. Shane has my password, and he's the one who watches all the time. These recommendations are for him."

"Is that your excuse in case there's weird shit?"

"Yes. Yes, it is." He slides me a look and grins. He's not relaxed by any means, but he doesn't look like he's bracing himself to take a punch anymore like he did at dinner. My news didn't ruin things.

Lightness fizzes upward inside me like I just rolled down a soda machine and someone unscrewed my cap.

"How 'bout this?" he asks. It's a rom-com I saw a long time ago.

"Sure." There's no way I'll be able to focus, anyway.

Brandon starts the movie and hops up to clean the popcorn. He disappears into the kitchen and comes back with more, this time still in the bag, and two more beers. He sits down closer than he was before he got up and puts his arm around my shoulder. We both stare at the screen intently. He munches away.

"I can't believe I told you I had herpes, and you ate popcorn and looked it up on the internet," I say, not looking over.

"I didn't want to say something ignorant," he says. "And I didn't want to ask you shit when you were upset."

"And you were hungry."

"I'm always hungry," he says.

We fall quiet and watch for a while. Well, he watches. I take the opportunity to really look around his place. There aren't any pictures on the walls or tchotchkes, but it's clean. There are stripes from the vacuum on the carpet.

The first floor is open concept, although the sink and stove are on a far wall that you can't see from the living room. There's a breakfast bar with nothing on it except for his keys and wallet, and the counters I can see are bare. It'd look like a model apartment except for the big-ass home gym in the dining room area and the "Cable Workout" poster taped to the wall with a bunch of illustrations of a man doing different exercises.

I feel Brandon's eyes on me, so I stop gawking at his place and focus on the movie. There are some kind of wacky hijinks going on. I guess we should be laughing, but neither of us has made a sound.

Brandon coughs, and then he asks, "So, we can have sex with condoms, right?"

The leather couch is overstuffed, but not enough to swallow me whole, which is what I wish it'd do. My heart pounds, and my face flames. I *do* want to have this conversation, but I also want to disappear down the crack between the cushions like the snack wrappers that Tamblyn sneaks.

"Yeah. There's always a chance you can catch it, but it's safer with a condom, and if I'm not having an outbreak."

"Okay." He waits a minute—to give me time to stop wanting to die, I guess. "I don't, uh, have anything. That I know about."

I blow out my cheeks and nod.

"I don't want to assume anything, you know, but—" There is a very, very long pause. I don't know where he's looking. I'm staring straight at the screen. "Do you want to?" he finally asks.

I'm shell-shocked, terminally embarrassed, terrified, and raw as hell, but theoretically yes. Very much. For a long time now.

I chew my lip. "Yeah."

"Okay, fuck, yeah," he says, and before I can blink, he turns, plunging a hand into my hair, and kisses me with all he's got. He doesn't stop, bowling me over onto my back, pressing me into the couch with his weight.

He tastes like beer and popcorn. He tastes *hungry*.

Oh, shit. I didn't know he meant *now*.

What do I do with my hands?

He raises up on his knees and grabs me by the waist, resettling me higher up on the couch so he can cover me with his whole body, and all the while, his tongue and teeth coax me. *Open up. Open wider. Lick me back.* I never liked French kissing before, but this is different. He's not trying to see if he can choke me with his tongue. I'm letting him in, and he's exploring, and vice versa.

It feels trusting. Like confiding, saying the things neither of us can say out loud.

I want this. I want you. This is everything. This is only the beginning.

I don't have to worry about my hands. Brandon draws them above my head, pinning them to the cushion, interlacing his fingers with mine. He wedges his knee between my thighs. My skirt is caught between his leg and my pussy, and it twists at the waist, digging into my soft middle. I've sunk into the couch. He uses his elbows to keep his weight off my chest, but his hard hips grind against mine, his cock poking my belly.

He's breathing so hard. His eyes are closed, and his arms shake, but not from holding himself up. He's swept away. I peek, captivated by the look on his face. He's lost. Lust drunk. I made him feel this way.

He knows everything about me, and he wants me, and the idea is so big, it leaks out my ears.

This started fast, but he's not taking it further. His hips rock, tugging my panties tight over my clit, and my overwhelm clears enough so I notice the pressure, and it feels good. He moves to kiss my neck and nip my earlobe with his teeth, and that feels good, too, but none of it feels as good as his weight. I'm caught, and that's how he wants me.

He lets go of one of my hands so he can shove one of his under my sweater. I clutch his hair. He groans and lets my other hand go. My fingers fly to his shirt buttons. I pop them open, and it's like I've given him the permission he's been waiting for. He moans and drags my top over my head. I push his shirt off his shoulders.

A grumpy whine escapes my lips. There are still clothes. He pulls the white tank top off one-handed. I splay my palms on his chest. His skin is hot. The leather is cool against my bare back.

We pause, breathing hard, staring at each other. It's not a check in. I want to look at him. I want to track his gaze as it travels from my breasts to my face to my bare thighs and back again like he can't pick. My hands rest on his shoulders. He grabs them, urging them around his neck.

"Hold on," he orders. I hardly have time to tighten my grip, but I don't really need to. He's got me, his hands cupping my ass, lifting me as he stands. I wrap my legs around his waist the best I can. He carries me to the bottom of the stairs, kissing me the whole time.

He raises a foot to the first step and grips me tighter, his muscles flexing.

"What are you doing?" I ask, breathless.

"Carrying you upstairs."

He hikes himself up the first step. He blows out a breath like the guys at the gym when they deadlift.

"Put me down. I'll walk up."

"No." He places his next foot, grunts, and hauls us up the next step.

"Come on, Brandon." I wriggle. "Let me down."

"No." He hoists me up to the next step.

I uncross my ankles and let my legs dangle. "This isn't romantic. You're gonna put your back out."

"I am not. I can deadlift two thirty-five." He grunts and up we go again. It takes a little more effort than the last step.

"I'm not impressed."

He takes two more steps. "You should be. This is very fucking impressive," he huffs.

My lips quirk, and I bury my face into the crook of his neck. "You're not gonna have any energy left by the time we get up there," I mumble into his shoulder.

"Just you watch," he says, making a final push up the last few steps and then striding down the hallway, breathing heavily but not at all slowed down. He opens his bedroom door with his foot and lays me on the bed, following me down, his hands and mouth everywhere.

He rolls me onto my stomach. Unhooks my bra. Kisses and nips down my spine until he hits the waistband of my skirt, and then he rolls me back over, unzips the skirt, tugs it off, and tosses it behind him onto the floor. He kneels above me, his spread thighs bracketing mine, and unbuckles his belt, staring at my breasts like he's got plans, serious plans, and our clothes need to get out of the way.

He shucks his pants. Then he hooks his fingers in the sides of my panties, starts to pull them down, but he stops before he bares my pussy to glance up at my face.

I watch him back.

I can't believe Brandon Kaczmarek is kneeling over me, naked. His chest and shoulders are a lighter tan than his forearms. He's got one of those Vs pointing between his legs, a thick, dark thatch of hair, and a thick, veiny cock. It twitches, straight up against his carved abs.

My heart races. It's Brandon, but he's also a gorgeous, ripped, naked man with a massive hard-on wearing the most smoldering expression I've ever seen. The Brandon I know is cool and collected. He doesn't say much, but he's steady.

That Brandon isn't going to go further until I give him a sign that it's okay no matter how much he's smoldering. Shivers race down my spine and prickle the back of my neck. My nipples harden into itchy, achy points. Blood rushes through my veins, a kick of pure adrenaline, because *this* new Brandon looks like he could shake off steady Brandon in a split second and fuck me like a rag doll.

Am I ready?

I've never been with anyone but Tyler, but I'm not going to think about him right now.

I'm scared.

What if Brandon changes his mind when he sees me? What if he looks real close at my pussy for a long time to make sure there's nothing wrong with me?

Nausea joins the other clenching and fluttering in my belly. My gaze flies to his face. He's calmly looking back at me.

"Scared?" he asks, his voice so low and gruff that it sends another round of shivers zipping from nerve to nerve.

"Yeah," I whisper.

"Me, too," he says, his thumbs stroking circles on my bare hips. Excitement swells in my chest. Or maybe panic.

Maybe both.

"Why?" I ask.

"I don't want to scare you off."

"Why would you do that?" I ask, breathless.

His voice drops even further, the hunger in his expression burning even darker. "Because I want to fucking wreck you."

My eyes widen. "What does that mean?"

"Say yes, and I'll show you," he says.

"Okay," I agree. 'Cause what else would I say?

"Okay," he repeats, and he kind of surges forward, over top of me, reaching for his night stand while he kisses me again like he just got let out of jail.

A drawer slides open. Foil crinkles. He bites my bottom lip and then captures a breast, raising it to his mouth, and suckles, rough and demanding. He's not gentle, not with how he holds me or how he sucks and lashes my sensitive nipple with his tongue. I cry out, and he rumbles, pleased. Self-satisfied.

Every move he makes is swift and assured. My panties disappear. I don't have time to think or worry. He flips me onto my stomach again, using his arm like a crook to hike my knee up, opening my pussy to him. Breathing hard in my ear, he pushes into me from behind, slowly but surely splitting me, filling me. A sound I've never made before slips from my lips. It's a startled squeak that somehow ends in a demanding wail. He grunts, even more satisfied.

He reaches around my waist and delves between my legs, finding my clit like it's a homing beacon, circling it with his two middle fingers. He cups my throat with his other hand, not hard enough to cut off air, but firm, so I'm held in position while he rides me, fucking me so hard my teeth would rattle if his palm wasn't holding my jaw shut.

His hair brushes my cheek. "You like this?" he asks.

I can't answer. I'm coming already, my stretched channel somehow clenching as a wave of release crashes through my belly, hot and bright and deliciously sharp. My whole body shudders, electrified. My legs flail. My heart slams in my chest. I press my palm between my boobs to calm it down. Oh, please, don't let it blow.

This has *never* happened before. It takes concentration for me to come. I have to focus, but with Brandon, my brain can't even follow one thought to the next. It's mush. He's leading, and I'm following, but I'm not entirely sure my body can take it.

He keeps thrusting, slower but unrelenting. I'm still spasming, and it feels so, so good. The intensity dwindles, but the pleasure doesn't fade. It mellows, lapping in lighter and lighter waves like ripples in a lake. I whine like an idiot. I can't help making these noises, and each time I make one, Brandon touches me differently, better, more.

As my trembling finally stops, he lets my knee go, smooths his hand over my hip, and murmurs, "You're so fucking beautiful when you come. I want to see you do it again."

He draws his cock out, and I whimper. He laughs low, flips me over, and slides back inside me on the next beat, his hips not losing time. He pumps like a machine, but a machine that knows exactly what rhythm I need and exactly which angle lets his pubic bone rub against my clit.

My knees fall open. My inner thigh muscles are putty.

Brandon cradles my face, kissing me, nipping my nose and chin, lowering his head to lap and suck my nipples like he can't bear to leave them alone for very long, stopping every few seconds to mutter dirty, bossy things that banish every single, self-conscious worry that tries to rear its ugly head.

"Feel how wet that pussy is for me. You're soaking my sheets, aren't you, Angie? You're making a mess on the sheets, aren't you?"

I whimper. I am. I'm dripping, and every time he thrusts, he smears my wetness up my belly.

"Let's see," he says, withdraws, and flips me again, propping me on my hands, knocking my knees apart and slamming into me, hands gripping my hips, jerking me back when he thrusts forward so he goes even deeper. I'm looking straight down at the wet spot. "See the mess you made with that pretty, wet pussy?"

He teases my clit, his breathing heavier and heavier, but his pace doesn't slow, doesn't ease an inch. I had no idea, but this is exactly what I need. Hard and long and greedy. I can't ruin anything. I can only hold on for dear life and go along for the ride.

"Can you feel me, Angie?" he pants.

I whimper. That's not good enough for him.

He pulls my upper arms back so my chest goes flat to the mattress, holding my elbows behind me as he spreads his thighs to open me wider. It feels like a yoga pose. My knees are bent and splayed like a frog.

"How about now, Angie?" He drives into me, and he should be hitting my cervix, he's so deep, but he's not. He's scratching some weird, wonderful place that I didn't even know itched.

"Yes," I gasp. "It feels so good."

"What feels good?" he asks.

I don't know what to say. Tyler just panted during sex, and I've heard dirty talk in porn, but damned if I can remember anything that they said right now.

"Does my cock feel good in your pussy?"

"Yes," I moan. Bingo. That's the answer.

"Where's my cock?" He pounds that spot he found, and each time he hits it, pure satisfaction bursts through me, an exquisite relief that somehow ratchets higher and higher, which isn't how satisfaction and relief are supposed to work. It's magic. "Where is my cock, Angie?"

"In my pussy," I slur.

"Say my name."

"Brandon," I sob.

"Say it again," he demands.

"*Brandon*." I'm demanding, too. He needs to finish what he started.

"I've got you," he says, thrusting a few more times like he can't help it. Then he hooks me around the middle and hauls me up so my back leans against his chest. While he pistons his hips, nailing the same spot from a different angle, he grabs my fingers and shoves them between my legs. "Play with yourself."

His hand stays on top of mine like he wants to learn how I do it. For once, I'm not worried about whether I can get there, or how much longer I have, or if I should go ahead and fake it now. I'm riding high, and I know he's not going to stop.

He pinches a nipple and scrapes his teeth along the crook of my neck, and it's exactly what I need. My orgasm rises like a tsunami, hovering on a knife's edge for an excruciating moment before it crashes down, washing every last brain cell away. I scream.

He groans, exultant, like he's freed himself from under the weight of a car, and bucks wildly. I'm a rag doll, so I just flop, taking everything he gives me. Then his body tenses, and he wraps his arms around me tight. He shudders and holds me up as we both gasp for breath.

At some point, he tips us over, and we land on our sides, spooning. The sheet is damp against my face.

"Shit. Sorry," he says and works his arm under my cheek so I can rest my head on his bicep instead of the wet spot. I'm happy he did because I can't move. I'm as limp as a dishrag.

The seconds tick past, and the rise and fall of his chest slows against my back. His hand roams, stroking my hip, smoothing over my belly, cupping my breasts. Every so often, he kisses my neck.

There is nothing I need to do, nowhere I need to be but here, and if there's something I should be worried about, too bad, because my brain is a sieve, and it can't hold on to worries.

"Hold on for a second, okay?" he says, rising from the bed and disappearing into the bathroom. I hold on. What else can I do? My legs sure as hell don't work.

A toilet flushes, and the sink runs. The mattress dips, and then he's back, nudging my knees apart so he can gently wipe me with a warm washcloth.

Should I be embarrassed? Probably, but I don't have the energy.

When he finishes cleaning me up, he balls the washcloth and shoots it at an open hamper across the room. He makes it.

"Two points. No net," he says, rolling onto his side to face me.

My mouth curves. I'm too tired to giggle. He's such a dork.

For a second, I float in the afterglow, soaking him in while he gazes into my eyes like he lost something there. His bicep flexes as he props up his head. His muscles are freaking amazing.

His brown hair is a sweaty mess. His abs still have ridges even though they're doing no work at the moment. Somehow, as I watch, his dangling dick stiffens. My surprise must show.

He glances down at his cock and flashes a playful grimace. "Yeah, I'm kind of impressed, too. I jerked off like five times today. It should be out for the count."

I can't believe Brandon Kaczmarek just admitted to jerking off. "Five times?"

"I wanted to last. You know. If things went, uh—" His words fail him, and his expression reverts to the tough-guy mask that I'm used to. My heart swells. I love his poker face. I've seen what's under it now, so I know what he's been hiding. His hard face makes the truth sweeter. Underneath, he's crazy about me.

My pulse spikes. It feels like winning the lottery when you're behind on the rent.

What happens when the crazy wears off?

When he realizes now that he's had me, he doesn't want me, and he's gone ahead and slept with a woman with herpes without thinking it through, and that actually wasn't a risk he was willing to take?

My stomach aches. I draw my knees to my chest. Where did my underwear go? I want my clothes. I'm too naked.

Brandon frowns. He reaches across the space between us and rubs his index finger between my eyebrows. He must be smoothing the line that shows up when I'm upset.

I tighten my arms, tucking myself into a smaller ball.

Brandon sighs, stretches his arm flat, and lays his cheek on his bicep to stare at me.

"Remember that time on the Henry McCarthy?" he asks.

"Yeah." It was a long time ago. Before Ivy. Tamblyn was a baby. The McCarthys are tugboat operators. Every fourth of July, they invite business associates and their families to cruise and watch the fireworks from the middle of the harbor.

Folks bring their own snacks and coolers, spread out blankets on the deck, and enjoy the best view in the city. I'd gone once before, when I was really little, before my dad left. He was a marine surveyor, so he knew the McCarthys that way.

The time that Brandon's talking about, I was Madison's plus one, and she was tagging along with Randy who knew the McCarthys from the port. I didn't know Brandon was coming. I didn't notice him until well after the boat had launched.

Miss Dawn was watching Tamblyn that night, and Tyler was away on a whitewater rafting weekend with his boys. I hadn't been out in months. I drank two hard seltzers, and I was three sheets to the wind. It was hot as the seven hinges of hell, but I was blissed out just being nineteen years old and having a break from the constant vigilance. Tamblyn was in her grab-it-and-put-it-in-your-mouth phase.

Brandon stops rubbing away my stress wrinkle and pries away one of my hands to hold it.

I squeeze it tight. "Why do you ask?"

"I was thinking about that night. You were leaning against the gunwale with your neck craned back, watching the fireworks, your face lit up, grinning ear to ear. For a whole half hour, you were smiling."

"You were watching me?" I was with Tyler then. If you'd

asked me, I'd have said I was in love. I never stopped to ask myself why love felt like shit.

"Yeah. I was skulking by the wheelhouse so you didn't see me."

My mouth softens. "I was wasted."

"You were beautiful, and it fucking broke my heart."

"Why?"

"Because I hadn't seen you smile like that for years, and I was so busy trying to act cool around you, I hadn't realized."

"You tried to act cool around me back then?"

His lips curve. "I tried."

"I didn't know."

He lifts our joined hands so he can smooth the line in my forehead again with his thumb. "I was a dumbass kid, but I thought if I ever got a chance with you, you were gonna smile like that all the time."

"There were fireworks. You can't have fireworks all the time."

"Beg to differ," he says, smirking and casting a glance down at his dick. It's not as hard as it was, but it's not soft either.

I roll my eyes.

"I know that," he says, serious again. "But whatever went through your head just now that made you curl up like you got kicked? I'm not having it. So you might as well tell me what you're thinking, and we'll sort it out."

"You're not having it?" Until tonight, I had no idea that Brandon had any bossiness in him. Maybe it should piss me off, but it doesn't. It makes me want to close my eyes and fall back like it's a feather bed. Like an acrobat's net.

"You know what I mean. What was that, Ang?"

I'm so used to making nice and smoothing edges for a man that my brain is already supplying me with convenient lies—I got tired all of a sudden. I got cold. My stomach hurts. Cramps. I was thinking about something that happened at work. The girls. I could pick any one of those things, and say, "It's nothing. I don't want to talk about it," and I'm one hundred percent sure that Brandon wouldn't believe me, but he'd drop it because I asked.

I don't *have* to trust him.

But I could.

I could try.

I'm so used to clinging to something flimsy to keep myself from drowning. What would it feel like to grab onto something solid?

I swallow, and then I say, "I'm scared that once you have time to think, you'll regret that you got carried away, and you won't want to risk being with me."

He nods. He doesn't argue. It takes him a long time to speak, but for some reason, my stomach doesn't sink, and my heart doesn't climb into my throat while I wait. Somewhere along the line, he won my sympathetic nervous system to his side.

"I'm scared that by some fucking miracle, Tyler is going to smarten up and beg you to take him back, and you'll do it for the girls." He guides our clasped hands to press between his pecs, right over his thumping heartbeat. "I'm scared that you're gonna finish your glow up and realize you can do better than a guy like me. I'm scared that I'm a rebound, and you're only with me 'cause I'm familiar. You're fucking *it* for me, Angie. If I'm your rebound, it'll kill me." He tilts his head back and stares at the ceiling. "It'd kill me, but I still wouldn't regret this," he says to the light fixture. "Not ever."

I curl my fingers around his thumb, squeezing tight, and inchworm until I'm plastered to his body. I throw a leg over his and hook my foot around his ankle. He exhales and presses my head to his chest. We're fully tangled now.

"I guess we can be scared together, then," I say.

"Or we could relax."

"What's that?" I joke.

Chuckling, he rolls me onto my back and grins down, drawing my hands above my head. "Or we could do the fireworks thing," he says.

"Okay," I agree, lifting myself to capture his lips and steal that smile.

His weight comes to rest on me, and we start at the beginning all over again, eyes locked, hearts pounding.

I didn't know that you could feel this close to another person, or this safe and happy. I didn't know that love could feel like something other than wanting and longing and wishing.

It can be having. And holding.

A fresh start. A moon shot.

And yeah—

Fireworks.

12

BRANDON

“You expecting titty pics?” Shane asks over his shoulder as he squats beside an SUV, rips its hubcap off, and throws it through the car’s busted-out rear window. “You know they’re paying us to lash these here cars, right?”

I flip him off, shove my phone in my pocket, and make quick work of lashing the car in my row to the deck. Doesn’t matter how much I dick around, I’m still ahead of him. He’s slow as shit.

Angie hasn’t answered my text yet. It’s been three hours. She’s at work, too, but she usually has no problem finding time to get back to me.

She’s mad. That’s good. I just have to keep reminding myself that.

I knew Tyler was an asshole, and I assumed he was a terrible boyfriend, but I had no idea that he’d done such a number on her. She’s got opinions on shit, but you have to pry them out of her. Everything is always fine. Step on her foot by accident? It’s fine. My dick slips, pokes her in the ass, and she jumps ten feet and her eyes tear up? It’s fine.

Forget about her mom, make a bad joke about meth heads, and her face goes white as a sheet? It’s fine.

She's trained as well as a whipped dog, and it fucking hurts my heart. She won't fight back. She just gets real quiet, changes the subject if we're talking, and then she'll do something nice for me—like freshen up my beer or stroke my neck with her spider fingers—like I wasn't the one who made her feel bad.

Apparently, between the two of us, *I'm* the one who knows how to be in a healthy, functional relationship. It's ridiculous. The longest I've ever been with a woman was a six-month situationship where she ghosted me because she found another guy, and I didn't pick up on that fact until I ran into her a couple weeks later at the bar, and it was awkward, and I had to figure out why.

I did have parents who loved each other, though, so that's my leg up. I know that it isn't normal for a woman to be agreeable all the time. It's unnatural.

She needs to understand that she can get pissed and let me have it. I'm not perfect, and neither is she. We've been going out for four months now, and they've been the best months of my life, hands down, but in some ways, we're still stuck at the starting gate.

I'm not Tyler Reynolds. I don't need her to be anything other than herself, and I don't need her to soft-pedal it when she's mad because my ego can't handle a woman talking back.

It makes my skin crawl when she pretends like she's fine when she's not, and it makes me fucking nervous. If a woman feels that she can't be straight with you, it's gonna come out of left field when she's done with you. I've never had that experience personally, but I've sat next to plenty of guys down at Donovan's while they cried over their beers. ILA Local 249 isn't exactly known for emotional intelligence.

"Hey, how was Broyce's?" Shane finishes with the SUV and moves on to the next vehicle, stopping to struggle with the knot of lashings that he grabbed off the rack like a kid grabbing candy from an unsupervised bowl of Halloween candy. He's been doing this as long as I have, and he still hasn't figured out that if you take them by the hooks and then lay them out flat, side by side, you don't need to untangle them like Christmas lights later.

I pick up a single strap from my neat line and mosey forward. In general, I hate lashing, but it's pouring rain today, so I don't mind working under cover, even though the deck is stifling and the fumes are thicker than usual because of the humidity.

"Fine." I kneel, pop the hubcap, throw it in the back seat, wind the strap through the wheel, and secure it to the deck before Shane gets a strap free from the rat's nest he's made.

"What'd you get?" he asks.

"Steak."

He snorts and gives up trying to make conversation, at least for a minute or two.

Angie's salty about dinner last night at Broyce's. Or about me pushing her when she was obviously pissed and said, "It's nothing" when I asked her what was wrong. Or both. No reason it can't be both.

She did say Broyce's was too fancy for little kids. I figured she just didn't want to be a bother, but I've got money. I can tip enough that no matter what the girls spill by accident, the server won't act bothered. And we were never going to get there again if we waited for Tyler to take his parenting time so we can have a date night. I wanted Angie to have a nice dinner. I wanted a redo.

So I told her to get everyone dressed up for a nice surprise. When I pulled up in front of the restaurant last night, she sure as shit was surprised.

I didn't think our first date could be topped for awkwardness, but I was wrong. She spent the entire meal watching the girls like a hawk, dabbing every crumb and blotting every drop that fell on the tablecloth, moving their water cups away from the table edge each time they took a sip, ducking under the table every time their napkins fell off their laps.

At least Angie ate this time. She shoveled a fifty-dollar filet into her mouth like there was a prize for finishing first. Then she made herself smile and thank me when she was clearly miserable.

I didn't have much time to talk to her afterwards. When we got to Mom's house, she sent the girls ahead, but Mom was at the Seahorse Inn, so they had to wait on the porch for Angie to come with the keys. We had just long enough for me to ask her what's wrong, and for her to say "nothing," and for me to say, "bullshit," and for her to say "I said it's nothing, so I don't know what you have to be mad about" before she slid out the truck door with her nose in the air, huffing all the way down the front walk.

Now I've got our first real argument memorialized in a text message chain, and she's left me on read.

angie call me back

i know youre pissed

I'm not pissed.

talk to me. if I was pissed at you, id talk to you about it.

Dots. Minutes and minutes of dots. And then—

I told you I didn't want to go to Broyce's with the girls.

yeah, you did

Yeah. I did.

i didnt get that you felt that strongly about it.
i wish you wouldve said.

I did say.

i just dont get whats so bad about it

You don't take two kids under five to a fancy restaurant.

whats so bad about it?

No one looks at you if the girls make a mess or if they're noisy.

they were fine

I mean, for kids that young, they were great. Only one glass of water got knocked over. They both left most of their steak on their plates, but they demolished the bread basket, and it's my money to waste. Tamblyn got a little loud and whiny toward the end, but she wasn't near as loud as the blowhard at the bar who was a few martinis deep.

That old couple beside us kept looking at me all judgy.

i didnt notice.

I know.

why do you care what they think? what anyone thinks?

Easy for you to say.

could be easy for you too

K.

you shouldnt let what other people might be thinking ruin your night

dont let other people get in your head so much

angie?

come on angie

There were so many dots, so many long pauses when she must have deleted what she was going to say. I called. She didn't answer. Finally, she texted back.

Sorry. It's really no big deal. Don't worry about it.

It's my bad.

I'm going to bed now. Goodnight.

goodnight beautiful. well talk tomorrow.

As soon as I woke up, I texted her good morning like usual. I still haven't heard back.

Her "sorry" makes me feel like shit. I don't want "sorry." I want what she gives me in bed and when we're hanging out alone or with the girls, having fun or just relaxing, when she lets her guard down, and she's like she was when we were younger, before she started hiding herself away.

I want her to trust me. With *all* the stuff.

But how do you make someone trust you? Especially when they're gun-shy.

I'm lucky she told me about the herpes and didn't just hold me at arm's length forever. I know she still worries about it, but she's really uncomfortable when I bring it up. Unless we're deep in the thick of it, she doesn't like me looking at her pussy. She won't let me go down on her, and she won't talk about that, either.

She hasn't had an outbreak since we've been together, and as far as I know, I haven't caught it. If I do, I'll cross that bridge when I come to it.

Honestly, mathematically, I *should* have it by now. The internet says twelve percent of people have it, and they say maybe like ninety percent don't even know it. I haven't fucked *that* much in my life, but statistically, Angie can't be the first woman I've been with who's had it.

And that twelve percent doesn't even count mouth herpes, which can be spread to your junk. Fifty to eighty percent of people have that. That's wild. Like what else do eighty percent of people have in common?

And yet, it's like this huge secret that no one talks about except to make jokes. Even Angie and I can't talk about it amongst ourselves.

I get that it's different for a woman. Worse. Everyone still jokes about the time Big Will from Sterling's gang got crabs from a chick he picked up at the Cancun Cabaret—and *he* still laughs his ass off about it, too. But then back in high school, there was a rumor—just a rumor—that Michelle Papadakis had something, and no one would date her. I haven't seen her around in years, but I run into her brothers all the time.

When you think about it, that's some scarlet letter shit. It's the 21st century. We've got AI talking to you in the chat box. You can pay to go to space. You can get literally *anything* delivered to your door, but a disease about as bad as poison ivy can ruin your life. That's crazy.

I never really thought about it much before Angie. I thought STDs were nasty, but they weren't my problem because I always used condoms. It's my problem now. If I want my woman totally comfortable in bed, I've got to figure out a way to undo the mindfuck that's got her acting like her pretty pussy is gross. And that's secondary to figuring out how to convince her that she's allowed to be mad at me when I fuck up. Girlfriends are hard.

"Hey," I call to Shane as I snug up the lashing. "How do you get a woman to talk to you when she's mad?"

"You mean, like, how do you get her to stop throwing shit and talk?"

"No, like if she won't talk about it. How do you get her to tell you what's on her mind?"

"That's really a problem? That she's *not* bitching at you?"

I shake my head. "I don't know why I asked."

Shane snorts. "I don't know why you did, either. No woman has ever had a problem telling me what I'm doing wrong."

We finish the rest of our row in silence. At the meal hour, we pick up subs and eat together in my truck to listen to the Gonzaga game.

The afternoon goes slow. The drivers are running behind, so we have to stand around a while with our dicks in our hands. I get paid regardless of whether the operation runs smoothly, but I don't have the chill some of the old guys have yet. They'll straight up slow-walk the work to get another hour or two. I've got a life. Yes, I want to get paid, but I also want to finish while I still have feeling in my legs. The steel decks are hell on your feet no matter what insoles you've got.

I get anxious when the dinner hour comes and goes, and there are still vehicles coming up the ramp, and I'm still on read.

Angie has class tonight at the community college, so we don't have plans, but I'm not about to leave this be. Thankfully, at eight, the port captain calls the operation. We're finishing tomorrow. I have thirty minutes to get to my truck, book it across the terminal, drive two miles to campus, park, and meet Angie when her class finishes.

I know where the building is because we went to campus the day before her first class so we could scout the place out. It was a good day. The girls ran around the quad, and I showed them the hill I used to sled down when I was a kid and we still had blizzards in winter in Maryland.

I make it with no time to spare. It's dark and raining when I step into Angie's path. She's making a beeline for her car. She doesn't recognize me at first. Her eyes round, and she stops short. She's got a big black umbrella, and her black jacket is zipped up to her chin. She's loaded like a pack mule with a backpack, a laptop bag, and her purse.

"Brandon?"

Like every time she says my name, my lower abs tense, and my dick twitches.

Like every time we see each other, our feet bring us together until she has to tilt her neck back, and I have to drop mine forward. She raises her umbrella to cover us both. I slide her laptop bag off her shoulder and sling it over my own.

"What are you doing here?" She's flustered, but she's not hostile.

"Checking on you. You left me on read." My face is cold and damp despite my hood, but my cheeks burn. I sound whipped. I guess I am. Why should I hide it from her?

She dips her eyes, shy and sweet, and her mouth curves. "I was busy."

"You were mad," I say as gently as I can. She lifts her gaze. There's a struggle there. I wish I could fight it for her.

"I didn't want to take the girls to Broyce's." She curls her free hand into a fist and hides it up her raincoat sleeve.

I nod. I keep my mouth shut. I make my face look like I'm listening so that she knows I am.

"It was stressful, worrying the whole time about how the girls were gonna act. I don't like people looking at me."

I want to tell her that she doesn't have to worry, that she can choose not to care—I sure as hell don't—but I already said that, and she did not take that advice on board.

I open my mouth to tell her that she should have told me that she didn't want to go, but I already said that, too. And as she already pointed out, she did tell me, and I didn't listen.

So what do I say?

Do I tell her that I just wanted her to have a nice dinner? That she can pick the restaurant next time? That sounds logical, but it doesn't feel like it's the right thing to say either.

She gazes up at me, braced, ready to duck back behind her defenses. Why is this hard? I need to stop ragging on Shane for being a dumbass because apparently, I am, too.

I want her to be honest with me.

So when she's honest, I have to be cool.

I have to listen, but I already fucked that up, and I can't reverse time.

She blinks, the hopefulness that broke across her face when she recognized me fading.

Out of desperation, I blurt out, "Yeah, I get that it sucks having people judge you and stressing about spills and shit when you just want to enjoy your meal." I basically just repeat what she said to buy time.

"Yeah. It does suck." Her expression softens.

"I'm sorry I didn't get that earlier."

"It's okay," she says.

"It wasn't okay, but it is now," I say as gently as I can, taking the umbrella so I can hold it higher. She huddles closer.

"You're soaking wet," she says. She pulls her shirt hem out of her sleeve and wipes the rain off my face.

I did it. I said the right thing. I made it better. I'm a god among men.

"I'll listen better next time," I say with the full knowledge that I had no idea that I *wasn't* listening until I'd already done fucked up. We talked it out, though. We're on the same page again. "We good?" I ask, just to be sure.

"We're good." She smiles.

I kiss her. She sinks into me, her breasts crushing against my chest. Raindrops patter on the fabric above our heads and the pavement beneath our feet. Except for the lamps lighting the pathway, the darkness is deep like it gets at night in spring when the cloud cover is thick.

We're alone. The rain has dropped a curtain on the world around us. Angie sighs, and I feel like the luckiest man alive because she gazes up at me, and she's happy. I did that. And that makes me pretty fucking happy, too.

"Ready?" I say. "I'll follow you home."

She nods.

"Let me take this." I slide the backpack off her shoulders and onto mine. She grabs my hand.

I don't expect anything else, but when we're almost to the car, she glances over, squeezes my hand, and says, "I love you."

"I love you, too, Ang," I say back. It's the most natural thing in the world, and also, the most amazing thing that's ever happened to me.

It feels precious.

It feels right.

And as delicate as glass.

13

ANGIE, A FEW MONTHS LATER

It's a good thing that Brandon postponed our plans for today. We were supposed to go hiking at North Point, but he has to work, so we're going to meet up for dinner. Tyler just called, and he wants to bring the girls home early. He had a convoluted story about Duck and a throttle replacement, and how he owes Duck for a chain adjustment from last year. Long story short, Tyler's ditching the girls to go dirt-bike riding.

It's okay by me. I'm never going to get used to weekends without them, and the girls don't seem to mind coming back early. The plan at the beginning was every other weekend, Friday evening to Sunday evening. Now, it's more like once a month, from whenever Tyler feels like getting them to whenever his mom brings them home on Sunday.

I leave off packing boxes and go hang on the front porch to wait for them. Tyler called from down the street. I don't know what he would have done if I wasn't home.

It sucks that Brandon and I aren't going to have all weekend together now, but I really did need the time alone today to go through stuff. The girls and I are finally moving to our own apartment in two weeks. Brandon wanted us to move in with him, but I want to be married first. I learned my lesson. The next time I cohabitate with a man, both our names are going to be on the lease or the mortgage or whatever.

Besides, Brandon and I haven't even been going out for a year yet, and we only said "I love you" a few months ago. It's going good—really good—and it physically hurts not to be able to sleep beside him every night, but I also feel like I need to stand on my own two feet.

He understands. He doesn't like it, but he gets it, and I've grown to the point where I don't get unbearably anxious when a man doesn't like something.

I didn't realize how much like a frog in a pot of boiling water I was with Tyler until I got out. His wedding vows were the biggest favor he could have done me. I see that now.

Overall, I'm feeling fine when Tyler rolls up with his dirt bike in the back of his truck. The weather's sunny, and I'm still achy and glowing from Brandon rocking my world last night. We were supposed to go out to the movies, but like always, when it came down to it, we decided to stay in. We watched about fifteen minutes of a comedy special, and then we got distracted touching each other, and he plowed me until I passed out from exhaustion while he was still finishing.

The man has the stamina of a jackhammer. I never thought that's something I'd want, but I love getting my mind blown. It feels good to stop thinking for a while.

I guess I must be wearing a goofy little smile as I head over because when Tyler sees my face, his expression sours and his eyes narrow. He gets really prickly when it looks like I'm in a good mood. He takes it like I'm trying to mock him or something.

He usually stays in the truck and lets me help the girls

out, but today, he puts it in park and hops down. Immediately, my stomach knots. He struts around the hood to stand on the lawn with his hands on his hips. He makes a show of checking me out, head to foot, and smirks.

My hair is thrown back in a ponytail, and I'm wearing pajama bottoms with an old T-shirt and no bra. I was doing laundry while I packed boxes, and I wasn't planning on seeing anyone besides Miss Dawn. I hunch my shoulders to hide my boobs the best I can.

Tyler glances at the two cars in the drive. "Where's lover boy?"

I shrug and reach up to lift Ivy out of the truck. The girls are quiet, but they don't seem upset. More tired than anything. Tamblyn climbs down herself, carrying her and her sister's overnight bags. The original duffel never turned back up, so I bought them kid-sized carry-ons with wheels when they went on sale after Christmas. Tamblyn's has ladybugs, and Ivy's has unicorns.

When Tamblyn hits the walk, she pulls up the handles and rolls both bags the rest of the way to the house like the world's smallest, most jaded flight attendant. Ivy trudges after her. Neither says goodbye to Tyler, but he doesn't notice. He's too busy sneering at me.

"You know, free advice, it's a little early for you to stop making an effort. Maybe wait for a ring first." He folds his arm, pleased with himself.

He's showered and shaved, wearing a spotless motocross jersey and aviation pants. I hope he doesn't think that I didn't notice the girls' hair wasn't brushed, and they were both wearing yesterday's outfits, which I bet they slept in. Of course, I don't say anything. I wouldn't dare. Don't poke the bear. Don't make problems bigger. Those are the rules for a peaceful life, right?

I say, "Well, I'll catch you later," and head for the house.

Every step I take, a coal in my chest burns hotter and hotter. I'm not this person anymore. Why don't I say something? I don't let people talk to me however they want.

Or do I?

No one ever talked to me like shit except Tyler, and his mother, I guess. I *think* I'm different now, but am I? Here I am again—taking it. Every single time—taking it.

I stop in my tracks and turn, my gaze catching on the brand-new dirt bike in the back of his truck. I never even confronted him about cleaning out the joint checking account. I told myself *lesson learned*, and opened a new account in my name only. When Madison asked about it, I said I'd dealt with it. I hadn't.

Have I changed? Or am I just ignoring the issues like I always have? Is it really okay with me that Tyler treats the girls like his last priority? Or do I just accept it because that's all I ever was, and I don't have the backbone to demand more for myself or them?

That dirt bike money was theirs, not mine. That was for *their* needs.

"Hey." I square up. "I have something I want to talk to you about."

Tyler hasn't made a step toward his truck. When I turn around, his eyes light up. He's spoiling for a fight. "What?"

"The money you took out of our account—when are you going to pay it back?"

He draws his head back like I've said the most out-of-line thing he's ever heard. "What the fuck are you talking about?"

That's always his first defense—act like I'm crazy, or I don't know what I'm talking about.

"Back in November. You spent three hundred and fifty-two dollars from our joint account at Thom's Cycle. That was money for the girls."

I can see him weighing whether or not to keep playing stupid and then the exact moment when airing his perpetual sense of grievance wins out over the habit of gaslighting me.

"Bullshit," he says. "If it was money for the girls, you would have spent it on food and clothes and whatever. You were using it as your personal petty cash."

"I was not." That doesn't even make sense, and besides, he could see where I used the debit card just as easily as I saw that he used his card at Thom's Cycle. If he had checked the statement, all he would've seen was Food Lion, Dollar Tree, and Wal-Mart. "I was saving for Christmas."

He snorts. "Don't lie."

I'm not. I'm not a liar. He knows that. My eyes burn. "You owe me that money."

For a second, I think I'm panicking because my chest feels so tight, but then I realize that this isn't panic. This is *fury*.

I don't ever get mad. My body doesn't know what to do. I'm holding myself stick-straight, joints locked, fists clenched. If I don't hold myself down, I'm not sure what I'll do. Swing on him? Kick him in the balls?

I take a jerky step toward him. "You owe me, and you know it, and you better pay it back." My voice is rough and scratchy and strange to my ears.

His blue eyes blaze, the pupils telescoping into tiny specks. Dread swamps my sad little moment of righteous anger. I freeze.

I'm no competition for him when it comes to meanness. I brought a knife to a gun fight.

His lip curls, and my body responds on cue. Panic surges through my veins, sweeping away the anger. I cringe, shrinking in my skin. My shoulders bunch. I stiffen every muscle so he can't tell that I'm shaking. He's meaner if I shake.

His face looks like a close-up in a scene from a wildlife special where the predator roars in slow motion. His neck cords. He bares his teeth. His nostrils flare.

"Oh, you think you're hot shit now, don't you? 'Cause you've dug your claws into some other dumb fucker to bleed dry. Goddamn, Angie. Aren't you ever gonna get tired of being a user? Grow up."

He pivots like he's going to leave, but it's a fake out. He does it to up the drama. He turns back around slowly, a movie monster who was heading out until he heard a muffled sound. His moves are so predictable. Why do they still tie me in knots?

"You know, I actually *pitied* you," he says. "Your junkie mom was sucking off dudes behind the Quick Mart, and you had basically no friends, and I was nice to you *once*, and you just wouldn't fucking let go. Like you were gonna off yourself if I told you I wanted to see other people. I was a *teenager*, Angie. I didn't want 2.5 kids. I wanted a *life*. But you didn't care what I wanted, did you? As long as Angie gets what Angie wants, who cares about anybody else?"

I want to cover my ears. Cry uncle. Scrub myself away with an eraser. Every word he says is true.

I did cling. I would have done anything so that I wasn't alone. It was so lonely watching Mom slip away. Hot tears fill my eyes.

Another man would stop. For Tyler, tears are a cue to go harder. "You know, it was a complete *asshole* move to find your pride at the fucking altar at the last fucking minute, but I was actually *happy* for you. Did you know that? What you did was selfish as hell, but I thought, hey, maybe she'll *finally* grow some self-esteem. Focus on being a mother. Make something of herself. But you'd rather suck the life out of another poor bastard. How long 'til you 'accidentally' get yourself knocked up by this one, eh, Angie?"

It *was* an accident. The condom broke. He was there. He said, "Shit. Guess I need Magnums." I said we should get Plan B, but he didn't want to spend the money, and I didn't have it. He said it'd be fine. I decided to believe him because it was the path of least resistance, and really, deep down, I wanted a baby so bad. I didn't want to be alone anymore.

I *am* selfish.

My anger drains away. Every word out of Tyler's mouth flays me in strips. I know he's the enemy, but I can't summon up my defenses. I take the blows. I deserve them. I always have.

"Do Brandon a favor though, would you? If you're just gonna bail at the last possible second, don't be begging him all the time to buy you a ring. It's pathetic. Don't waste his money as well as his life." He sneers, drops his metaphorical mic, and strides to his truck, swinging himself into the cab like he just won by TKO, and he's the heavyweight champion of the world.

His engine roars as he peels off, a black plume of smoke rising from that stupid stack.

I feel like a worm.

Even though it's sunny and cool, and birds are chirping in the trees, no one but me is outside. The sky is a hard blue. The sunshine is a spotlight.

I'm an embarrassment. A leech. Too weak to stand up for myself. Pathetic.

I creep back to the house, schlep myself up the steps, and skulk inside. Please let the girls be into something already. By some miracle, the tears have stopped, but if I have to put on a smiling face for them, they're going to come flooding back.

The door to the basement is open, and voices from the

TV filter up the stairs. Miss Dawn is futzing around in the kitchen. I duck into the living room to collect myself. It'd be easier to collect sand in a sieve. I collapse on the couch.

I thought I was good. I was happy. Am I deluding myself again? Am I forcing things with Brandon because I can't take being alone?

But I love him.

Do I even know what love feels like? Or is this desperation? A drowning man loves a life preserver, too.

My head hurts. My heart is skinned. I sink onto the couch. My phone rings.

It's Brandon.

"Hey," I answer, trying to sound normal. There is a lot of noise on his end. He's calling from a ship.

"Hey. Listen. The operation is going long. I'm not gonna be able to meet up tonight. I'll have to catch you later," he says. Loud. No hesitation. No hint of disappointment.

All of a sudden, it feels like all the blood in my body rushes to my head. I can't breathe. I don't have lungs.

A voice from deep, deep inside me says with total confidence, with *glee—he's not disappointed because you're a burden. A clinger. He'd rather work than see you. He won't admit it—he's in too deep—but that's the truth. He doesn't really want you. You trapped him.*

What twenty-five-year-old wants a woman with herpes and two kids who lives in his mom's basement?

Vaguely, somewhere way out in the farthest reaches of my mind, I recognize that these are intrusive thoughts, but what does that matter? Where's the lie? What's the difference between an intrusive thought and a truth you don't want to be true?

Metal clangs and clanks in the background, and Brandon shouts, "Angie? Did you hear me?"

I heard.

"Don't worry about it," I say.

"We can hang tomorrow."

"Don't worry about it," I repeat. My voice is cold. Mean.

"Ang?"

"Just don't worry about tomorrow. I've got the girls. And I've got things to do. I'll catch up with you later."

"Angie, what's going on?"

"I said later." Why won't he listen? I'm giving him an out. Why is he pushing? "I just need space, Brandon. God. Can't you get that? Why do you have to push? Just *let it go*."

I end the call and drop the phone in my lap. Immediately, it vibrates. I power it off.

Whose voice was that? Mine, but it didn't sound like mine. What the fuck just came out of my mouth?

My hands shake. I shove them under my thighs and stare at the dark TV screen. The room is bright and silent. Competing voices float in from the kitchen and downstairs —Miss Dawn humming, the girls chatting amongst themselves.

The blood drains from my head. In the vacuum left behind, my thoughts bump into each other, drunk and blindfolded.

What am I doing?

How am I even here in this house?

Except for the flat screen and couch, nothing much has changed since I first came over as a little kid. The pastel patterned curtains and valance with pom-poms are the same. The same mirror with the paint-speckled frame hangs on the wall. These are the same end tables with racks for the newspaper. Miss Dawn keeps her Sudoku books there now.

When Mr. Mike was on hospice, they put his hospital bed in here since it wouldn't fit in their bedroom. Mr. Mike wanted the TV on 24/7, and Miss Dawn complained that she couldn't sleep with the noise, but for those weeks, there was always bedding piled in a laundry basket in the corner. She camped out on the couch every night anyway.

The first months after he died, I couldn't sit in this room without thinking about him. It only crosses my mind every once in a while now. Like when I drive past the Tremont Motel. Sometimes I catch sight of their vacancy sign and surprise myself with how many times I've driven past without remembering that Mom died there in room eighteen.

It's a small town. If you stay, there's no such thing as a clean slate or a fresh start. You have to make peace with the ghosts, one way or another.

And the boogeymen.

In the kitchen, the landline rings. I tense. Miss Dawn gets it, but she doesn't call out to me, so I guess it's not Brandon.

I lean forward, my elbows digging into my thighs, and stare at that dark screen. There's something I didn't think of, something I missed, but I can't quite put my finger on it. It's just out of reach.

And then, inside me, I feel a nudge. It reminds me of when we're at the pool, and Tamblyn is paddling her heart out toward the wall, and she's so close, but she's about to give up, so I take her gently by the waist and glide her forward. Her hand touches the tile. Bam. Got it.

Connection made. I've got a grip on it now.

Everything Tyler says is backwards.

Focus on being a mother? He dropped his kids off early to go mess with dirt bikes.

I bled him dry? I made him dinner every night after I got home from work. I paid my half of the bills, and I cleaned the house and did the laundry and dropped the girls off to Miss Dawn and picked them up and did the grocery shopping and made sure we never ran out of Mountain Dew, salt and vinegar chips, and Captain Crunch, and *I* need to grow up?

I'm a user? I'm selfish? Everything he calls *me* is true about *him*.

And I *knew* all this. I've *known* he's a gaslighter. But there's knowing it in your head, and knowing it in every part of yourself down to the bone. Every part of me has a grip on it now—I am not what he says I am, what that lonely, abandoned girl inside of me believes.

My heart races. I'm in the Matrix now. I've slowed down time, and I'm bending in half backwards, and the bullets are flying past me.

All the shit Tyler says isn't *true*. It's what I'm *afraid* of. What's the unwanted girl scared of the most?

Being a burden.

Being unwanted.

I'd say he's an evil genius, but he's not. He's a dumbass, but he's mean, and I swear mean is a form of intelligence.

Adrenaline kick-starts my muscles. I pop to my feet, dropping my phone to the carpet. I'm going after him, and I'll scream in his face that I'm onto him now, and he can fuck himself, and then I'm going to punch him in the face, and I bet he'll go down and stay down like he did when Brandon hit him.

Oh. Brandon. Shit.

I didn't mean it.

I need to take it back.

I bend over, fumbling for my phone, but before I can power it back on, I hear the girls' footsteps on the stairs. They pad into the living room with long faces.

"Snuggle puddle," Tamblyn grumps, grabbing my hand and pulling me back down to the couch. The girls curl up, burrowing into my side.

Even though it's the middle of the day, they've changed

into their pajamas. Ivy has a stuffie tucked under her arm, and Tamblyn has Chickie wrapped around her shoulders like a cape.

"Whatcha doing, Mama?" Tamblyn asks.

Ivy lays her head on my lap and winds her thin arm around my thigh.

"Just thinking," I say, smoothing Ivy's hair. It's going to be a bitch to get the knots out.

"About what?" Tamblyn stretches to get the remote from the end table.

"Nothing important." Just how your dad set me off, so I was an asshole to the man I love. He thinks the sun rises and sets on me, but I agreed with your dad that no one can *really* want me since my mom OD'd and my dad left. I didn't really believe anyone could actually love me until this very moment. That's all.

Tamblyn turns on the TV and starts surfing from channel to channel, looking for something. "Is Brandon coming over?" she asks.

My heart twinges, dread rising in my chest. Did I ruin things? Did I dump him? I can't remember exactly what I said.

"No," I answer. "He's working today."

"He'll come by later then," she says.

"He probably has to work late." And he's probably pissed and confused. How do I explain? All of a sudden, I'm not so desperate to talk to him.

At what point does all my shit become too tedious?

"Then he'll come over tomorrow," Tamblyn says matter-of-factly, smiling as she comes across the channel she was looking for. It's the Orioles game. They're singing the National Anthem. Ivy perks up and climbs to sit on my lap.

When did the girls get into baseball?

They both begin to sing along, the lyrics indecipherable

until the end when they bellow “O!” in unison with the rest of the stadium.

“You’re supposed to shout ‘O,’ Mama,” Tamblyn informs me.

“Okay. I will next time.”

We snuggle in to watch the game. I need to call Brandon, and I will, but I need to figure out what to say first. The last thing I want to do is make him even angrier when he’s operating heavy machinery.

I’m so pissed at myself. I’m a stupid fish, jumping for the bait yet again, and this time, I managed to drag Brandon down with me. I’m not going to do that again.

He’s a good man, and dammit, I’m a good woman. We have a good thing going. I’m not going to let anyone—including me—mess it up.

“See this guy? Number two?” Tamblyn asks when a new player comes up to bat.

“Yeah.”

“He started slow last season, but he came through in the end. We think this is his year.”

“Who thinks that?”

“Me and Brandon.”

“I think that, too,” Ivy pipes up.

“His year for what?” I ask.

“Baseball,” Tamblyn says, like it’s a very silly question. I guess it was.

Around the third inning, an amazing smell begins to waft in from the kitchen, and Miss Dawn comes to join us. She collapses into her easy chair with a huff and cranks the footrest.

“It’s too hot in this house,” she says, fanning herself.

“What’s cooking, Miss Dawn?” Tamblyn, my sugar monster, asks.

“Blackberry cobbler.” Miss Dawn, the original sugar

monster, grins over. "It's a little early in the season, but blackberries were BOGO this week. Who's winning?"

"O's," Tamblyn answers.

"You girls remind me to check on the oven in twenty minutes. I don't want the juice running over and ruining all that hard work your mama did scrubbing it out."

Miss Dawn keeps a tidy house in general, but she only runs the self-cleaning cycle every blue moon, and it really needed a once-over with vinegar, baking soda, and elbow grease.

We watch the game together in silence while the whole house fills up with the scent of warm cobbler. It's the best smell, but I can't enjoy it. The need to make things right with Brandon is climbing up my throat.

I need to call him now.

But he's at work. I don't want to get him any more bothered while he's operating heavy equipment. Longshoreman is a dangerous job. They can't even get regular life insurance; they have to get it special through the union. That freaked me out when I heard it.

If I don't call him, though, he'll think I meant it, and maybe it'll be the straw that'll break the camel's back.

But if I call him, how do I explain myself?

I'm so antsy that the girls abandon me for the opposite ends of the couch, but at least they've chilled out and got their playfulness back. Tamblyn wanders downstairs and comes back with her little fuzzy animal critters, and Ivy joins her on the carpet. Except for the anxious pit growing larger and larger in my stomach, it becomes an ordinary Saturday evening.

I make dinner while Miss Dawn and the girls finish watching the game, and when we're done eating, we all have a big slice of cobbler. Miss Dawn says it's not her best work, that the blackberries aren't at the height of sweetness, but honestly, with the amount of sugar in the recipe, you can hardly tell what kind of berries she used. It's delicious. I have to wash it out of both girls' hair during bath time.

After I read the girls their story and put them to bed, I wait until they're asleep and head upstairs to unload the dishwasher. Even though I tell Miss Dawn I'll do it, she always puts the kitchen to rights while I put the girls to bed. At least I can put away the clean dishes and set up the coffeemaker so it's ready to go first thing in the morning.

My phone burns a hole in my pocket.

I could call Brandon now. I really want to hear his voice, but I'm so freaking scared. What if he's really, really mad at me?

I'm used to a man being mad at me for bullshit reasons, and frankly, it's easier. All I needed to do with Tyler was kiss his ass until he got bored with punishing me, but Brandon isn't Tyler, and I'm in the wrong this time.

Brandon will understand if I explain, though.

Won't he?

He could still be working. He said the operation is running late. I should wait. I'll text him when I get back downstairs.

I take my time, wiping down the counters and the stove range, even though Miss Dawn already did a thorough job of it. I'm going to miss living here when we move. I can't say that Miss Dawn is like the mother I never had. That's not the relationship we have. We feel more like reluctant brothers-in-arms.

She doesn't let on that she's lonely, and I don't let on that I'm overwhelmed, and we face the day-to-day struggle together. We haven't lost yet. Some days, that feels like victory.

Once I'm done in the kitchen, I wander into the living room to check on her. Sometimes she falls asleep in her chair, and I'll cover her with an afghan. She's awake, though, watching one of her real-life mystery shows.

"All right, Miss Dawn?" I ask from the doorway.

She smiles, rousing in her chair. She must have been drifting off. "There you are. I need a favor."

"Sure."

"There's a covered dish in the fridge with some cobbler for Brandon. Will you run it over to him?"

I narrow my eyes. She narrows hers right back.

"He might be working late," I say.

"I'm sure he's home by now. I'll keep an ear out for the girls." She turns back to the TV. I'm dismissed.

She must've talked to him. He must not be too mad if she's giving me an excuse to see him. A weight lifts from my shoulders, and butterflies explode in my stomach.

I rush downstairs as quietly as I can, changing into the cute T-shirt, jean shorts, and white sneakers that he likes the best. Before I duck out, I check on the girls. They're conked out, sleeping like they always do—Tamblyn on her back like Sleeping Beauty, and Ivy on her stomach, arms and legs stretched like she's holding the fitted sheet down.

They were fine tonight. It doesn't seem to faze them when Tyler drops them off early. They don't take it as a rejection. Yet. It hurts my heart, though.

I don't want to wish he was a better father. I want to hate him.

I scoop Chickie off the floor, tuck him back under Tamblyn's arm, and tiptoe up the stairs.

I almost forget the cobbler, but I remember when I'm halfway out the front door and dash back for it. When I open the fridge, for some reason, my eyes catch on the eggs. Due to the daycare kids, Miss Dawn buys the eighteen count.

A memory pops into my head. High school. Shrunk

down in the passenger seat of Tyler's old Civic while he and his boys egged poor Mr. Prescott's house and his little car that they'd stuck up the gym roof for the senior prank. Tyler and his boys were mad that Mr. Prescott made a big deal about it.

The thing about Tyler is that he does what he wants, and if you complain, he gets worse.

The other thing about Tyler is that if you let it go, he gets worse.

On impulse, I grab the cardboard carton along with the cobbler and hustle back down the hallway.

Miss Dawn snorts a laugh from the living room. "No need to rush," she calls after me. "Take as long as you need."

Outside, it's cool, but not cold, and the sky is black like velvet. Only a few stars are visible, like poked holes.

To get to Brandon's, you turn right out of the cul-de-sac. When I get to the stop sign, I look over at the egg carton sitting on the passenger seat. What am I thinking? Egging a house is childish. It's not me. I've never acted out of spite once in my life.

I turn left. My heartbeat picks up, and my palms get sweaty. I crack the window. My nerves are too jittery to turn the radio on, so I listen to the wind.

Am I really going to do this?

I think I am.

I obey the speed limit all through town and into our old development. When I turn onto his street, I turn my headlights off, cut the engine, and drift to a stop in neutral. I reach overhead and switch off the overhead light. I've never done anything like this before, but it comes so naturally.

Lights are blazing in the living room, spilling into the front yard. Tyler's truck is parked in the short driveway. No one else is here. I'm surprised he's home. Usually when he works on dirt bikes with his boys, they go to the bar afterwards. Maybe the story about Duck and the throttle replacement was bullshit. Maybe he just got tired of watching the girls.

I get out with the eggs, holding them carefully, with due respect. An eighteen count is almost seven bucks at the Giant these days.

I leave my car door open and stalk quietly to the entrance to his driveway. The maple tree is gone, and there's a big hole where it used to be. What the heck happened? Did someone hit it?

There's other evidence that things are going to pot. My flowerbed is filled with the husks of last summer's annuals. For some reason, the kitchen trash can is sitting on the front porch. The HOA is going to get him for that.

I wish I could be angry. Not all the time. Not at the whole world. But this once. For my girls. And myself.

I close my eyes and hunt for the rage. I don't want Tyler to get away scot-free yet again. I don't want to be the person who *lets* him.

He ditched our girls.

He called me selfish and pathetic.

He cheated on me.

He treated me like a maid and then claimed I bled him dry.

He took advantage of me.

Where's my anger?

I'm holding an egg carton in the dark, waiting for a cleansing rush of righteous fury that'll wash away the past and all my mistakes, but there's nothing but the wind rustling the neighbor's hedge and the drone of traffic out on Route 1.

I screw my eyes shut tighter. I summon harder. I picture Mom, her cheeks sunken and her knees as knobby as the girls', sneaking in the house from a bender while I was getting ready for school. I think of Dad, the same handful of memories I can still conjure, half of them from photographs.

I don't want to beat myself up anymore over shit that other people did and that I didn't deserve.

I open my eyes, flip the lid of the carton. There are two white eggs missing. They're probably in the cobbler.

I am perfectly calm as I pick one up, draw my arm back, and pitch it at Tyler's truck. It cracks against the rear window. Yolk and whites drip down.

I've heard if you let the egg dry, you can't get it off without scratching the paint job.

I hurl another egg at the tailgate. And another. They crunch as they smash, dribbling down onto his back fender.

I'm still not mad, but my heart is speeding anyway. It's lifting.

I keep throwing. I cover the rear window. I nail that dumb smokestack. I miss his bumper and egg splatters on the driveway.

A rush washes through me, but it's not fury. I'm grinning like an idiot. The night air is sweet, I'm young, everything is ahead of me, and I have somewhere I want to go, someone I want to see. And it's not here.

I've got two eggs left. Could I risk climbing into the truck and dropping them into that stupid smoke stack?

I wish I could drop them into Tyler's big, fat mouth.

I pivot toward the house, aim, and wing one at the front window. Splat. Adrenaline surges through my veins. Kind of feels like winning.

The door opens. Tyler stamps out onto the porch wearing his gaming headset, holding a controller. He's in shorts, no shirt, and his black sliders with white gym socks pulled high. He squints into the dark.

"Angie? What the hell are you doing?"

He sees his truck.

"What the *fuck*?" His eyes careen from the rear window to the tailgate to the open, empty carton in my hand. "Are you a fucking *child*?"

I aim. I'm not athletic, but he's not very far away, and I'm warmed up. I take a deep breath, and on the exhale, I pitch the last egg at his stupid head. I miss. It goes splat on his bare chest. Yolk sprays, dousing his microphone.

"You *bitch*!" He bolts for me.

I'm quicker. I sprint for the car and leap into the driver's seat, tossing the carton onto the floor. I swing the door shut as I peel off, gasping for air to scream, "Fuck you, Tyler!" out the window. Then I burst out laughing.

It's a good laugh. It just keeps coming, shaking my belly until my abs ache.

I don't feel closure, if that's even a real thing. I'm still not angry, but I deserve to be, and I know it.

I deserve to be happy, too. We all do. And I'm going to go make it happen right now.

~

IT'S ONLY a fifteen-minute drive to Brandon's. I blast the radio, feeling young in a way I never actually was. This must be what sneaking out feels like.

The closer I get to Brandon's townhouse, the more my butterflies collect in my stomach, and the heavier my foot falls on the gas pedal. I'm not sure if I'm hurrying to get this over with or if I'm running to him.

I park behind his truck. His porch light is on. Before I even turn off my engine, he opens his front door and steps out. He's still in his work clothes, but he's barefoot. His head is high, his shoulders back. He's so handsome, but his face is hard. All of a sudden, I'm not in a rush anymore.

I undo my seat belt. Grab the plasticware from the passenger seat. Double-check that the car is in park. Step out into his driveway.

Which is when I notice the tree in the back of his truck. Budding branches hang over the side. It's a young maple. It's *my* maple.

"So where'd you get the tree?" I call to him softly.

His jaw tenses, and he crosses his arms, his biceps stretching his short sleeves. I love his arms.

"You know where," he says.

"Did you dig it up from Tyler's front yard?"

"I don't know. Did Tyler do something that made you wig out on me?"

I walk closer until I reach the bottom of the steps. "Yeah."

"Well then, yeah, I did," he says, glancing down at me. His brown eyes are carefully blank. My heart aches. I did that. I made him put his defenses back up.

He stole me a tree. I want to wrap my arms around him and hold on forever, but he's five steps above me, and I can't skip the part where I explain myself. Even though I think if I opened my arms right now and said his name, he'd come to me without a second's hesitation. Knowing that makes my insides glow.

I know him. He knows me. We love each other. It's crystal clear now without the static in my head.

This is my man. I didn't break things between us. We're stronger than that.

"I'm sorry," I say. "I didn't mean what I said, and I shouldn't have turned my phone off. It was a dick move."

"If you do it again, I'm gonna walk off the job and hunt you down. And then they're gonna have to fire me."

"I won't do it again." I step up a stair. "I'm gonna work on my communication skills."

"Yeah?" The straight line of his mouth eases into a faint smile. "You want to tell me what Tyler did?"

"I don't *want* to, but I will." I go up another step. "He brought the girls back early so he could ride dirt bikes, and I started with him about money, and he said a lot of mean shit, and I spun out."

"You know that everything that comes out of his mouth is total bullshit, right?"

"Yeah." I step up again. "I'm working on knowing that."

His eyes soften. "Do you want to tell me what he said?"

I shake my head.

"Do you want me to beat the shit out of him?" he asks, a note of hopefulness in his voice.

"No. It wouldn't be a fair fight."

He sighs. "True."

"Besides, I egged his truck."

"You did? When?"

"Just now."

He grins. I've managed to surprise him. "Attagirl," he says.

"I'm sorry that you have to deal with my asshole ex making me crazy." I step up one more time. I'm almost on the porch.

He shrugs. "It's part of the package. I wouldn't have you any other way than how you are."

My face heats, and I glance down at the rubber toes of my sneakers. I feel the same way, but there's nothing about him I have to overlook or deal with. He's amazing.

One day, I swear, come hell or high water, I'm going to feel that way about myself all the time.

Brandon isn't making a move, even though he's getting impatient, scrunching and straightening his toes on the cold concrete. He's letting me come to him in my own time. Again.

Another rush of love floods through me. It's not a crash, but a swell, like in the ocean when you're swimming past where the waves break, where the water lifts you, and you're weightless. I smile, and it must be goofy as hell.

He grins back.

I step onto the porch. He lowers his crossed arms. I pad forward until we're so close that I can feel his warmth and hear his breath.

"I don't want space," I whisper.

"Neither do I." He grabs my waist and tugs me to him. I circle my arms around his neck, bumping him in the back of the head with the plasticware. "Is that my cobbler?"

I murmur, "Yes."

"Hold onto it tight," he says as he lifts me into his arms.

He kicks the door open and steps over the threshold. Our mouths slam together. I drop the cobbler. His knees hit the floor. I push him over, straddling his waist, scrabbling at his clothes. I get his shirt half-up and his pants half-down. He gets my jeans down around one ankle.

"Oh, shit. Wait a sec," he says, doing a sit up while he maneuvers me so that I'm leaning left so he can get his wallet from his right pocket.

He grabs my ass with one hand and hoists me forward so he can roll on a condom, and then he moves both hands to my waist to lift and lower me onto his thick cock. His groans mingle with the moans from the back of my throat.

"Hold on, hold on," he pants, pausing his thrusts for a second and scooting us toward the door. I hear a thud.

"Was the door open?"

"Not anymore," he says with a grin and goes back to pumping his hips. I ride him again, back arched and breasts bouncing, my knees digging into the carpet.

He lies on his back in the foyer, mesmerized, like he's never seen anything like me before and doesn't want to miss a second. I don't want to blink either. He's gorgeous, and he's mine.

"I'm gonna come," he gasps. "Are you close?"

I shove a hand between my legs, find my clit, and catch up quick. "Yeah," I say, breathless, folding forward so I can kiss him. He grips my ass and helps me keep rhythm as I lose focus on everything except the pleasure swirling and tightening inside me.

"You are the most beautiful thing in the world," he says, staring up, apparently distracted by my face. He groans. His body tenses and then shudders, but he doesn't break eye contact. He watches as I fall apart, too.

Afterwards, I collapse on top of him and stare dumbly at the boots lined up against the wall and the upside-down cobbler container. He wraps me in his strong, steady arms.

"We didn't make it past the foyer," I mumble, still trying to restart my brain.

He chuckles. "Give me a minute or two to catch my breath. I'll carry you up to bed, and we can do it again."

I push up on his chest so I can look at his face. He's smiling, his brown eyes crinkling. "You're beautiful, too."

He smiles wider, cradles my head, and guides my mouth down to his. It's not our first kiss, but somehow, it feels like one.

Careful and hopeful and so very, very sweet.

Like love.

EPILOGUE

BRANDON

THE RING IS BURNING A HOLE IN MY POCKET.

We've been here for three hours, long enough to catch a decent catfish and a white perch and throw back a cownose ray after the girls had a chance to squeal over it while it swam around the bucket awhile.

I need to do it. The girls are gonna get bored or hungry soon.

We're alone on the pier except for an older gentleman crabbing with a string and a hunk of ham. The bridge rises above us. Tamblyn says it looks like a brontosaurus with its head dipped down to drink. It's a fair description.

Fort Armistead has a bad reputation, but I've never found it anything but peaceful during a weekday. Angie works twelve-hour shifts, three days a week, now that she's a CNA, so I've been working doubles and taking off Mondays so we can take the girls on day trips. Summers are short, and there's so many places I want to take the three of them. We haven't even gotten out on a boat yet this year.

But first things first. I've got to propose.

It's not going to come as a surprise. Angie and I have talked it through, backwards and forwards. She's big into sharing her thoughts and opinions now. Kind of a course correction from Tyler. I love it. No secrets, no hiding her worries. If something's bothering her, she tells me, and I fix it. Unless it's Tyler. There's no fixing that asshole.

Best we can hope for on that front is that we maintain the status quo. He had to sell the house since he couldn't keep up with the mortgage on his salary alone. He's back living with his parents, which is good. We feel better knowing his folks are around to keep an eye on things and make sure the girls are fed.

He's down to about maybe one sleepover every other month, and an evening here and there. It's not a lot, but he's been consistent, and the girls seem cool. He's also learned to keep his mouth shut during pick up and drop off. I taught him that one the day after I dug up his tree.

Tamblyn's bobber ducks under the water, and she shrieks. Ivy pops to her feet. The bobber pops back up. The girls hold their breath. It keeps floating. They sigh and groan.

Angie sings, "The one that got away." She's been doing that all afternoon, cracking herself up. Happy Angie is the prettiest thing in the world. I need to just do this.

She's going to say yes. Hell, she's probably guessed that I'm going to ask today. We picked the ring out together two weeks ago.

I ran the whole thing past the girls, too. They are beyond excited. They want to be flower girls and ride a pony down the aisle. I might have said yes while carried away by the moment. I haven't shared that detail with Angie yet. Might make it a surprise for the wedding day.

The sun is sinking behind the cranes at Seagirt, and the river water's turning a deep denim blue. If the Imperial Manila is on schedule, it's just left port. I'm gonna have to do this thing with the crabber looking on. He might be asleep, sitting on his milk crate. He's wearing mirrored sunglasses, and he hasn't moved in a while.

Angie sits on the edge of the pier with her legs dangling, her arms resting on the railing. Tamblyn and Ivy are snuggled against her sides. All of them have their hair thrown up in buns. I couldn't say whose is messier. The evening breeze whips strands from all three heads.

They're mine. That's my woman, and those are my girls. I'm gonna be a good dad—to them and whatever babies come in the future. I know how it's done. I had the best. He taught me everything I know.

I join my little family and say, "Make room."

Tamblyn wriggles over so I have a space to sit. I swing my legs over the edge, wrapping my arm around Angie's waist. The girls are wearing the biggest grins. They know what I'm about to do.

"Brandon, did you forget where you put the ring?" Ivy stage-whispers.

"No. I've got this," I say, reaching into my pocket and taking out the diamond solitaire framed with tiny emeralds for Tamblyn and amethysts for Ivy. The girls giggle and clap, squeezing in to get a closer look.

Angie smiles, her eyes meeting mine. I fall—like I have a hundred thousand times before. My nerves disappear.

"Will you marry me, Angie Miller?"

Her smile reaches her ears. "Yes, I will, Brandon Kaczmarek."

I kiss her, and the girls shriek, hopping up and racing off down the pier, hooting and hollering their excitement. The crabber startles. Guess he was asleep.

I kiss my woman again. This time, like I mean it.

"Is it exactly what you wanted?" I ask her as she holds up her hand, watching the diamond sparkle in the evening sun.

"Exactly," she says. "Perfect."

She reaches for me. I take her hand.

We sit there, quiet and content, listening to the girls laugh and play as the shadow of the bridge grows long.

A few minutes before we pack it in to go home, the Imperial Manila sails past on its voyage across the Atlantic. Angie's eyes are closed, her head resting on my shoulder. If her eyes were open, and if she looked at the right place on the top forward deck, she might recognize a familiar, ass-ugly truck. She wouldn't be able to see the dirt bike tossed in the bed, but I know it's there.

I don't disturb her, though. I preserve her peace and let it sail by.

I'm going to tell her as a first anniversary gift.

Better start thinking now about what I'll do for the following sixty or seventy.

~

IF YOU LOVED Angie and Brandon's story, you might also enjoy *Charge*, the story of a down-on-her-luck single mom and the biker next door.

ABOUT THE AUTHOR

Cate C. Wells writes everything from motorcycle club to mafia to small town to paranormal romance. Whatever the niche, readers can expect character-driven stories that are raw, real, and emotionally satisfying. Cate's into messy love, flaws, long roads to redemption, grace, and happy ever afters, in books and in life.

She lives in Baltimore with her family and resident cat, Cat C. Wells.

Want more CCW? Subscribe to her newsletter at www.catecwells.com.

Made in the USA
Columbia, SC
27 May 2024